Who Rules the Night?

Four figures moved out of the shadows.

"We want your head, pretty boy. And your nice leather coat."

Val showed his teeth in a hard smile. "Come and get them, then. If you can."

The gang moved as one. *They've done this before*, Val thought. *Well, so have I.*

He folded his disciplines around him—and swept into action. He flowed into the midst of his opponents, hardened claws sinking deep into soft flesh as the dark street became a hell of blood and organs and displaced bones. . . .

THE WORLD OF DARKNESS

WEREWOLF
Wyrm Wolf
Conspicuous Consumption

VAMPIRE
Dark Prince
Netherworld
Blood Relations

MAGE
Such Pain

WRAITH
Sins of the Fathers

Strange City (an anthology)

Published by HarperPrism

THE WORLD OF DARKNESS
Vampire

Blood
Relations

Doug Murray

HarperPrism
An Imprint of HarperPaperbacks

This is a work of fiction. The characters, incidents, and dialogues are products of the author's imagination and are not to be construed as real. Any resemblance to actual events or persons, living or dead, is entirely coincidental.

HarperPaperbacks *A Division of* HarperCollins*Publishers*
10 East 53rd Street, New York, N.Y. 10022

Copyright © 1996 by White Wolf Publishing
All rights reserved. No part of this book may be used or reproduced in any manner whatsoever without written permission of the publisher, except in the case of brief quotations embodied in critical articles and reviews. For information address HarperCollins*Publishers*,
10 East 53rd Street, New York, N.Y. 10022.

Cover illustration by J. Chandlee Stowe

First printing: April 1996

Printed in the United States of America

HarperPrism is an imprint of HarperPaperbacks.
HarperPaperbacks, HarperPrism, and colophon are trademarks of HarperCollins*Publishers*.

❖ 10 9 8 7 6 5 4 3 2 1

DEDICATED TO MY WIFE PAM—WHO IS
VERY MUCH LIKE MARIANA (EXCEPT THAT
SHE CAN'T USE A COMPUTER),
AND NOT ENOUGH LIKE ACQUIEL. . .

I *don't belong here.* Anneke's eyes moved from wall to wall, alley to alley. *New York City of all places!* Her shoulder blades tingled as a pair of eyes fell on them. *The stronghold of the Sabbat!* She shrugged, pulled her coat tighter, and sighed. *Can't be helped, though.* She checked over her shoulder, her movement nonchalant. The spying eyes were invisible. *This is the neighborhood the message stipulated.* She glanced into the darkness, eyes easily reading the numbers on the shadowed doors—168. *Half a block or so this way.* There was a rustle behind her. Just a whisper of sound, but there. *Fool! Can't he see* . . . Another rustle.

Anneke moved. She had reborn with a incredible degree of celerity, and, as she aged, had honed the discipline to an incredible degree. In a kine heartbeat, she was in the shadows, behind the clumsy Brujah, whose movements had been so obvious. Anneke's hand fell on the childe's shoulder. "Fool!" she spit into the other's suddenly frightened face. "I am not prey!" She regarded the leather-clad creature before her. Perhaps this was the one the message promised? *No. He's much too young.* Anneke looked at the frightened face. *I could destroy him.* That would effectively eradicate this source of information about her visit. She sighed and shook her head. *No. Someone would know she had been here*—and it would do no good to give *that* one an extra hold on her.

1

I'll just give him a hint of who he's dealing with. Anneke tossed the childe aside, his weight no strain. She chuckled as he landed right in the spot she had picked—a pile of greasily messy garbage. *The stain will remind him to avoid his betters!* As the childe scrambled away she grinned, then strode confidently back into the street, glancing at the sky to gauge the time. *It's late.* There'd been too many delays along the trip here. She could feel the sun, just over the horizon. *Not here yet,* she thought. *But soon.*

She sped her pace. *Just a few more doors . . .*

There! This was it. Anneke hurried up the short flight of stairs and knocked on the door. The sun was higher now. Just below the horizon. *I have to hurry!* She knocked again, harder.

Anneke heard movement inside, quiet footsteps approaching. *About time!* The door opened. "Is it ready?" Anneke glanced back at the sky. *Still under the horizon, I've got a few more minutes.* She stepped in. "Well?"

"Of course." The dark figure holding the door nodded.

Anneke glanced around the room as the door closed with a solid thump. "Where?"

"This way." Anneke followed the dark figure down the hall, through another, nearly invisible opening. The inside of the house was black as midnight, but Anneke knew it was an illusion. *The sun is rising!* She tightened her grip on consciousness and continued walking, down a short staircase, around a bend into a larger room. Anneke's eyes darted from wall to wall. It was totally dark. No windows. None.

Anneke nodded. *Specially prepared.* The place had a palpable hush, not even street noise. *Soundproofing.* She nodded her head. *My host has been very thorough.*

"Over here." Anneke's eyes darted in the direction her companion indicated. *Yes, there it is.*

"My mistress says to consider this her gift to you."

Anneke nodded again. She knew what was left unsaid. *There'll be a price. There's always a price.* Aloud: "How old?" Anneke caught a glint of a smile in the darkness by the door.

"Old enough. Fifth generation."

"So!"

The dark figure moved through the doorway, pulling the door closed behind him. "My mistress says to take your time. There's a bed in the corner, and no light can penetrate this room." That grin again. "And I'll be on guard. Nothing can hurt you here. You're under the mistress's protection."

Anneke nodded at the closing door, then turned to regard her gift. *Fifth generation. Good enough.* She smiled. *At least, for the moment.*

The figure before her was obviously in torpor. He had to be. No one, kine or Kindred, could experience the kinds of injuries this one had suffered and still retain consciousness. Anneke's hands ran over the man gently, lovingly, assessing. Both arms gone, stumps turned into black knotty things by open flames. Anneke's face was suddenly lit by a smile. Her fingers had found the tiny bud of a hand. A *strong one!* Anneke's black snake of a tongue ran over her lips as she bent over the helpless, unbreathing figure. *This one should last a very long time.* . . .

New York was full of nightclubs. Some had been around for decades, catering to the rich, growing more exclusive and more stuffy by the year. Others sprang up overnight, open to anyone who could afford the cover charge, disappearing as tastes, and rent levels, changed.

In recent years, "themed" clubs had appeared. Places designed to pander to the tourist trade. Little Disneylands, offering exotic furnishings, elaborate entertainment—and high prices. The Playboy Club had been the first of these, its success spawning such diverse competition as Planet Hollywood, Jekyll and Hyde's, and the Hard Rock Café. Each specialized in a different form of entertainment; each catered to one, very specific, clientele.

In Greenwich Village, the Blood Club appeared. A dingy-looking dive that catered to the oddest of human tastes, supplying those who wished it an opportunity to sample the salty red stuff from the comeliest of containers.

Blood dolls were the Club's stock in trade. Women into the "Vampire" scene, who got off on others taking a sip of their "elixir vitae," be it from a cut on the arm or a fang in the throat.

It was the place to be if you were a Goth.

Or a vampire.

"I don't know, Tessler." The young-looking man scuffed at the street in front of him, frowning. "It seems so juvenile . . . . "

Tessler grinned at his cousin. "You feel like hunting tonight?"

"No."

"You gotta feed, don't you?"

"Well . . . "

Tessler's grin widened. "Hey, you'll be doing these bimbos a favor! They *like* it! That's why they're here!"

Val looked around. "Well, it *is* part of Elysium. . . . "

Tessler nudged his companion, forcing him to step a little to one side. Ahead of them stood a large wooden door, with a line of young men and women waiting patiently behind a velvet rope. "Just wait until you see the kind of quality they have inside. Not like those uptown dives—all class." Tessler grinned at his cousin. "Just like you!"

Val shrugged off the flattery and followed his cousin toward the door. "I hope you're right."

"I am." Tessler casually strolled past the line of people, slowing only when a well-dressed tree of a man stepped into his path. "Hey!" The tree grunted. "Wait in line like the rest of them."

"Are you talking to *me*?" Tessler's voice was calm, almost casual, as he glanced from side to side. "You must be. I don't see anyone else close enough."

The tree poked a finger toward Tessler's chest. "Yeah, wise guy, I'm talkin' to . . . Umph." Tessler's hand moved, iron fingers closing on the other's wrist, squeezing.

Val heard bones touch and shook his head. Tessler's temper was legendary, and the tree was clearly a mere human. This could get ugly. *Can't let it happen.* He moved forward. *We're supposed to be inconspicuous.*

Val stepped forward. Shaking his head in disgust. "C'mon, Tessler. Let him go."

Tessler grinned. "Sure thing, cuz!" He released his grip on the tree's wrist. "Whatever you say."

Val shook his head and turned to the tree. The man was rubbing his bruised wrist hard, trying to alleviate the pain. Val reached into himself, touched his disciplines: a little Presence should do the trick, he thought. He allowed a smile to cross his face. *It'd better!*

"Are you all right?"

The tree looked toward Val—and was lost. "Y-y-yes, sir. I just thought . . . "

Val caught Tessler's muttered: "I doubt that's possible."

The tree didn't hear a thing. All his attention was on Val, eyes shining with adoration. "What . . . what can I do for you, sir?"

Val sighed. "Just let us in. There's a good man."

The tree reached blindly for the velvet rope, tripping over the supporting stanchion in his haste. "Yes sir, this way, sir."

Tessler strutted past the man, stepping over the fallen support, never looking back. Val sighed again—*He'll never learn!*—then took a second to nod and thank the fawning gatekeeper. The tree's answering look of admiration was almost too much to bear. Val hurried through the door and into the Club, sparing one last glance at those still waiting outside. He saw several emotions on the human faces staring at him; anger and annoyance were obvious, but beneath, Val detected more. Desire. Lust. He turned away. *Inconspicuous. Sure!*

Tessler was waiting inside the door. "You should have let me break him, cousin." The man's grin showed sharp canines. "Teach him how to treat his betters!"

Val shook his head. "It just would have started more trouble."

"No trouble at all!" Tessler laughed. "Not from cattle! Just more fun!" He grabbed Val's arm, pulled him toward the staircase ahead. "But let's forget about it now." He laughed again. "And do some hunting!"

"You can relax." Mariana turned away from the canvas. "I'm finished for the moment."

"How is it coming?" Acquiel bounced off the cushions she'd been sitting on. "Can I look?"

Mariana smiled as her model padded up to her. "Not

just yet. I'm having trouble with the light." She shook her head. "Haven't gotten it yet."

Acquiel smiled slyly. "Well, we can fix that right now, can't we?"

Mariana raised an eyebrow, amused by the other's forthrightness. "Well, we could . . ." Her hand reached out, fingertip tracing the slightly rouged tip of Acquiel's breast. She laughed at the blonde's sharp intake of breath. "I thought you wanted to go to the Blood Club tonight."

Acquiel moved closer, angling like a cat for a proper pet. "It's still early. . . ."

Mariana turned to the window. "Early enough. Still a few hours until dawn." She reached out a hand again, cupping the offered breast. "But there might not be enough time for both." She moved her fingers, smiled at the answering gasp. "Which would you prefer?"

Acquiel fought for control. "If we go to the Club first . . ."

Mariana shrugged her shoulders. "We *might* have time for something before dawn."

She withdrew her hand. "Of course, it all depends on whether you can dress quickly enough."

"I will!"

Mariana grinned as she watched the girl flash into the bedroom. *So young. So full of life.*

Her grin disappeared. *I used to be like that.* She looked at the painting on the easel and shook her head. *Technically, it's perfect*, she thought. *Yet, it's no good at all. No life to it.* She took one more look. *It's the light. . . .*

Mariana heard herself giggle—and bit down hard on the sound. That way lay madness. *Of course the damn light is wrong!* She turned her dark eyes toward the limitless night that filled the loft's one big window. *There's no sun in it. No warmth.*

Mariana rubbed her face. *I haven't seen the sun, been warm, in how long? Years? Decades? How can I paint in darkness?* The giggle came again. No! she thought, biting down hard, feeling the saltiness of blood ooze into her mouth. *I won't stop! Won't let it destroy me! I'm still an artist! I see with an artist's eye, it's just that the work is so . . .*

Mariana turned away from the night and stared at her easel. *Dead!* She tore the canvas from its support, shredding the tough fabric with razor-sharp claws, panting with the effort. She had to do something to find the light again, anything. *Maybe I should go back to working with woods—at least they were alive. Those inlays I did had something going for them. . . .* She tossed the remains of the canvas into the waste bin. *No.* She shook her head. *That would be hiding from the problem. It's what's inside me, not my medium.* She sat down, cradling her head in her hands. *I've got to find a way to add life to my paintings.* She glanced toward the bedroom. *Acquiel's right. I have to get out. Touch life. Taste it.* The blonde's singing grew louder, happier. Mariana walked down the hall, tongue touching dry lips. *I think I'll start right now!*

As usual, the Club was packed. Humans were packed wall to wall in the main bar, drinking and talking, their noise adding to the din of the Club's exotic sound system. Val shook his head. *I hate this kind of music!* All around him, the less-than-dulcet tones of Concrete Blonde bounced and echoed. *It's nothing but noise!* He tried to tone down his hearing, block out the noise. The music dimmed—and he began to hear the voices. Conversation after conversation came thundering into his brain:

"Did you hear about Simmons . . . ?"

"What's a nasty girl like you . . . "

" . . . Every night, and twice on . . . "

Tessler grinned at Val's expression, and shrugged touching his own ears. There'd be no quiet talks here that was for sure.

The Club did have other uses. Tessler motioned Val toward one of the corner rooms. They entered a smaller area, the Mask Room. Here, the walls were covered with the death masks of famous people, many of whom, to Val's certain knowledge, were actually quite *undead*.

Tessler pulled at Val's elbow, pointing him to the room's shadowy corners. Several blood dolls were there, lounging with various paramours. Val could see the occasional flash of a razor blade, followed by the rich smell of blood, red and fresh, trickling from a soft arm.

Val snorted. The kine were such fools. *Playing at being Kindred!* He glared at the girls, eyes squinting in appraisal. *Tessler's right, though.* His gaze ran over a red-head on the couch. *Some of these are quite attractive.* His tongue touched dry lips. *And I do have to feed. . . .*

Val turned, looking for his cousin, but the other had left the Mask Room, heading for another darkened alcove on the other side of the bar. *The Treasure Room,* Val remembered. *Okay.* Val shrugged. *All the more for me.* He took a second to adjust his leathers, a second more to call up the proper attitude. *Confident,* he decided, *with just a touch of arrogance.*

Val strode deep into the Mask Room, instantly grabbing the attention of every sentient being in range.

And inconspicuous. He sighed. *Right!*

*   *   *

Lady Ambrosia smiled as she watched the scene in the Club through the eyes of one of her thralls. "I see that the boy has arrived."

Her servitor bowed, a slight smile touching his face. "As you planned, Mistress."

"An old plan." There was a flash of needle-sharp teeth in the gloom. "But they're always the best."

She grew silent for a moment, concentrating on the bar, making her thrall turn from side to side, scanning, peering into corners. "It appears the girl hasn't arrived as yet."

"She should be there soon."

"And then, it begins . . ." The Methuselah allowed herself to fall into a huge pile of cushions, her smile growing. "Soon the city will be mine!"

"As you say, Mistress."

A soft sound filled the darkened room. It might have been a laugh. "Always."

"Goddamn straps always leave marks!" Acquiel rubbed at the red lines on her slim wrists.

"But you do love wearing them." Mariana grinned.

Acquiel touched the studded collar that surrounded her aristocratic neck. "Only when they're tight!"

"And tight straps always leave marks."

Acquiel sighed, still rubbing. "I guess you're right, but still . . ."

Mariana laughed. "Don't worry, sweet, nobody at the Club is going to look at your wrists—not with the outfit you're wearing!"

Acquiel grinned, looking down at herself. She knew that Mariana was right; the skintight leather dress she was wearing, cunningly cut to show bits and pieces of creamy flesh, was definitely hot. Acquiel moved a bit, watching as the flesh shifted in interesting ways, pink bits showing at the most intriguing times.

Mariana laughed again. "Hey! Don't waste it out here!" She gestured at the crowd ahead of them. "Wait until we get inside."

Acquiel nodded, moved to stand alongside the other girl. "Whatever you say, Mistress!"

It didn't take Val long to sate himself. Tessler had been right—these were quality kine—purebreds. Val smiled for a moment. *Maybe we should start our own special version of the 4-H Club. Breed the cattle for quality rather than quantity.* The thought made him laugh out loud. He could just picture some Kindred prince judging kine at an annual fair. *As if the Camarilla would allow such a thing!* He laughed again. *Still, the advertising would be interesting. . . .*

But not inconspicuous.

Val leaned back, pulling the girl next to him onto his lap, gently sucking a bit more blood from the little cut on her neck. *For vitae like this, it might be worth it!* He noticed small scars on her arms and wrists where she had been cut by the tiny knives and razors the blood dolls preferred. He snorted. *As if real vampires would leave such obvious marks!* He felt her move closer to him as he took another tiny sip from her veins. *I won't leave anything to mar this lovely flesh.* She shivered as his tongue touched the welling blood. He felt her heat grow. *She's on the edge of orgasm!* he realized. *Just from the touch of my teeth.*

Cattle.

Val suddenly found himself filled with distaste. *I've*

got to get out of here. He stood as the girl spasmed, caught in her own world of desire. *Got to get away from all these unthinking, unfeeling animals!* He laid the girl onto the seat next to him, carefully licking her neck to remove all signs of his attentions. She moaned again, her body shaking with the aftershocks of her ecstasy. Val recoiled, and left the little group of women, heading into the center of the Club. *I'll find Tessler and tell him I'm leaving.* He looked around. *I didn't want to come in the first place!* A slim arm reached out to him. He pushed it away.

He had barely reached the bar when *she* appeared in front of him. He started to brush past, then realized that the woman in front of him was no kine. *Kindred!* He stopped, curiosity filling him. *One I've never seen before.*

She turned to him, her dark eyes meeting his lighter ones. Val felt a spark leap between them. *I can almost read her mind. . . .* He turned away, shaking his head.

Impossible! He thought. *And yet . . .* He felt the need to look at her again, touch her. *No!* He shook off the feeling with a conscious effort of will. *Kindred are* not *ruled by emotion!* He kept repeating that, over and over, as he forced his body to walk away from her. *I've got to get out of here!* Something inside kept shrieking at him to turn back, to look into this woman's eyes forever. He fought the instinct down, covering it with a litany of Kindred thoughts, pushing it deep into the basement of his mind. He reached the staircase, started up. *Got to get out of here*, then he stopped, sighing. *As soon as I find Tessler!*

God, what a boring night! Mariana sighed. *No, be honest. It's not the Club.* She turned away from the bar. *It's me.* She started to move toward the back rooms, looking for Acquiel. *Time to go home. . . .*

She took a step—and *he* was there. *Kindred! And so familiar. . . .*

Mariana found herself frozen, unable to move. *I know him! But . . .*

Her body began to tingle, just from his nearness. *It's impossible!* She tried to shake herself but found she was trapped, unable to move. *Kindred don't have feelings like that!* Her whole being ached, yearned for one look, one touch . . . *Phillipe?*

She blinked, and he was gone.

Mariana's eyes scanned the room, searching. *There he is!* Halfway across the room, striding toward the staircase, pushing the kine out of his way as he regained the outside world.

She went cold, strength ebbing as he disappeared. *Get hold of yourself! That couldn't have been Phillipe. Phillipe is dead!* Her eyes misted. *I saw him die!*

People were looking toward her. *I must have said that out loud!* She glared at them, forcing their eyes away, down, to the bars, to their drinks. *Cattle!* she thought. *As if you could ever hope to judge me!* She giggled, caught herself. *Me who's lived two of your lifetimes!* The giggle came again, Mariana stifled it, trapped it in her throat. *Got to get hold!* Her mind raced. *Can't lose control. Not here!* She straightened on her seat. *Not now.*

Mariana turned back toward the staircase. *He's gone!* She sighed. *I wonder who he is. . . .* She shook her head. *No! I don't want to know!* She looked around. The drinkers all around her were lost in their own worlds again, deep in meaningless conversations, working at routine seductions. All the things that made up their short and mundane lives. *Fools!*

Where's Acquiel . . . At the thought, she looked to her side, eyes narrowing as they searched the gloom for her companion. Nothing. Mariana rose from the bar, gliding through the crush, touching no one, allowing none to touch her. *She must be nearby,* Mariana thought. *She never wanders too far.* . . .

Mariana finally spotted Acquiel in the main room. Leaning against the big bar, tormenting the human server with every breath. Mariana sighed. *I wish she wouldn't play games like that.* There had been occasions when she had caused problems—Mariana hated trouble. It made her show a side of herself she didn't care to show. She forced all thought of her encounter with the other Kindred to the back of her mind and sauntered to Acquiel's side. *Time for a little discipline.* A smile crossed her face. *Acquiel will like that.*

"Not much of a meeting!"

Lady Ambrosia released her thrall, relaxing against the cushion. "There was more to it than met the eye." She reflected for a moment. "Enough, I think." She turned to her big window, gazed into the heart of the night. "We Kindred are a romantic lot." She smiled a humorless smile. "Even if we lack the means for consummation." She laughed softly, a bare exhalation of breath. "Given the proper impetus, the boy and girl will come together."

Her mouth tightened. "He did show more strength than I expected, breaking the contact so quickly."

"Too much strength to serve our plan?"

"Impossible." Lady Ambrosia stroked her cheek in thought. "Perhaps, though, we should make this night especially memorable for him."

The retainer showed his teeth. "I will arrange it immediately."

Lady Ambrosia turned, let her eyes wander across the city while her busy mind worked to fit tonight's moves into the Great Game. Finally, she nodded. "Yes, do so. And make it something very special. . . . "

Her laugh filled the room.

Val dragged Tessler out of the Club. He'd finally found the other Kindred sprawled on a couch in one of the little upstairs lounges. Tessler had been surrounded by a crowd of blood dolls, and, if his appearance was any indication, he'd been having a whale of a time.

Val soon discovered that Tessler had imbibed a bit too much—sating himself with blood loaded with alcohol and drug toxins. It would be some time before his cousin could think (or walk) straight. Val thought about calling for a cab, but decided that a walk through the streets would be better. Maybe the sights and sounds of the city would help Tessler come around. *And help me forget!*

At first, that seemed a good decision. The early winter winds were blowing, turning the night air fresh and cool, pushing the litter and pollution of the city out to sea. That seemed to help; Tessler quickly recovered enough control to walk on his own, although he still leaned heavily on Val for balance. Val sighed and trudged on. Dark eyes had taken up residence in his mind, demanding his attention, asking for his love.

As *if* I could *love* . . . Val shook his head. He didn't have time for that now. It was late. Only an hour or so before dawn. He glanced at the eastern sky. No light yet. Just the stars. . . . Val smiled. I *used to love looking at the stars.* His mind wandered. *Lying in a field, trying to see the bulls and bears and centaurs.* He laughed. *Never could quite make them out.* He stared at the night sky—and dark eyes stared back.

He would welcome his dreamless sleep *this* day.

The night changed. One instant, Val and Tessler were alone, the only moving things on the darkened block. Now, suddenly, there were others. Silent figures gliding through the shadows.

Some other clan? Val stiffened, glancing at the street signs. *But I'm still in Elysium.* He shook his head at the thought. *With the Sabbat running the show, does that mean anything?* He kept track of the movements, watching out of the corner of his eye as he and Tessler stumbled along. *They're too clumsy to be Kindred. Punks?* That didn't make sense. The human gangs must know it was unhealthy to hunt in this part of town. Val tried to look more closely. *Could they be anarchs?*

That would mean trouble. He might need help from Tessler. Val glanced at his companion. No, he was still out of it. No help at all if it came to a fight. *He doesn't even realize that we're not alone!* Val kept walking, ignoring those around him. *Maybe they don't have anything to do with us at all.*

"Hey!"

No such luck! Val noted that the voice came from an alley to his right. *The others'll stay to the left.*

"Pretty boy!" Val kept moving. "You think that leather outfit of yours makes you tough?"

Tessler stirred, just a little. *Not enough.* Val looked for a place to make a stand. *Over there, where those two buildings join.* Val saw a shallow alleyway. . . .

"Maybe you swish the other way?" That came from

the left. At *least two*. Val sped up, pulling Tessler along. *Just a little farther . . .*

"This is our turf, pretty boy." Behind him. And so slow. *They're kine!* Val shook his head. *Don't they know who they're fooling with?*

A third voice. Still behind, this one to the left: "And you ain't gettin' through without payin' us the toll!"

They don't know!

"That's right!" Four of them. Val quickened his steps a bit more. "The toll, man!"

Fools! Val got ready to make his move. *Still, I'll be careful, they might have guns.* Consciously holding his pace down (there was still the Masquerade to be considered, after all), Val broke into a run over the final few yards to the tiny alcove. Reaching it before the punks could react, he dropped Tessler into the opening and whirled, just in time to see the gang burst into the open.

"You think we gonna let a little wall stop us, pretty boy?"

"You so wrong!"

Val could see five of them now, all young, all dressed in the motley of the street. He looked for arms, saw two—no, three knives. He shook his head. *They are fools! Don't even have guns!* He set himself, putting an arm back to ensure that Tessler was firmly braced in the little alcove behind him.

"Are you sure you know what you're getting into?" Maybe he could get them to talk—avoid killing them. After all, he'd already sated himself. *I'd just be wasting good*—he looked the gang over, appraising them—*well, at least viable blood.*

The punks seemed surprised by the question—and the calm way it was asked.

"What the hell you mean, man?" one of them spit. "We supposed to be afraid of one asshole in leather?"

They were closer now. Val marked the positions of the three knives. Those would hold as much danger as this group could muster. *Don't get overconfident*, he told himself. *Handle them first*, then *laugh at them*. "You *do* know that this is a protected area?"

"Protected by who, pretty boy?" Val marked that one as the leader. Marginally older than the others, he was dressed in newer clothes and had one of the knives. "Pigs?" He snorted. "Ain't no protection but what you make for yourself!"

Val quietly flexed his muscles, preparing . . . "Remember *you* said that."

Val moved. With all the speed his Discipline could muster, he drove himself forward. Just short of the closest of the punks, he set his left foot hard and pivoted on its toe, transferring all his leverage and weight to the right foot, which he swept up and into the knee of his opponent.

Bone shattered.

In the blink of an eye, the punk was down, his knife clattering into the gutter. Val, still moving at incredible speed, let his right foot come down just over the punk, then pivoted, his left foot coming up and around.

Directly into the temple of his second armed opponent. *This is fun!*

The punk's skull shattered with an explosive crash.

Val rolled with the impact, going over the falling body of his foe. He hit the pavement, continued his roll for a split second, them came to all fours, eyes searching for his next target.

He smiled in exhilaration. *It's been too long since I had a real hunt!*

To the other three punks, their prey seemed to disappear, replaced by a blurred figure that shimmered over their friends, leaving nothing behind but limp bodies.

Shock slowed their minds, hampered them as they tried to regroup, try another, more powerful, attack. Stumbling into one another, they formed a rough triangle, Val "trapped" in the middle. They moved in slowly, trying to keep their courage up by yelling and cursing.

"That some fancy fighting, pretty boy!"

"Yeah. Bruce Lee stuff!"

"But Bruce Lee dead, man—just like you gonna be!"

The one on Val's right raised the last knife. "Then we drink your blood!"

Val smiled at them, planning his next move. He was confident now, ready to finish them. One last knife, and then this charade would be over. He leaned slightly forward, shifting his weight, and . . .

Exploded into action!

Val feinted toward the knife wielder, pivoting at the last instant from the awkwardly backstepping punk, turning toward the advancing body on his right. He didn't kick out this time; instead, he drove the flat of his hand into his opponent's jaw, putting all his speed and weight behind the blow.

The punk's neck disintegrated. His head, torn from the body, catapulted across the street, hit the wall opposite, and fell to the street with a sickly, wet sound.

Val twisted, ready to turn to the punk on his left, but his foot skidded in a puddle of blood, throwing him off-balance. He tripped forward, tried to keep his balance, failed. Desperately, he threw himself into a forward roll, half succeeded—and found himself tangled with the headless corpse of the punk he'd just finished. Val sprawled, balance gone, caught in the embrace of rapidly cooling flesh.

"We got you now, bastard!!" The voice was shrill with mindless fear—and close. Too close. Val tried to move—and found he was trapped under the limp body of his victim. He tried to roll out from under, tried to get his feet under him, but the punk's body blocked his every move, its lifeless weight just limp enough to hold him down. Val's neck tingled as he heard the sound of a knife slicing through the air.

No! With speed and strength he had never realized he possessed, Val threw himself forward, lifting the body up and into the thudding blow of the knife. He heard the punk curse, felt the man struggling to pull his weapon free.

Val smiled a hard smile, pushing himself up from the ground, the headless body a shield now. Val shoved the dead flesh into the face of the knife wielder, driving the punk before him.

The punk tried to move to one side, tried to get the knife free, but he never had a chance. Val pushed out from under his limp burden and, again pivoting on firm footing, drove his right hand, fingers extended, into the eyes of his opponent. The punk squealed like a slaughtered pig, knife forgotten, as he clawed at Val's iron grip.

Val's smile widened as he drove his fingers deeper, felt them penetrate soft tissue, cut into the punk's brain.

His opponent sagged, cries cut off.

Val pulled his fingers free, taking a second to wipe off the gore on the corpse's shirt before turning to his one surviving opponent. The punk's eyes darted from side to side, searching for an attack that might succeed—or a way to escape.

Val didn't give him either.

Again moving with speed and grace, Val feinted toward his opponent's knee, then, twisting away at the last moment, he snapped the man's neck like a twig, watching as the body fell, first to its knees, then, lifeless, to the ground.

"Did I miss something?"

Val whirled around, ready, every nerve and muscle tense.

Tessler scratched his forehead. "You do all this yourself?"

Val nodded. "No sweat. They're all cattle—stupid ones at that!" He saw one of the knives at his feet. Odd! He bent to pick it up. *This looks like* . . .

Tessler nudged one of the bodies with his boot. "I see what you mean." He took a step forward. "Hey! This one's still with us!"

Val looked toward the limp body at Tessler's feet. It was his first opponent, still trying to move, although that knee would never work again. Val's right hand shot forward, the knife arcing between Tessler's feet, biting through the right eye of the instantly stilled figure lying there.

"Not anymore."

Tessler pulled the knife out of the skull. "Remind me not to get you mad."

Val nodded. "I will." He took the knife from Tessler. "Notice anything unusual about this blade?"

Tessler leaned forward. "Should I?"

Val turned the knife over, showing the carefully, intricately inlaid hilt to his cousin. "See that?"

Tessler nodded. "Toreador sigil—an artist?"

Val shrugged. "*Someone* with talent. Strange to find human punks with such a thing, though."

"Very."

"I think Don Cruez will want to know about this."

Tessler nodded, then pointed over his shoulder at what little horizon was visible. "I agree—but maybe we'd better get home and out of the light first."

Val smiled. "Whatever you say, cousin."

The two hurried down the street.

"No!" The whimper was high-pitched. "Please, no more!"

Mariana grinned, bringing the riding crop down on Acquiel's red rump again. The girl was loving it. The louder she got, the better she liked it.

"Oh, God, Mariana, please—"

"Please what, baby?"

Acquiel tried to turn her face toward her mistress. It was hard. Mariana had tied her facedown, arms and legs pulled out to their fullest, each limb tied back and down to the legs of the bed below. Still, Acquiel tried, turning her head as far as it would go, trying to get the soaked rags of her hair out of her face. "Please don't use that thing anymore!'

"I thought you loved the crop."

Acquiel nodded. "I do, but right now I really want—really need something else."

Mariana's hand moved down, stroking the other girl's straining bottom. "And what might that be?"

Acquiel moaned. "You know . . ."

Mariana stroked lower, index finger exploring. "No, dear, I don't know."

"Don't leave me like this!"

Mariana reached behind her, pulling a leather and rubber contraption from the wall. "You're giving orders now?"

Acquiel shivered. "Oh please . . ."

Mariana removed her hand from Acquiel's soft places. "I think it's time you were quiet."

"Oh no, Mariana, not that!"

Mariana popped the rubber ball of the gag into Acquiel's mouth. "Yes, that." She tightened the straps, making sure that everything was properly secure.

Just the way Acquiel liked it.

"Now that we have that settled . . ." Mariana selected a new whip from the wall. Leather, with nine tails. She swished it experimentally through the air. "I *will* try something different."

Acquiel whimpered.

Mariana smiled. And brought the lash down precisely where her hand had rested a moment ago. She felt Acquiel shudder with pleasure and pain. *Yes, this is what you want, little one.* She looked out the window—still lots of time before dawn. She pulled the whip back again. *I just wish I was as clear about what I want. . . .*

Val walked down the busy streets of the Lower West Side and sighed. *Everyone's in such a hurry!* He looked up. *Such a pretty night, too.* Last night's wind had blown itself out—and cleansed the city at the same time. *Just beautiful!* It was a perfect night for strolling with a pretty girl. *Which I plan on doing once I find a willing one!*

Val was bumped by a man in a gray suit. He reached out, ready to teach the kine some manners, then thought better of it. *Fool! Where is he rushing?* He looked around, snarling at the whole street full of rushing feet. *Stupid herd animals! Rushing to get home from work. Why?* Val smiled grimly. *So they can watch their stupid TV shows until they doze off on their couches! And then? Do the whole thing over again tomorrow.*

Didn't they realize that they were wasting their lives? He swerved to avoid two older women, watched as they strolled by, oblivious to everything else on the street. Hmmm. He thought. *Think they own the street. Just like the old days.* His thoughts drifted back. . . .

He was nineteen, proudly wearing his uniform for the first time—and he wasn't the only one. The streets were filled with military men, many of them proudly displaying newly acquired women along with their newly acquired uniforms. It was a brilliant sight, a patriot's dream colored in all the hues of the rainbow.

Val, however, had been in too much of a hurry to fully appreciate that. He'd only managed a three-day pass, then it was off to the war—and, he hoped, glory.

I was so young!

Like all the others rushing to taste life, he hurried through the streets, determined to reach home early, surprise his mother and father before they sat down to dinner.

They'd been surprised all right—and delighted by the appearance of their son. "You look fine, son," his father had said with deep pride. "All grown-up—and ready for the good fight." Val had been touched by his father's sincerity, pleased by his obvious approval. It reassured him that he had, in fact, done the right thing.

His mother's reaction, sadly, had been different. She'd never liked the idea of his joining up, certainly not at his age. To be face-to-face with the reality of his service—and the realization that he was leaving almost immediately for a place so far away she couldn't comprehend it—well, it had nearly been too much for her. She had tried to be brave about it—had avoided crying in front of

Val, but he knew she was bothered. He hadn't been sensitive enough to realize how deeply, but he'd been young.

And blind.

Val's mind snapped back to the present. He found himself chest to chest with a pimply teenager. The kid was wearing leathers—and had a real attitude. *Not to mention lousy flossing habits,* Val reflected.

"You listenin' to me? I told you to get outta my way!"

For Val, the world began to move in slow motion. *Two fights in two days.* He sighed. *And I'm supposed to be inconspicuous!* He shook his head, eyes scanning his opponent. *Look at this fool!* Val smiled a crooked smile. *He doesn't know who he's facing, and isn't smart enough to find out before he starts trouble.* He noted the faces of those around him. Most were trying to ignore the confrontation, assuming it would go away if they didn't see it. Others were watching, but surreptitiously, from the corners of their eyes. Those were the ones who would tell the police all the details, even though they hadn't really seen what happened—and wouldn't understand it if they did.

Val sighed. *I was like that once.* . . .

Val had stayed with his family as long as he possibly could. He had until dawn on Sunday to return to his outfit, and it was nearly ten when he left home. He knew he could make it—he'd been careful to plan things out beforehand. There was a coach leaving from Marble Arch at midnight that would get him to Spithead in plenty of time. *I'll make it back to camp with an hour or more to spare.* He smiled. *Even if I fail, it's been worth it!* For the first time in his life his father had actually treated him as an adult! *If that costs me a few hours of extra guard duty or a couple of days of potato peeling, so be it.*

Val grinned. That wouldn't happen, though. He'd make it back. He had enough time.

The streets were crowded when he reached Leicester Square. Evening theaters were letting out, filling the streets with strolling men in uniform and their ladies. True, these uniforms had gold braid, and these ladies were wearing silk and brocade rather than cotton and twill, but it all added up to the same thing—congestion.

Val decided that he'd be better off going through one of the side streets, ducking the crowd. He headed into an alley he was sure connected with Piccadilly. He was halfway down its shadowy length when he bumped into someone. "I'm terribly sorry," he blurted out. "All my fault." Then a pair of viselike hands grabbed him, held him immovable, while two red, glowing eyes appeared before his face. It was the first time Val had ever seen one of the Kindred—and it terrified him. He's *going to kill me!* The realization had come out of nowhere, echoing through Val's mind, forcing all other thoughts from his head, leaving him a paralyzed shell, unable to run, unable to scream.

Val knew helplessness then, for the first time. He was totally unable to do anything to save himself.

But the other didn't kill him. Those eyes bored in, seemed to laugh at Val's fear—and then disappeared, along with the viselike grip. Val found himself alone and free—and he ran like a scared rabbit, racing toward the light at the end of the alley. Light that filled his soul with the hope of salvation.

Val found himself next to the fountain, staring out at passing traffic. It was utterly, eerily normal. A street filled with gaudily dressed gentry, fresh out of the theater and determined to parade their finery for all to see.

Val forced himself to stop and sit on the edge of the fountain. He took a minute to regain his breath—and his sanity. He was sure that he'd faced death in that alley—and just as sure that he'd never feel comfortable in darkness again. He finally gathered enough courage to stand, but was unable to face the long tunnel of tall buildings that stood before him. Instead, he spent the last of his money to hire a hansom to drive him the rest of the way to his coach. Despite the cabby's odd look, Val also kept the little lantern in the passenger compartment on throughout the trip.

He needed the light. All around him, he could see the night move, swirling with life. Life Val had never noticed before . . .

Movement.

Val swept back into the present. Pimple-face was moving, left arm coming up to push Val away, right reaching into a pocket for a knife or gun. Val let him continue the move, remembering what it had been like for him, all those years ago. I *won't kill him*, he decided. *I'll just scare him a little*.

As Val had been scared.

It was a knife the boy came out with. Val smiled. It wasn't even a particularly large one. Perhaps a six- or seven-inch blade . . . *There's something familiar about that*!

Val sidestepped the punk's first thrust. He reached out with his right hand, closed iron fingers on the pressure points of his opponent's thumb, and caught the weapon as it fell from numbed fingers. His left arm hooked behind the thug's back, pushing him forward and past.

The punk hurtled by, barely under control. Val took the time he had gained to look at the weapon, turning it over in his hand. *Inlaid hilt*. And the sigil. *Same as last night*! He pocketed the blade. *Something is* definitely *wrong*. Val shook his head in resignation. *I'm going to* have *to see Don Cruez about this*!

Val patted his pocket, making sure that the little knife was safe, then turned to finish his laughable confrontation with Pimple-face. The teenager had finished his move, his right hand still thrusting forward, empty, into what should have been Val's stomach. Val shook his head. The breather still didn't realize that Val had moved! *Ah well.* . . .

Val flowed in beside the other, grabbed the knife hand hard, and pushed the wrist down. As the hand dropped, Val pressed his hip into the teenager's side and let gravity do the rest.

Time flowed normally again. Pimple-face, disarmed, flew across Val's hip, landing hard, butt first, on the concrete. The teenager's eyes were glazed, just now realizing what had happened. Val stepped forward, reached down to pick up his erstwhile foe. Pimple-face found himself dangling in the air, swimming helplessly, as Val held the collar of his jacket.

Utterly helpless.

"You're a lucky boy." Val let anger flash in his eyes, felt the other's bladder void—and laughed. "Next time, you won't be. Understand?"

The teenager nodded, Adam's apple bobbing. "Y-y-yeah!"

Val tossed him, *Gently now*, into the wall. There was the soft splat of flesh meeting concrete. "Good. Now—get out of my sight!"

Pimple-face scrambled away, not even waiting to get his feet under him. Val smiled. It would be a while before that punk tried anything. He looked at the breathers around him—they were doing their best to look the other way. *Yes*, he thought. *Some things never change.* . . .

*   *   *

Some things never change! Mariana tossed her brushes into the jar, staring dolefully at the painting before her. *Technically, it's perfect.* She sighed. *But there's nothing else there.* She shook her head. *I should be used to this by now. It's the price I pay for being alive without living. Is it worth it?*

Her mind reached back. . . .

Her childhood had been idyllic. Her parents had been French aristocrats: educated, intelligent, wealthy. *They encouraged me to paint from the first time I used a finger painting set.* She giggled. *What was I? Four?*

By the time she was ten, she had a private tutor teaching her all the tricks of artists through the ages. Showing her how to use the tools of what would obviously become her trade.

My folks were so proud! The memory warmed her. *They beamed at my work, always kept the best to be framed and hung and shown to the relatives and neighbors.*

At fourteen, she was given an exhibition at the Palace of the Arts. *That was quite an honor,* Mariana remembered. *Especially for someone my age.* She was declared a savant, and the world was hers for the having.

Then the war came.

At first, it didn't touch Mariana or her family. Oh, her father was concerned as the Nazi army marched through Poland and Belgium—but, after all, those *were* rather minor republics. Peasant states, really, where the people did not even speak a civilized language.

France would not be that easy to conquer. After all, she had the Maginot Line—and behind that, the Allied armies. *The Germans were not able to reach Paris in the First World War,* he had told his wife and daughter. *They're certainly going to do no better this time!*

Mariana's father was wrong. The Germans were

going to do much better. In a matter of weeks, they bypassed the vaunted Maginot defenses, defeated the Allied armies, and, within months, their jackbooted troops were pounding through the Arc de Triomphe. France was defeated. *And I was terrified!*

Time passed—and things did not seem to change. School went on as usual. *I stopped being afraid*, Mariana remembered. *Everything seemed the same; I read, I studied, I painted.* Art was still Mariana's life—and art was flourishing, even under the Third Reich. Hitler and Goering were art collectors. Who would harm a simple artist?

I was so naive. . . .

Mariana had learned just how much things had changed when she tried to walk home from the conservatory late one evening in 1941. Normally, her father would arrange for a car to pick her up, but rationing had become very tight as the Germans planned their invasion of Britain. There just wasn't enough gasoline to drive Mariana to and from school. *Besides, I was an adult, eighteen years old.* She shook her head. *Eighteen . . .*

The school was on the bus line, and Mariana had assured her parents she was perfectly capable of walking the half mile or so to the bus stop.

And so, eighteen, naive, and beautiful, Mariana had walked, without thought, past a pair of German soldiers . . .

They grabbed me without thought, without effort. . . . The memory was dull in her mind. *Before I could scream, I was flat on my back, skirts hiked over my shoulders. . . .*

Mariana's eyes went hard. *I cried when the first of them forced himself into me. Begged with him, pleaded, threatened . . .*

None of it did any good. The soldiers were members of the Master Race. The cries of a French girl meant nothing to them.

I thought they'd kill me when they were done. I wanted them to kill me. They didn't. Just pulled Mariana to her feet and shoved her toward the bus stop. *They laughed. Told me I shouldn't miss my ride home, told me I should stop again tomorrow, that they'd wait for me. . . .*

That was the beginning of the terror. It got worse. Two weeks later, her father failed to come home from the office. Her mother had applied to the police for help. *They told her it was a military matter. The Germans never answered questions about military operations.*

A month later, the two women were thrown out of their home. A German colonel needed a field headquarters, and, after all, two women didn't need all that space, did they?

Mother and I moved what we could salvage into the gamekeeper's cottage, on the edge of the estate. It was tiny. . . . It was also warm and dry.

Time passed. The conservatory closed. *Not enough fuel available to light and heat it.* Mariana stayed at home and continued to paint, using anything she could find as her canvas. Her new art was dark, disturbed. She didn't quite recognize the world in those paintings, but she knew it was closer to the real world than the sunny illustrations she had done earlier.

More time passed. Mariana's world narrowed down to her canvases, one after the other, each darker and more frightening than the one before. *I thought perhaps I had gone insane. Thought that the rape had unhinged me.* She shook her head. *I was still naive. . . .*

She kept painting, until, finally, even that was taken from her.

"I'm sorry," the clerk had told her. "But there is no paint left. None at all."

"But what am I to do?" Mariana had been shocked. There had always been paint. Always.

The clerk sighed. "I don't know what to tell you. It's the war." He'd rubbed his forehead. "The war . . ."

Mariana had gone home and cried—for the first time. *I didn't cry for my father, or for my virginity. But this . . .*

She had lost her art. *What was left?*

Then Phillipe arrived.

Phillipe! Mariana's thoughts raced. *That man in the bar was so much like Phillipe!*

"Mariana?" The voice seemed to come from far away. Mariana heard it, recognized it. *Acquiel? But how . . . ?* Then she snapped out of the reverie, found herself in the cold loft, staring at the dead canvas. . . .

"Mariana! Are you all right?" The other girl was hugging Mariana tightly, standing on tiptoes to look into her mistress's eyes. "Talk to me, Mariana! Please!"

Mariana shook her head, willing herself back into the present. "I've got to find him!"

"Find who?"

"Phillipe!"

Acquiel stepped back, looking at Mariana with puzzled eyes. "Who's Phillipe?"

Mariana reached out, pulled Acquiel to her, reveled in her warmth, her *aliveness*. "Don't worry, pet, he's just an old friend."

"One of you?"

Mariana nodded, smiling. "Yes, one of us."

"Cool!" The other girl's hand reached up, cupping Mariana's breast, warming her still more. "And I like the picture."

Mariana laughed, bending her lips toward Acquiel's

pliant nudity. "It sucks." She licked her lips. "And now it's time for me to do the same!"

The blood doll laughed.

"It begins, milady."

"Just as I planned!" There was the rustle of coverings as Lady Ambrosia changed position, pushing away the thrall she had been dining on. "Let us watch through the eyes of our cat's-paw!"

The retainer frowned microscopically. "I do not have that power, milady."

He recoiled at the flash of irritation in Lady Ambrosia's eyes. "Fool! Do you think I don't know that!" She gestured to a seat alongside the door of the sanctum. "Take your seat and I will link my mind with yours." A hint of a smile touched her lips. "My power will more than suffice for this task!"

The retainer sat. "As you say, milady."

"Always."

They called him the Idealist, a name that, to some Brujah, would have been an insult.

To Don Cruez, though, it was only the truth—a comment on who and what he was. The tall Kindred believed in only one thing—the Traditions. He would do whatever was necessary to keep those Traditions pure and active. Anything.

That's why the Brujah had named him as their Justicar.

That's what made him the most dangerous being

in the city. Even if those of the Sabbat didn't know it yet.

Don Cruez had quietly moved into an abandoned movie theater on the Brooklyn side of the East River. It was perfect for him. Large, near the city which he studied, defensible against any force, and, of course, dark— the old theater had no windows. None.

Val walked slowly up to the door. He hated to visit Don Cruez on official business; it made him feel like he was taking advantage of their relationship. This time, though . . .

Val activated the knocker, waiting for the summons to enter. *I've got to talk to him!* he thought, fingering the two knives in his pocket. *Too much has happened.* He pulled the knives out, turning them over in his hands. *They're beautiful, works of art.* He touched them gently. *And familiar somehow. As if I knew the artist.*

Val shook the thought off. *Silly,* he told himself. *I don't have a jot of Auspex! Can't let my imagination run away with me!*

The door opened. Val found himself looking into the chest of Topper, the Justicar's chief retainer. "Come in, young Percival." Topper's voice was deep and slow, like a bell tolling somewhere in his chest. "Don Cruez is expecting you."

Expecting me? Val's thoughts raced. *But how could he know I was coming?*

Topper answered in the same breath, as if he had been reading Val's mind. "The tale of your problem has preceded you." The big man's face creased in what must have been planned as a smile. "As has your cousin."

Tessler! Val relaxed. *Of course!* His cousin loved a fight—and if the Sabbat were actually trying to use the city's gangs in a pogrom against the Brujah . . . Val's face set. That would start a fight that would be remembered for a long time.

If anyone survived to remember it!

Topper led Val into a smallish room, lined on two sides with framed posters from classic films. The Justicar loved films and the stage—so much so that there were those who whispered that he had started life as an actor.

"Percival!" Don Cruez's deep, beautifully resonant voice added weight to the rumor. "Please, have a seat!" He waved to several overstuffed chairs placed in front of a wide desk. "Perhaps you'd care for a drink."

"No, thank you." Val took a seat, nodding at Tessler, who sat nearby. "Good evening, cousin."

Tessler looked a bit sheepish. "I thought the Justicar should know as soon as possible, and as my haven is closer than yours . . . "

"Of course." Val took the two knives out of his jacket, placing them on the Justicar's desk, careful not to mar its beautiful finish. "These are the knives in question."

Don Cruez picked up the weapons, cradling them in large, capable hands. "I was under the impression that there was only one?"

Val sat back in his seat. "I had a second . . . encounter."

"Again!" Tessler leaped out of his chair and began pacing, coming within millimeters of bumping into Topper, who was entering with a carafe and glasses. "Twice! That proves it, sir! The Sabbat are aware of our presence and are using kine gangs to attack us! We must counterattack—at once!"

"Sit down." Tessler stopped in his tracks as the Justicar's gaze transfixed him. "Only I say what must and must not be done!"

Tessler sat. "But—"

Don Cruez turned away from Tessler, effectively shutting him up. He gestured to Topper, who poured a little ruby red liquid into a glass and carefully placed it before his master. The Justicar picked it up as he transferred his attention to Val. "Certainly this story of yours is disturbing, and if true . . ." He took a careful, measured sip of the drink, then nodded. Topper moved to fill the others' glasses. " . . . must be dealt with."

Tessler found his voice. "Of course it must!"

The Justicar put the drink down, his long tongue darting out to blot up a tiny drop left at the corner of his mouth. "But first we must make sure it *is* true."

Val sat forward. "Do you doubt my word?"

Don Cruez shook his head. "Never." He smiled grimly. "But sometimes, things are not what they seem."

Tessler started to get up, then thought better of it. "What do you mean?"

The Justicar made a gesture. "Such an act could mean many things. Perhaps the Sabbat have become aware of our mission here and wish to make their displeasure known." He looked at the knives and shrugged. "Or perhaps, more simply, a gang of kine stumbled upon the haven of one of the Kindred and found these knives inside."

I *hadn't thought of that*! Val considered it, then: "Is that possible?"

Don Cruez nodded. "Although I think I would have heard of such a thing by now."

"Someone would have." Tessler nodded.

"Then, of course, there's always the possibility of"—the Justicar took another sip of his drink—"a Methuselah."

Tessler leaned forward. "One of them!"

Val's mind raced. *Of course! One of their damn games!*

Don Cruez turned to Tessler, taking another sip of his drink. "As you can see, anything is possible." He carefully set the little glass on his desk. "That is why we must be very sure before we act."

"But how *can* we be sure?"

"We will use the sigils on these blades." The Justicar's fingers caressed the steel. "With them, we can find the Toreador who did this work, and from him . . ."

"We can find out why it was done!" Tessler did get up now. "I'll start on it right away!"

The Justicar's glance turned cold. "You'll do nothing but sit down! I want Percival to investigate this."

Tessler's face showed his puzzlement. "Val? But . . ."

"Percival is not as hotheaded as other members of the Brujah." Again Don Cruez's gaze burned into Tessler. "And not as willing to start what might be the last war." He turned to Val, holding one of the knives out, hilt first. "Are you willing to undertake this?"

Val took the weapon, nodding slowly. "If you wish it so."

The gaze warmed more, an approving warmth. "I do, my son." Topper appeared, signaling an end to the interview. "Report to me when you have some answers." Don Cruez nodded at Val. "Until then, beware of the gangs—and the Sabbat."

"So. Cruez suspects the truth."

"Will that cause a problem?"

"Don't be silly. The boy will meet the girl, and then . . ." The darkness reverberated with the old one's laughter. "All will happen as it should!"

*   *   *

Dieter Kleist was lounging in the depths of the Club's Treasure Room when Mariana found him. He was not one of her favorite Kindred. *He's always after something.* She sighed. *But this time, so am I.*

"Dieter?" She kept her voice low. "May we talk?"

He nodded, eyes not rising from the little screen he was holding on his lap. "Certainly, Mariana. Just give me a minute, if you please."

Mariana nodded Acquiel toward the bar, watching casually as the little blonde sauntered away. *I don't know why she bothers with clothes,* Mariana thought. *She certainly doesn't leave anything to the imagination.* Acquiel sneaked a peek back at her. *And she knows I'm watching! I wonder if I have her too close to the edge.* Mariana frowned. *Close enough to give her a touch of Kindred discipline, perhaps . . . ?*

There was a soft *snap!* behind her as Kleist closed the lid of his laptop.

"So, Mariana." She turned toward the soft, carefully controlled voice. "To what do I owe the pleasure of this visit?"

Mariana looked at the tiny rectangle in his lap. "What's that you were playing with?"

Dieter smiled. "Just a little job for one of our brethren." He reopened the cover of his little machine, showing her the tiny keyboard. "They get smaller all the time, don't they?"

She nodded, then grinned as she realized the opening he'd given her. "Are you talking about the computer? Or . . ."

Kleist got it. He nodded, a touch of anger creeping into his voice. "Of course, what else? With this little laptop, I can tap into any net in the world!"

Mariana gestured. Even at this early hour, the Club was crowded. "Why do it here, with all these people around?"

Dieter smiled, pulling a little wire out from under his feet. "The cattle make good camouflage—and when I use the Club's phone line, nobody can trace me back to any of my havens."

Mariana smiled and nodded. N*obody* wanted their haven threatened. "Smart."

"Of course it's smart!" Dieter put his hands behind his neck, letting his body drop deeper into the softness of his chair. "Enough of this mindless banter—you want something from me. What is it?"

Mariana sat down next to Kleist, bringing herself level with him. "I met someone the other night. . . ."

Dieter looked at her, eyes quizzical. "Kine?"

She shook her head. "No. Kindred."

He sat up a bit, interest sparking. "So what's the problem?"

She looked down at the hands linked in her lap, happy to see that they were quite still. "I want to see him again."

"So see him."

She gritted her teeth; this was the hard part. "I don't . . . don't know who he is."

His laugh filled the little room. "And you want *me* to find him for you!" He looked at her now, mouth showing a broad smile that never for an instant touched his eyes. "And just how do I do that? Do you have a photograph? A license number?" He shook his head in disgust. "Anything?"

"Well, I do have this." She pulled out a piece of paper with a carefully accurate drawing of Val's face on it. "It's as close as I can make it."

Dieter stared at the drawing. "It *might* be enough." He

took it from her. "Of course, there's always my fee to consider. . . . "

"Yes, I expected that." Mariana looked him in the eye, mouth set. "Knowing you, you'll already have something in mind."

"As a matter of fact"—Dieter grinned, confident now that the deal was all but done—"I do. Something simple." His eyes drifted toward the bar. "Who knows, she might even like it!"

Mariana followed his glance, saw Acquiel undulating to the music in the main room. "You want Acquiel?" Her mind locked for a moment. "Permanently?"

He shook his head. "No, of course not." His grin widened. "Just for a few . . . sessions."

Mariana nodded slowly. Dieter was known to have odd tastes. "You won't hurt her."

He chuckled. "Well, that depends on whose definition we use, doesn't it."

Mariana stood up. "Nothing permanent."

"Never."

Mariana started toward the bar. "Then I believe we have an arrangement."

Dieter opened his laptop, plugging the phone line in. "Come back here in two, maybe three nights."

"So soon?"

He grinned at her. "My dear, if I don't have the answer by then, I'll never have it."

"Kleist's back on the Internet. Second time tonight."

Dim light glinted on the edge of a sharp smile as Lady Ambrosia stretched. "Is that something new?"

"Not really." The retainer hesitated. "But his usage

pattern is rather odd. He seems to be doing an all-out search."

Lady Ambrosia came upright, smile gone. "A search for what?"

Another moment of hesitation. "If I read his parameters correctly—"

"Spare me the techno bullshit!" Red eyes flashed as the Methuselah came to her feet. "What is he looking for?"

The retainer backed up half a step, took a breath. "I think he's trying to find a Kindred's haven."

Lady Ambrosia turned toward the huge window, eyes flashing into the night as she integrated that bit of data with all the others she worked with. "That could be dangerous."

"Should I ensure his failure?"

She turned back to the retainer, eyes still calculating, mind still leaping from possibility to possibility. "No." Her voice showed the slightest hint of uncertainty. "Not yet." She motioned to one of her thralls. "Have him watched, though. And find out just who he's looking for. We don't want him interfering with any of our little . . . endeavors."

"I'll see to it." The retainer backed out as his mistress began feeding.

Val woke up seconds after the sun disappeared over the horizon. It was quiet in his haven. *Quiet as the tomb!* he thought humorlessly. He had a task to accomplish—and not a single idea how to go about it. *I'll have to be careful how I handle this,* he thought, *because if the Sabbat really are trying to destroy us, I could end up playing right into their hands.* He got up, pulled clothes together. *I need a starting place, someone I can talk to. Who do I know who might be able to help . . . ?*

He stood in place, half-clad, silent. Thoughts flowed through his brain; ideas came, were tested, and set aside. Someone, somewhere, could lead him to the creator of those knives; he only had to ask the right people the right questions.

But who were the right people? And what were the right questions? He didn't know, and the more he thought about it, the more confused he became.

This isn't helping. He sprang into action, pulling the rest of his clothes on. *I'm no good at thinking these things out.* He grabbed a jacket from his rather sparse closet. *Maybe I need a solid meal.*

Val headed for the street.

It was cold out. The wind swirled through the man-made canyons of the New York skyline. *Tough night to hunt.* Val sniffed a hint of snow in the air. *Worse later—especially if it starts snowing.* He smiled grimly. *Good! I could use the challenge. Things have been too easy around here lately!* He looked around. Which way to go. Downtown? Into the Village? Lots of possibilities there, blood dolls, street people, gangers . . . He thought of the two knives. He'd gotten them downtown. *Maybe there are more of them*—he could search around, find somebody actually holding one of them, question him.

No. *Tessler'll be down there. Trying to beat me to the prize.* Val smiled tightly. *Show me up in front of Don Cruez, prove he's more capable . . .* Val nodded to himself. *I don't want to deal with that tonight.* Uptown then. The world of brownstones and brick, where the rich and powerful looked down on the rest of the world.

Uptown! Val's smile widened, showing sharp, ready teeth. *Where the livin' is easy!* He licked his lips. *And the blood is rich!*

* * *

Mariana arrived at the Blood Club an hour or so after sundown. Acquiel hadn't been too keen on the idea of being loaned to another Kindred, so Mariana had taken the time to show her why she should do it.

For both, it had been time *very* well spent.

Now, just for good measure, Mariana led Acquiel into the club on a leash, the tight collar around the blood doll's neck giving her very little choice in the matter. The blonde was on a short chain—and loving every minute of it.

"Kleist come in yet?" Mariana asked Andy, the Toreador actor who amused himself by playing "Graves, the Butler."

"Down there." Graves pointed into the Treasure Room. "He's pretending to be engrossed in that damned machine of his." Andy smiled at her. "But he keeps asking whether you two are here yet."

"Thanks." Mariana started toward the staircase, Acquiel obediently following.

Graves's huge hand stopped her. "Be careful with him." The butler glanced around, making sure there was no one in sight. "People have been asking questions."

"People?"

Graves nodded. "People you don't want to get involved with."

Mariana's mind flashed back:

Germans kicked down the door to the cottage she and her mother had worked so hard to make livable. Mariana had been caught in the living room, painting. She screamed when the men marched in. No one came to help, and the Germans seemed to enjoy the sound! These were different from the other Germans she had met. Not soldiers. No uniforms. These were hard men, quiet, alert. All dressed alike in long brown leather trench coats. Not an insignia or patch among them. They seemed colorless, monotone.

Brown and flesh.

They hadn't said a word to Mariana. Just pulled her away from her easel, jerked her arms behind her back, and handcuffed her. *I didn't even have time to run!*

Her mother tried to stop them, fight them off. They just brushed her aside like some kind of annoying insect. Mariana was dragged to their waiting car. *I never even got to say good-bye.*

She never had another chance.

Mariana's memories of the following days were mercifully dim. The brown men drove her to the Rue Madeleine, headquarters of the dreaded Gestapo. *It was the dark world I had spent so much time painting.*

Chained in place, she was stripped of clothing and dignity. Naked, she was given to the guards, who were encouraged to rape her, over and over. *They just grinned. Never said a word. Just grinned and thrust into me.*

Centuries later, she was carried into a brightly lit chamber where more guards, still grinning, took turns beating her. First with their fists and belts, later with whips and bits of wire. *I never knew why they were hurting me. They never asked me anything. Nothing at all.*

She was beaten for hours, day after day, then thrown back into her cell to recover. Mariana's mind wavered under the constant torture. *I would have told them anything to stop the pain.*

She tried. Screamed out confessions, begged them to listen to stories that weren't even marginally true.

Nothing satisfied them.

Finally, after an eternity, she was strapped, nude, to

a wooden chair. One of the brown-leather men—this one unsmiling, sat down next to her.

"So, Fräulein." His face twisted at her smell—she hadn't been allowed to bathe since her arrival. "Are you ready to talk to us?"

Mariana's head spun. She had been trying to talk to them all the time! "Wh-what do you want to know?"

The unsmiling man leaned forward, eyes burning. "We want to know where Phillipe is!"

"Phillipe?"

His hand thundered into her face, rocking her head back, stunning her for a second. "You think you've been hurt? You know nothing of pain! I could make you beg to tell me—scream to die."

Mariana shivered. She knew, far back in her cringing brain, that what he said was true. But Phillipe? What could she possibly tell them about him?

"I don't know where he is." She started to cry. "Really, he just came to our house, I don't know anything about him!"

The unsmiling man's mouth cracked open, showing teeth in what might have been meant as a grin. He gestured. "You will tell us, Fräulein." Two of the grinning guards appeared, new instruments of torture in their hands. "Believe me, it is only a matter of time."

They started again. Hot pokers, torches, pincers. I *thought* I *was in* Hell!

Mariana had screamed, begged, promised, done everything she could think of, but they kept hurting her, hurting her. . . .

Finally, when she had fainted for the fourth time, they freed her from her seat of fire and took her to a cell. "Have a nice rest, Fräulein." They laughed as they tossed her onto the stone floor. "We'll be back. . . . "

She lay there, without the strength to move. *I wanted to die. Anything to stop them from hurting me again.*

I couldn't even faint! Mariana wept then, bitterly. Wept for her pain, her life.

My art . . .

"Mariana?" The voice was dim, far away. "Mariana!"

Mariana climbed back into the present. *Never again!* she thought. Below her, the music had started. Mariana looked around. Graves was no longer in sight. *I was dreaming that long?* "Come on, Mariana!" Acquiel was pulling at the leash. "Let's go down!"

Acquiel was trying her best to reach the staircase, while being careful not to open her collar. Mariana sighed. *At least she's still showing some discipline.* Then smiled. *Too bad. It would be fun to punish her!* Still . . . "All right, little one. Just a minute."

They started down the stairs, Mariana's eyes immediately going to the dark entrance of the Treasure Room. Her mind filled with memories and Andy's warning as she sought Kleist. What had he meant?

People you don't want to get involved with . . .

"I have discovered what Kleist is looking for." There was a touch of pride in the retainer's voice.

"*You* discovered?" Lady Ambrosia stirred from her pillows, eyes fastening on the face of the man. "I was under the impression that Kleist was the best techno hacker in New York."

"That is so."

The air went suddenly electric as Lady Ambrosia's eyes flashed red lightning. "Don't play games with me, worm!" Her hand shot out, instantly sprouted claws gripping the retainer's surprised neck tightly, drawing a slow welling of blood. "Never with *me*!" The claws loosened, drew back, a tiny drop of blood disappearing onto a long tongue. "Now report properly!"

"Yes, milady!" The voice was shaken. "I caused the telephone lines into the Club to be monitored . . ."

The air tingled with fresh energy, more lightning. "You meddled with the Blood Club!"

The voice lowered, its owner shaken. "Only to protect milady!" The voltage drained fractionally.

"The Blood Club has a special place in my plans. It is never to be compromised." Eyes now hard as stone bored into the retainer. "Remove all monitors immediately you leave my presence—and never do such a thing again . . ." Lady Ambrosia paused for a heartbeat, new possibilities running through her mind. Finally, she nodded: " . . . without my express order."

The retainer's voice showed his relief. "As you wish."

"Now . . ." The hand-turned-claw gestured minutely.

"I monitored Kleist's communications until I had a significant sample, then ran a simulation on our mainframe."

Lady Ambrosia's expression reflected her hatred and distrust of computers—the same distrust she had for anything beyond her control. Still, one had to make do. "And?"

The voice strengthened. "As I suspected, it showed he was running a search for a Kindred haven." He bent forward. "But not that of any elder, primogen, or prince."

The Methuselah allowed her puzzlement to show. "Who then?"

"Our subject!" The retainer allowed himself a short chuckle. "Kleist is acting as an agent for the girl—looking for the boy!"

"Are you sure?"

The head nodded. "Absolutely positive."

Lady Ambrosia turned away, mind flashing through the possibilities this might present. "Has Kleist succeeded in his search?"

"Not yet."

"See that he does."

The retainer stood and moved to withdraw from the dark room. "Yes, milady."

"And as soon as you complete your task—"

"Milady?"

"Remove all monitors—immediately!"

"It shall be done." The door closed, locking with a clearly audible *thunk*.

Lady Ambrosia stared at the closed door for a moment, mind running through moves and countermoves. "Yes," she nodded to herself. "It had better be!"

Val took the subway (*so proletarian*) all the way uptown, getting off in the east eighties, just a few blocks from the Metropolitan Museum of Art. He walked past the ornate front of the building, noting a party just starting at the uptown end. *Must be in the Egyptian temple they transplanted a couple of years ago*. He stopped at the corner as the light changed, watching guests walking into the big greenhouse that was built around the limestone monument.

And remembered . . .

The same temple, not under glass now, under the sun, baking in the sands of the desert. *Just like me!* Val's mind filled with the heat, the dry, kiln-hot air. Once again he felt the sun burn away at his skin, slowly leeching the water out of his body. Killing him. . . .

I was too stupid to fear it then. He shook his head. *It was just the sun. I saw it every day. . . .*

It'd been his first pass since he got to Egypt. *Eighteen hours they gave us. To see the wonders of the ancient world.* He smiled. *They knew Napoleon was coming. Knew he outnumbered us three to one, so they let us have a last look at life.*

Her name was Miriam. . . .

They'd rented camels that afternoon, riding through the worst of the day's heat. *She told me I had to see the pyramids at dusk, with the sun setting behind their stone faces.*

He'd been willing to do anything she wanted.

They'd finally come bumping over a rise, him cursing the awkward gait of the animal, her laughing at his curses. . . .

And there they were! From a distance, they'd seemed perfect. Spearpoints arcing into the sky, edges hard and straight. *Just like the books described!*

Closer and he began to see the ravages of time. Oh, the stones were still carefully dressed, perfectly placed, but their limestone surface had been torn away, leaving the wall of the Great Pyramid jagged, like some great decaying tooth . . .

Forever, he'd thought. *They've been here forever.* He thought of the coming invasion. *How long do I have? Years? Months?* He glared at the pyramids.

Days?

His face must have reflected his thoughts because suddenly she was there, her soft lips covering his, driving all thoughts of tomorrow, all fears of death far away. His arms and body moved without thought, pulling her to the ground, joining with her, in the most ancient act of life, on that eternal plateau. . . .

"Are you all right?" Val snapped back to the present. There was a woman (a *girl*) standing about twenty feet away. She had a medium-sized dog on a leash; the animal was doing its damnedest to keep as far away from Val as it could. "I'm sorry." Val smiled.

"My mind was a thousand miles away."

He looked the girl over. Twenty-eight, maybe twenty-nine. *Pretty, well-off.* Val smiled. *Yes, she'll do.* He reached out with his mind and touched the dog, squatting down to pet the little animal as it trotted over to him.

"She likes you!" The woman seemed surprised. "She's usually afraid of everybody!"

Val scratched the top of the dog's head. "There's no reason for her to be afraid of me." The woman smiled at him, moving closer. Val stood up. "You know, this isn't a safe place at night. Can I walk you home?"

The woman and dog both looked at him, four animal eyes filled with lust. "All right."

He'd sated his thirst before they reached Fifth Avenue.

"You haven't found him?" Mariana leaned forward, uncomfortable on the room's overstuffed couch. Acquiel, still on a short leash, knelt quietly in front of her, back arched, breasts out as far as she could push them. Kleist couldn't keep his eyes off the collared blonde. And Acquiel was making sure he had something to see!

Mariana was getting angry. "Kleist!" This was getting her nowhere. "I thought you could find anyone!"

Kleist shrugged, forcing his eyes to drift from the blonde to his laptop screen. "This one is smart." He shook his head. "And has friends who are almost as good as I am."

Mariana sighed and got to her feet. "Then I guess I'll

just have to try someone else. Perhaps one of the Nosferatu."

Kleist's eyes glinted at Acquiel as she wriggled upright. "I'll keep trying, and if I do find something . . . "

"Our deal still stands."

Mariana started out of the room, Acquiel heeling to one side—just close enough to rub a hip against Kleist as she passed. "Wait!"

Mariana turned. "Yes?"

Kleist was punching keys, calling up information, screen after screen scrolling in front of his eyes. "I've got something!"

"Come on." Mariana looked doubtful. "You're expecting me to believe that you found something just this minute?"

Kleist looked up at her, face serious. "I'm not trying to trick you! My tapeworm just now found what it was looking for." He tapped more keys. "Look!"

Mariana looked into the little LCD screen—right into the face of Phillipe. . . .

Please stop crying.

She started, shocked at the voice. She was in her cell, near death, her body covered with cuts, bruises, burns—every breath a separate torture. . . . *I'd given up hoping. I just wanted to die. Prayed to die. I thought the voice was in my mind. . . .* It wasn't, though. It was inside her cell, behind her.

Phillipe's voice.

"Phillipe." Mariana tried to sit up, tried to turn, but her body wouldn't move.

"It's all right. Just lie still."

She felt him sit down on the side of the bed, felt his face touching her neck. She relaxed into the embrace. *Phillipe is here. It's going to be all right.*

"It's going to be all right." His words aped her thoughts. "Just relax. This won't hurt."

There was a slight sting in her neck, almost unfelt in the midst of her other agonies. Mariana began to feel euphoric. The world swelled and ebbed, the horror moved away from her. Farther and farther away. Something touched her mouth. She swallowed automatically, tasting sweet saltiness.

She died.

"That's him." She looked at Kleist. "That's Phillipe. Do you know where to find him?"

Kleist nodded. "It's all here. But first . . . "

She motioned Acquiel to her, knelt her in front of the other. "As we agreed." The little blood doll shivered, whether in fear or anticipation, Mariana couldn't tell.

The uptown woman, Christine, was a patron of the arts. One of those who found the theater fulfilling. Val took a moment to glance through her collection of posters and mementos while she slept.

Langella as Dracula! Val smiled. *Swishing around the stage like . . .*

Of course! Val's eyes widened. *Why didn't I think of him before?* Val grabbed his coat, headed for the door. There was a Toreador who *might* be able to help him. *If I approach him properly . . .* Val glanced at his watch; the timing was just about right. Val would have to kill about an hour. He turned toward the bedroom. The uptown woman was still in there. Val grinned and changed direction.

The wind was still blowing when he finally went back onto the streets. Not as strongly now, with the nearby park to dissipate much of its force. Val stuck his hands into the pockets of his jacket and headed for Midtown. He strolled into the park, glancing at the glass-enclosed Egyptian temple to his left and the beautiful people milling around it.

Val shook his head in disgust. The Egyptians had built these temples and pyramids as vaults to ensure their eternal protection. *Eternal. There's a big word.* Val grinned ruefully. *The "eternal" temple in there lasted less than a millennium!* Then the cattle moved it here, thousands of miles from its native soil—and the souls it was supposed to protect.

All to satisfy the curiosity of a bunch of half-witted gawkers.

What a waste.

Val shrugged. *It's not my problem.* He turned his back on the Egyptians, *and my little Uptown Girl.* He found himself suppressing a laugh as the Billy Joel tune threaded through his head. *Stupid!* he thought as he headed into Central Park. *She didn't look at all like Christie Brinkley.* He shook his head. *That's a pity!*

He strode into the park, the girl's blood rushing through his veins.

And stopped almost immediately. *There's something happening up ahead!*

Old reflexes took over. Val glided into the skeletal bushes on the side of the path, noiselessly flitting through their dry branches. *Just a little farther.* He listened again. *Near the middle of the park.* Val moved cautiously. *In the zoo! How quaint!* It might be another gang, maybe with more of those damn knives, although he doubted it. *That would be too much of a coincidence!* Still, stranger things had happened.

It *was* gangers. Although they didn't have Toreador knives. What they *did* have were three of Val's uptown girls, although in their current state of (un)dress it was hard to tell. Val worked his way closer to the scene, trying to see what was going on. *I really should leave. None of this is any of my business. . . .*

The leader of the gang was a small man, five feet tall, perhaps 105 pounds. What he lacked in size, he made up for in attitude. He had one of the girls—*the prettiest,* Val noted—backed up against the polar bear enclosure. Her flesh was goose-bumped from the cold, Val could see, and her eyes were wide with fright. *This is not some sort of kine gang initiation.*

"So, Mama! You tryin' to walk through Trey's territory without payin' the toll?"

"Toll?" She was shivering now.

"Yeah, Mama—toll!" He slapped her casually, almost gently. "Don't you know nothin'?"

"Please, we're just working girls tryin' to make a couple of bucks at the museum . . ."

"Big party, eh?"

The girl nodded.

"Lots of big shots?"

Another nod.

The little man edged forward, eyes never leaving his prey, "Then why wasn't Trey invited?"

The girl stared blankly.

Trey turned to his followers. "So, we got these hookers tryin' to take a little shortcut through our park. What we gonna charge 'em to do that?"

The punks holding the other girls started to laugh. One started dancing around, hips grinding suggestively. "How 'bout we have a little party of our own!"

Trey nodded, a nasty grin on his face. "Yeah, we *gonna* have a party—but that ain't no toll—I need to charge these 'hoes a toll to teach them not to mess with me."

Another punk, a big man with a nasty scar running

down his bare chest, waved an arm at one of the girls. "This one's knocked up—why don't we feed her baby to the bear."

Trey's eyes lit up. "Feed the baby to the bear?"

The big man pulled out a knife. "Why not? Ain't nothin' to it."

Don't do that.

Trey turned back to the other girl. "What you say, Mama? That a good enough toll for you—you remember that? Tell it to all your friends?"

The girl's shivering was more intense now. "Please, don't hurt us. . . . "

Trey slapped her again, harder now. "Hey, Mama—you don't never tell Trey what to do—he tells you—and you better obey, dig?" Trey pushed the girl down on her knees. "Stay there, now, until I give you somethin' to do!" He turned to the big man. "You can get the baby out?"

Teeth glinted as the punk nodded.

Please don't.

Trey shrugged. "Then do it." He draped himself on a bench across from the bear cage. "I ain't never seen no baby cut out of no uptown mama before."

The knife flashed in the darkness.

Damn.

Val was there before the blade could touch flesh, snapping the man's wrist and taking the knife before the big man realized he had company. His howl of pain came just as Val was pulling the knife from the chest of Punk #2. The three other punks holding the girls were dead before #2 hit the ground.

That left Trey.

"Go home, girls." Val advanced toward the paralyzed gang leader. "And don't come this way again."

He didn't have to tell them twice. The three women,

still shivering and sobbing, gathered up what was left of their clothes and disappeared.

None of them looked at the five bodies scattered around the zoo grounds.

Val waited for them to leave, then he turned to the gang leader.

Trey screamed when he saw Val's smile.

Dieter Kleist surprised Mariana by asking her to join them. He escorted the tall Toreador and her leashed doll to "one of my havens." An abandoned pier on the East Side waterfront. Outside, it looked like all the other piers—dilapidated, rotting, ready to fall into the ocean. Inside . . .

Inside it looked like Toreador heaven.

"This is a Renoir, isn't it?" Mariana stared at the painting, carefully hung under a precision spotlight.

Kleist nodded. "There's another over on that side, near the Van Gogh and the Manet."

Mariana wandered around, staring at the various pieces of art, some by well-known artists, some by lesser, but no-less-talented, figures. "Frazetta?"

"And Whelan. You can *feel* the action!"

Mariana looked around, eyes wide with wonder. "I've never seen some of these before." She turned to Kleist. "They're not in any of the books."

Kleist smiled. "They don't exist. Not officially." He moved to the middle of the big room and gestured. "You see, these were all hidden away to be used as a hedge against inflation."

"Hidden by whom?"

Kleist's smile grew broader. "You don't really want to know that—suffice it to say he was not one of us."

It was Mariana's turn to nod. "A kine."

Kleist just kept smiling.

"How did *you* find them?"

"He filed their locations in his computer system." Kleist sneered. "All password protected and secure."

Mariana looked around, troubled. "Aren't you afraid of an investigation? If the FBI found them, it might lead them to the Masquerade."

He shook his head. "There'll be no investigation."

"But surely when whoever owned these dies . . . "

Kleist shook his head. "He's already dead. And I made sure his computer files died with him."

Mariana looked around her at the wonders on the walls. "Maybe I should take up the computer."

Kleist laughed. "Maybe you should!" He motioned toward Acquiel. "But for now . . . "

Mariana had been holding Acquiel's leash in her hand as she explored the room, but now she handed the lead to the other Kindred. "An agreement is an agreement."

Kleist nodded. "Thank you. Please, make yourself at home while I . . . prepare this one."

Mariana smiled at the sudden uncertainty in Acquiel's eyes. "Go ahead, little one. That is *my* wish."

The blood doll nodded, then followed along as Kleist strolled to a door on the far end of the gallery.

Mariana continued to study the hanging works. The big room was broken into sections, she found. Old masters on one side, modern painters on the other. She strolled around, eyeing the collection, wondering at Kleist's good fortune in locating it.

Then she saw it.

It was at the end of one gallery wall. A single piece—at first, Mariana thought it a painting, but, on closer examination, she found it to be a print. Odd, she thought. It's the only print here. Why . . .

"Ah." Kleist had appeared out of his room. "I see you've found my guilty secret."

"This?"

He nodded. "Tell me what you think of it."

Mariana turned to study the piece in more detail. It was a landscape of sorts, with a vivid sunrise over some sort of cemetery. "It's very good. The color usage is particularly impressive, and the depiction of the sun is wonderful!"

Kleist grinned. "Thank you."

Mariana was stunned. "You did this?"

Kleist nodded. "Is that such a surprise?"

"But the color! The use of the sun!"

"Difficult for a Kindred." He leaned back against the wall. "Nevertheless, I did do it."

Mariana stared at the print. "What's the medium? And why isn't the original here? Did you sell it? Lose it?"

Kleist laughed. "So many questions." He gestured to the room behind him. "Come with me and I'll give you the answers."

Mariana felt eagerness for the first time in years as she followed him through the door.

Val washed his hands in the zoo's rest room before continuing his stroll downtown. It was sort of a shame to waste this much vitae, but Val didn't want any of Trey's madness in his veins. They call us monsters! he thought. And yet they let creatures like that run free among them!

Val shook his head. He'd never understand the kine of this time. They'd gone completely mad, unwilling or unable to accept responsibility for anything. He sighed. *At least in my time, people paid their accounts.* Be it in money—or blood.

Val walked out of the park at Fifty-ninth Street, a few blocks from Lincoln Center. *I hope he's still there.* He crossed the street, moving quickly to avoid the rushing cabs, then strode through the huge open portico in front of the Library. The wind whipped around him, moaning as it pulsed over the broken windows that dotted Avery Fisher Hall. Val smiled. *That's the real* music of the night! He kept moving, ducking now and again to avoid a loose piece of paper or chunk of plastic. Anything that had been loose in the great city was now part of the wind. *Nature's cleanup crew.* Val saw a man drop a cigarette on the street. *A good thing too, or this city would be knee-deep in filth!*

Val finally ducked into the library entrance, then, allowing the building's side to shelter him, worked his way to the smaller Vivian Beaumont Theatre. He reached the box office just as the performance ended.

I was right! he thought, glancing over the poster, searching the cast credits. *He is here!* Val waited while the crowds of kine filed by, occasionally nodding when he sensed a Kindred among them. *We still like the old things best,* he thought, watching an obvious elder stroll by.

Finally, the last of the audience was gone. Val slipped in through the door before it eased closed, heading past the theater doors and down toward the dressing area. *I better hurry, he may slip out the back door.* There! The dressing rooms were over there. Now, which one was his—that one! Now . . .

"Peter Grimsdyke?"

"Yes." The Kindred that turned toward Val seemed ancient, face gaunt, dominated by razor-sharp cheekbones and equally sharp blue eyes. It was a face every movie- and theatergoer in America had seen time and again. The face of an actor who had made a career of character roles—a career that had spanned several centuries and three continents. "Do I know you?"

"Not really, although we did meet once—at the old Majestic in London. You were playing . . . "

"I was Poole, the butler." Grimsdyke's eyes glimmered. "And that fool, Mansfield, was doing the dual role."

"Until the Home Office shut you down."

The actor sighed. "That was the rumor—in fact, business was bad—and Mansfield was not the thriftiest of stars. . . . "

The glittering eyes turned to Val's face, studying his features. "I can't say that I remember you, sir. Were you in the company?"

Val laughed. "No! I met you backstage. Asked for your autograph."

"Really!" The actor smiled. "Did I give it to you?"

Val opened his hands. "No sir, you just brushed past me and headed for the Café Royal with your friends."

Grimsdyke nodded. "I was younger then."

"We all were."

The actor indicated a sofa in the little dressing room. "Well . . . "

"Val, sir."

Grimsdyke nodded. "Well, Val. What can I do to help you this time? I don't suppose you want an autograph now."

Val sighed. "Something a bit more serious, I'm afraid." He reached into his pocket and pulled out one of the knives, placing it carefully on the table. "Have you ever seen this workmanship before?"

Grimsdyke moved in close, studying the hilt with great care, then pulled out a magnifying glass to study the sigil at the base of the weapon more closely. "Fine work." His fingertips traced the sigil. "True artistry."

Val nodded. "A Toreador, do you think?"

"Absolutely. And recent work—this inlay is held in place with an adhesive that didn't begin to appear until well into the twentieth century."

"Could you give me any idea of who might have done this?"

Grimsdyke looked up, eyes measuring. "I might." The eyes went hard. "But first, I'd like to know what your interest is."

Val motioned toward the knife. "A gang tried to kill me with that knife just three days ago."

"A gang!"

Val nodded. "That's right. A gang of kine—with a Kindred weapon."

"Dear me, I've got to think about this." Grimsdyke looked at the clock on the wall. "Look at the hour! I haven't even had time to feed yet!" He came to a decision. "Could you meet me here tomorrow, around this same time?"

"Certainly."

The actor smiled, ushering Val from the room. "Splendid. I should have an answer for you then."

"Then you do know who made it?"

Grimsdyke smiled, then touched his nose with his index finger. "Perhaps. I certainly know someone who will know—and that's the same thing, is it not?"

"Yes, I suppose it is." Val smiled. "Until tomorrow then, sir."

"Good night, dear boy!"

Val strolled out into the windy canyon of Lincoln

Center, a new lightness to his step. He was closer. He could feel it. Tomorrow he would know who made the knife. *Then I can turn the whole damn business over to Don Cruez. Let him handle it!*

Val smiled as his mood lightened. He looked at his watch. The party over at the Egyptian temple would be breaking up soon.

Maybe I should walk back over there, find another uptown girl . . .

The room Kleist led Mariana to was quite remarkable. The walls (and ceiling) were painted a bright, almost neon, green. There were lights everywhere, mounted on tripods, set into wall fixtures, hung from the ceiling—all of them pointed to the center of the room.

In the center was a six-foot-tall stake, set, to all appearances, deeply into soil. Around the stake was piled a rather large quantity of wood, ready to light into a blazing bonfire. And in the middle of that potential bonfire was Acquiel.

The blond blood doll was quite naked now, arms tied tightly behind the post, the rest of her body pinned in place by carefully (and artistically) placed ropes. Acquiel couldn't move and was quite silent—the gag filling her mouth ensured that—but Mariana could see a quite genuine terror in the other's eyes.

"Like it?" Kleist was all smiles as he gestured toward the frightened girl.

"You promised not to hurt her."

Kleist's grin widened, showing dainty, and quite sharply pointed, canines. "Wouldn't think of it—she's going to be my best model yet!"

"Model for what?"

Kleist motioned Mariana to the side of the room. "Let me show you!"

Mariana followed Kleist, walking past Acquiel who, Mariana could see, was looking a bit less frightened now. Mariana grinned. The bound blonde was grinding her hips against the post behind her. *Just can't get enough.*

Mariana paused for a moment, taking the time to give the bound girl a quick caress. Her smile deepened as she noted the trembling this caused, but she didn't have time to do anything about it just then. *Later!*

Kleist gestured at a crowded table as Mariana reached him.

"This is the secret!"

Mariana looked the table over. She recognized the monitor and keyboard of a Macintosh computer, but the rest of the equipment there was foreign to her. "I don't see any art supplies."

Kleist's smile broadened again. "Sure you do! You just don't recognize them!" He stepped forward, hands resting lightly on the keyboard. "Let me show you!"

Behind her, the lights flared to life, illuminating the middle of the room with midday brightness. Mariana quickly shielded her eyes.

"Don't worry. It's fluorescent." Kleist touched several more switches. "Can't hurt us."

Mariana turned and watched as a camera lens moved in the middle of one of the light tripods. "There's a camera over there."

Kleist touched another button. "Right. Take a look at the CRT."

"The what?"

"The screen."

Mariana turned and saw that the screen was now totally covered with Acquiel's image, body undulating against the ropes. "So, it's a TV camera?"

Kleist shook his head. "Nope. Digital." He pressed another group of buttons. The light grew brighter. "Okay, now . . ."

He turned toward the center of the room. "Acquiel! I want you to fight the ropes hard—and look frightened!"

Mariana watched on the screen as Acquiel reacted to Kleist's commands; her movement stopped for a moment, then resumed with a different tempo, the thrashing body now seemingly trying to escape the ropes.

"Perfect!" Kleist pressed a button decisively. "I knew she'd be the one!"

"For what?"

Kleist sat down in front of the keyboard, fingers flying over the keys. "Just watch!"

As Mariana watched, Acquiel's image froze into immobility. "Yes," Kleist muttered, "this one should be perfect." The green background suddenly disappeared, replaced by plain black. Acquiel floated in the void, fighting her bonds. "And now . . ." A new background appeared. Angry people, dressed in pilgrim garb, were suddenly shouting their hatred at the struggling blonde. Mariana shrugged; she'd seen photo montage work before. "So what's the secret?"

"Watch some more." Kleist kept typing, sending directions to the computer. A fire appeared around Acquiel's feet, smoke drifted up, covering her loins. "I can add anything I want. . . ."

Mariana leaned forward. The illusion was amazingly precise. "Interesting. But it's still just trick photography."

Kleist grinned again. "Do you really think so?" He

touched several more keys—and the image changed completely. Suddenly, Acquiel was not tied to a post; rather, she was sunning herself on a beach, her nudity now covered by a rather ugly bathing suit. "Is that trick photography, too?"

"Well . . ."

He hit a few more keys. The cemetery scene was suddenly on the screen, exactly as Mariana had seen it in the gallery. "You did *that* on the computer?" Mariana was impressed.

Kleist nodded, then touched a few more keys. Now Acquiel was in the cemetery, on top of a vault that suddenly appeared in the foreground. She was nude again, but smiling now, making love to a marble angel. "This too."

The scene changed again. And again. Had they not been of places Mariana knew did not exist, she would have taken them to be photographs. "This is incredible!"

Kleist smiled again and pushed back from his screen. "And there's no limit to what you can do. With the mouse and the proper touch, you can draw right on the screen!"

"Show me!"

Kleist pulled another chair over. "Have a seat." It took Mariana several minutes to get the knack, but she soon found that she could, indeed, draw with the little mechanical device Kleist called a mouse. Afterward, she could paint the results with any colors she liked.

"It's not at all like working with oils," Mariana muttered several hours later.

Kleist grinned. "No. It's more like painting with little bits of the sun."

The sun! Mariana leaned toward the screen, learning

to paint with the bits of light. She had forgotten her depression, lost all track of the reason she had come.

Phillipe had disappeared from her mind.

Peter Grimsdyke wanted to stand up, wanted to pace. *I've always thought better on my feet. Asset for an actor.* He wasn't sure he was doing the right thing, and it made him uncomfortable.

"Mr. Grimsdyke?"

The voice from the darkness was supposed to shock visitors, but Peter Grimsdyke had been in the business of illusion much too long to be fooled. He'd noted the "hidden" door immediately upon entering the room, and had prepared himself for its use.

Of course, he had not expected so mundane a use. *The talents wither in some of the Toreador,* he thought wryly. "I'm over here, dear boy."

The Kindred who came through the door was good-looking in an average sort of way. The actor recognized him as Demetrious Slater, confidant and companion of the Archon.

"Where is Masika?"

Slater bowed. "Unfortunately, my companion is unable to attend you at present."

"Indeed?"

Slater's face showed an ingratiating smile. *Fool!* Grimsdyke thought. *As if I cannot tell true expression from false!*

"The Archon is away on other business." Slater dropped into a seat facing Grimsdyke's. "Perhaps I could be of some help?"

Grimsdyke hooded his gaze. *I dare not trust this one.* The actor's mind raced, trying and rejecting scenario

after scenario, until . . . *Perhaps, though, I can use him.* . . .
He smiled an open smile at Slater. "Mayhap you
can."

The other leaned forward.

"I had a visit the other night"—Grimsdyke paused for
effect—"from one of our Brujah brothers."

"A Brujah!" Slater tried to show surprise—and failed.
"What did he want?"

The actor smiled inwardly. This might be educational.
"He inquired as to the name of a certain member of the
Kindred."

"A Toreador?"

"He wasn't sure." Grimsdyke moved forward in his
seat, smiling conspiratorially. "Although, under the cir-
cumstances, he assumed so."

The other leaned toward Grimsdyke, clearly eager for
any information. "Why did he think that?"

"It had to do with some artwork. An inlay job."
Grimsdyke smiled. "And one which I believe I recognized."

Slater feigned ignorance. "Inlay?"

Fool! "Come now, my friend." The actor projected
brotherhood. "Surely you remember the special gifts
the Archon commissioned for his friends."

Slater showed uncertainty. "I'm sorry—"

"Knives!" Grimsdyke's hand suddenly flashed forward and down. "Knives like these!" A blade appeared,
as if by magic, vibrating in the chair arm inches from
Slater's hand.

The other recoiled.

Grimsdyke smiled. "Nothing to worry about." He
reached forward, pulling the knife free of the hard-
wood without effort. "I never miss what I aim at."

Slater seemed frozen in place, unsure of what to say.

Grimsdyke reversed the blade, showing the inlaid

hilt to the shaken vampire. "The Brujah had a knife just like this one—made, I am sure, by the same hand."

"Did you"—the mouth worked, trying to force moistness—"tell him who made them?"

The actor smiled, all affability. "Of course not, dear boy." The knife disappeared. "I wanted to speak to the Archon first."

Slater wobbled to his feet. "Good, you did the right thing."

Grimsdyke nodded. "Indeed. Now, what are you going to do?"

Slater turned, the smile back on his face. "I? I will do nothing . . . except to pass this information on to the Archon."

"When?"

The question seemed innocuous, but Grimsdyke wanted an answer.

Slater looked at the ornate grandfather's clock on the far wall. "Later tonight, I presume."

"The Archon will be back?"

Another smile of fatuous insincerity. "Of course."

Grimsdyke came to his feet. "Good! Then I will take no more of your time." He headed for the doorway.

"Ah, Mr. Grimsdyke . . . "

The actor turned, his face a mask of calm affability. "Yes, dear boy?"

Slater had regained all his composure now. "I . . . the Archon would appreciate it if you had no further contact with the Brujah about this."

Grimsdyke considered. "And how would you have me avoid him?"

Slater leaned forward. "Could you . . . disappear for a short time?"

"My dear boy!" Grimsdyke cocked his head in surprise. "I am appearing at the Vivian Beaumont!"

"Couldn't you . . . cancel?"

"Cancel!"

Slater looked surprised. "Yes, would that be so hard?"

The actor shook his head; the other had no clue. "Dear boy, it's just not done—after all, the play's the thing!"

"I really must insist."

Grimsdyke hardened his gaze, just a touch. "Insist?"

Slater backed off. "I mean, the Archon will *certainly* insist. After all, we don't really know what the Brujah are after, do we?"

Grimsdyke let his face show indecision. "I suppose not."

"Please." The imploring look was genuine this time. "Give the Archon time to look the situation over. I'm sure he'd be very . . . grateful."

Calculation this time. *He's awfully anxious.* Grimsdyke nodded. "All right, dear boy, I'll tell the director that some horrid family thing has come up." He opened the door. "But do tell the Archon that he owes me one? There's a good boy."

Slater's smile lit the actor's way out. "Of course, sir. You have my word."

Which isn't worth a red cent! Grimsdyke headed for one of his havens—dawn wasn't far off. *Still, this does promise to be interesting.* Certainly more interesting than that stupid cow of a director!

Val usually turned on his TV when he awoke—it gave him a quick overview of the world and showed him which parts of the city might be a little . . . unfriendly.

After all, I'm supposed to be inconspicuous. He laughed. *Although so far . . .*

Tonight, he was amused to see, one of the lead stories concerned a supposed gang fight in the Central Park Zoo. *They don't know what to make of it!* Police were promising a crackdown on gang violence and an investigation of several rival groups. *I guess the girls didn't come forward and tell what they knew.* He grinned again. *Not that they know much—can't be more than two or three hundred thousand guys in leather jackets around town!* It would clearly be safe to go uptown again tonight. Maybe he should hunt there again. He licked his lips. *Stay with the prime cuts for a while.*

Val was out on the streets and halfway to the subway when he *felt* someone behind him. He didn't look back, just kept walking until he came to a corner. Then he quickly ducked around it and, digging his fingers into the gaps in the masonry, climbed up the wall, finally stopping about fifteen feet above the ground. *This should do it,* he thought, waiting for his unseen companion to arrive. *Nobody looks up when they turn a corner.* No one came.

Val stayed in place for a few minutes, ready for anything—except the nothing that continued. Finally, he relaxed his grip and let himself drop to the ground, knees flexing to take the impact.

"Clever move."

Val whirled, rising onto the balls of his feet, hands curling into claws . . .

And found himself face-to-face with Tessler. "Damn!" He allowed himself to relax. "Why are you sneaking around behind me?"

Tessler grinned. "Staying in practice."

Val grunted, then tugged the tail of his coat back into pace and started toward the subway. "Play with somebody else."

Tessler fell into step beside him. "Nobody else gives me a challenge."

"Ask Don Cruez."

Tessler laughed. "No thanks. I plan to be around to see the new millennium." They turned a corner. The subway kiosk was just ahead. "Going somewhere?"

Val nodded. "Uptown."

"Out of your territory, isn't it?"

Val shook his head. "I'm still trying to find out where those knives came from."

Tessler grinned. "You haven't worked that out yet? Hell, let me do it—I'll have an answer tomorrow!"

"No. Don Cruez asked me to look into it." Val pursed his lips. "You know what that means. I've got to do it myself."

Tessler laughed. "It's not a homework assignment, you know; besides, it could mean trouble for all of us!"

Val stopped, glancing at his friend. "I know that. You haven't heard of another attack, have you?"

"No."

Val looked Tessler in the eye. "You're sure you would know if there'd been one."

Tessler nodded. "I'm sure."

Val turned back toward the kiosk. "That's interesting. Maybe the whole thing was a coincidence."

"Don Cruez doesn't think so."

Val watched Tessler out of the corner of his eye. "What do you think?"

Tessler shrugged. "I don't believe in coincidences."

"Neither do I." Val started down the subway steps. "I'll let you know if I need help."

Tessler watched his friend disappear into the bowels of the earth. "Do," he muttered, then turned away for his own hunt. *Let's see.* He looked downtown. *How about Italian tonight!*

*   *   *

Mariana woke alone for the first time in months. She had loaned Acquiel to Kleist for another session—in return, the techno had arranged for a Mac and associated hardware to be delivered to her studio. She looked in. *Yes, the equipment is all here!* She locked the door, hurrying outside. *I'd better feed before I start. . . .*

Mariana hunted quickly, not a hard thing in the East Village. *Cattle*, she thought, watching the eyes of the men follow her. *They think they own the world.* She licked her lips, picked one out. *How little they know!*

Later, sated, she rushed to the studio and began the lengthy and complicated process of uncrating, arranging, and booting the system.

By midnight, she had things running satisfactorily. Her mouse skittered across the pad, creating lines of green light on her screen. *It's not too different from using a pencil*, Mariana told herself. *Just another skill to be learned.*

All it took was time—and Mariana had plenty of that.

She turned things off just before dawn, letting her first piece of new art fall into the printer's hopper. She steeled herself against disappointment and picked it up.

It's different! She held it at arm's length. *The light! It's right!* Right! She sighed. *It's been so long.*

It was very close to dawn when she finally returned to her haven. Acquiel was already there, asleep in the big bed they shared. Mariana looked down at her companion. There were some new marks on the blood doll's silky skin. *Kleist was sloppy.* Still, Mariana was willing to forgive a lot of the Kindred who had given her back the sun.

I'll have to do something nice for him. She looked down at Acquiel, breathing lightly and regularly beneath the covers. *Have to do something nice for Acquiel, too. She deserves it.* Mariana lay down, feeling the sun cross the horizon outside. *Maybe I can do a painting of her as I see her. Full of life, bathed in sunshine. . . .*

She fell asleep with a smile on her face.

Val had no trouble meeting another uptown girl. The streets were full of people, rushing from store to store, buying something here, something there. *It's astounding that they put so much energy into acquiring things*, Val thought. *What are they going to do with all of it?*

Val also noted that there were more police than usual on the streets. *They're serious about cracking down on gangs.* He nodded. *Should have done it a long time ago.*

A lot of the cops were giving him hard looks, he noticed. *It's because of my leathers!* he thought with a shock. *As if clothes meant anything!*

He began to play mind games with the police, smiling at some, glaring at others. The ones he glared at tended to spend a great deal of time watching him, and Val realized that that might not be such a good idea. If one decided to take him downtown for questioning, he might end up locked in a cell until sunrise.

That would never do.

He avoided the police after that, until, just before ten, he came across a rather attractive female officer. He played the game one more time, with his smile this time, and drew her to him, just inside an alley.

It was the first time he'd ever dined with an officer of the law. *That's what life is all about.* He laughed to himself. *New experiences.*

Sated, he gave the napping cop a kiss, then continued

his trudge to Lincoln Center, timing the walk so that he would arrive just as Grimsdyke finished his show.

It was not to be.

When Val reached the box office, the first thing he saw was a large CLOSED sign across the cash windows. *Did Grimsdyke lie to me?* Val turned to the posters. *Matinee only on Wednesday.* Val glanced down at the big watch he'd worn for the last year. *Today is Wednesday.* Val stalked away, mind running at full speed. *Why didn't he tell me? Or did he just forget?* The subway was just ahead. *I'll have to come back tomorrow and find out for sure.*

Val stopped at the entrance to the station. *It's early yet.* He looked around. The streets were still full of people. *Maybe I'll walk around some more, see if I can find another new experience. . . .*

The summons to the sanctum had come as a surprise to the retainer. He had been busy with his own projects, moving them forward with the deft assurance that decades of association with Lady Ambrosia had taught him. He'd thought everything to be running properly. *What has gone wrong?* he thought, hurrying to the Lady's apartment. *And why do I not know?*

He bowed when he entered the Sanctum and was immediately shaken at Lady Ambrosia's positioning. *She's in the Chippendale!* It was the seat she reserved for judgments.

The retainer hesitated in the doorway for a moment, trying to think of something, anything he might have done to earn the Lady's displeasure; dozens of little disloyalties sprang to mind. *But she can't know about them!* He started as she motioned him toward another chair, before and beneath her own. *What is it? What have I done?* He tried to blank his racing mind before she could seize upon it, wrest all his guilty secrets from him.

"Why have you disobeyed me?"

The voice was ice. The retainer shivered. Death, final death, could be seconds away. "I have never disobeyed . . ."

"Silence!"

The retainer sank deeper into his seat, mind now blank with fear.

Lady Ambrosia's hand reached toward him, transformed into a claw, extended. "I gave you an order!" The claw gripped him by the neck, lifted him into the air. "Kleist was to give the girl the proper name, the proper haven."

"But . . ." He was dangling now, held at arm's length.

"He has not done so. The two have not yet found one another." Lady Ambrosia snarled, tightening her hold. "My plan has not moved forward!"

The claws penetrated the skin. He could feel blood welling out. Terror raced through him. *If she cuts my spinal column . . .* He tried to move, tried to break free.

"Be still!" The now-huge figure spit the words out, hurling the other against the wall with terrible force. Plaster collapsed inward, wooden beams snapped.

So did bones.

The figure that had been Lady Ambrosia loomed over her broken servant. "I will expect a report of success within one week."

The other moaned. A claw reached out, picking the broken figure up, setting it on already healing legs. "One week."

The retainer nodded, worked to keep his footing, careful not to move his chest until the ribs healed. "A week."

The claw released him. "No excuses."

* * *

"Come on, Mariana!" Acquiel's clever fingers moved over her mistress's body, tickling here, caressing there, trying to get some kind of response.

It was no use. Mariana was in no mood for horse-play. *Or any other kind!* The little blood doll rolled over, pouting, allowing Mariana to feed from her soft breast. "It's not fair!"

"What's not fair?" Mariana licked the breast, raising goose bumps as the tiny marks of her teeth disappeared. The artist rolled to her feet, quickly pulling black jeans over long legs.

"You don't spend any time with me anymore!"

Mariana stopped dressing, looking toward Acquiel and thinking. It was true that she now spent much of her time at the computer, exploring her newly discovered world of pixels and sunlit colors. In fact, now that she thought about it, she had spent *all* her time there in the last few weeks. *But I'm not ready yet. Not quite.*

"I *have* been a little busy."

Acquiel nodded. "I know. And I know that you're happy. Really happy."

Mariana looked into herself, surprised to discover that the other girl was right.

"But still"—Acquiel let herself fall back into the big bed, rolling into a ball on top of the covers—"I wish you'd *spend* some time with me."

Mariana nodded. Acquiel did have the right to expect some attention. *But this is not a good time!* Mariana thought about it. *Perhaps . . . yes!*

"Acquiel?"

The blonde turned over, looking sadly at her mistress. "Yes?"

"You're right. I haven't made enough time for you." Mariana saw the girl's eyes light up. "And I'm sorry."

Acquiel exploded out of the bed, tumbling into Mariana's arms, hugging her. "Then you aren't tired of me?"

Mariana laughed. "Of course not! I'm just . . . involved with that new program."

"3-D STUDIO?"

"That's the one."

"Why?"

Mariana was surprised by the question. *Why am I so obsessed about working with this new medium.* She shrugged. "I can't really explain it." She motioned Acquiel to sit down on the end of the bed, noted the gleam of interest in her eyes. "I guess it's all about the light."

"The light?"

Mariana nodded. "Remember all those paintings I did of you?"

"Sure! They're great!"

"No, they're not." Acquiel's eyebrows lifted. "Oh, it's not your fault, you're a beautiful model." The girl's quick grin warmed the room. "They're bad because of me."

"You?"

Mariana nodded again. "Great paintings need great light. The sun's light." Mariana turned away, found herself staring at the heavily draped window. "I can't see the sun anymore. Can't even picture it in my mind." She shook her head. "Without that light, my paintings are dark, lifeless." She sighed again. "Soulless. Like me."

Acquiel raced to her side, hugging tight. "You're not soulless!"

Mariana smiled in spite of herself. "All right. Lifeless only. But still wrong."

"And the computer can make them right?"

Mariana shrugged her shoulders. "I think so. You see, the computer paints in little electric dots called pixels."

"Like the cat in that Heinlein novel?"

Mariana laughed. "Yes, I guess that *is* where he got the name." She shook her head. "Only these pixels aren't alive—at least, not the way a cat is alive."

"Then what makes them so special?"

"It's what they're made of."

"Huh?"

"Think about it. They're particles of light." Mariana walked to the window, pulling the drapes open, revealing the world of darkness outside. "Pieces of the sun."

"And that makes them different?"

"Very different."

Acquiel raised her chin. "How long are you going to work with them?"

"Until I find something better."

"Oh."

Mariana laughed, taking the blonde into her arms. "But I'm never going to find anything better than you!"

Acquiel lit up. *She's like the sun too. In her own way,* Mariana thought. "Just give me a little more time. I'll make it up to you."

Acquiel kissed her. "Not too much more time."

Mariana smiled and kissed her back. "Not too much. I promise."

Val made still another trip uptown the following night, this time taking the subway directly to the Lincoln

Center stop. The winter wind was swirling again, roaring through the open plaza, scouring it of paper, leaves, anything that might mar the white marble of the place. Val strolled past the fountain, noting the brown, sticky mass hugging the bottom. *Thing's been turned off too long*, he thought, then smiled. *A good thing too, or the wind would be blowing this crud all over the place.* His smile grew harder. *Doesn't really matter, though, the mayor'll declare a water shortage this summer anyway.* He shook his head. *New York!*

The box office for the Vivian Beaumont was open when Val arrived. A rather thin girl sat behind the bulletproof glass. "Can I help you?" She looked up, and was instantly held in Val's gaze.

Val smiled at her, noting the increase in her pulse rate. "I'd like to speak to Peter Grimsdyke."

She swallowed hard, eyes never leaving Val's. "Mr. Grimsdyke's not here."

Val frowned. The girl shivered. "Not here?"

The girl tried to drop her gaze, but did not have the strength. "No, sir."

"Where is he?"

She swallowed again, the gulp almost audible. "I don't know, sir. Would you like me to find out?"

Val gestured—and the girl's gaze was released. She turned to a telephone at the back of the little office, her movements a little shaky.

Val turned away, glancing around the confines of the Center. *He's run away*, he realized. *Somehow, I scared him!*

There was a movement overhead. Val's gaze darted upward. *A nighthawk!* He watched as the raptor plunged out of the darkness, stooping toward a group of fat pigeons in the plaza. *Dinnertime.* Val licked his lips as the hawk lifted with his prey. *For me as well.* He turned back to the girl, still on the telephone. *No. She's a bit too thin for my tastes.*

As he watched, she hung the phone up and turned toward him. He smiled when he saw how red her cheeks were—and how hard she tried to avoid his eyes. "I talked to the director, sir, and he says that Mr. Grimsdyke had to rush home." Despite her best efforts, her eyes came up to meet his—and were caught. "Some . . . some sort of family emergency."

Val nodded. *Gone.* He smiled at the girl, touching her with a trace of his discipline, warming her. Then he turned away. "Thank you."

He felt her gaze on his back as he left. *Maybe I should feed here,* he thought. *She's certainly ripe for a little attention.* He hesitated for a moment, then looked back at the ticket booth. A young couple was standing in the spot he had just vacated, buying seats for the show. *No.* He chuckled. *She has too many tickets to sell.*

He turned and strolled through Lincoln Center, the wind swirling, catching at his jacket, chilling his face. *Besides, I still have to find the craftsman who made those damned knives.* He crossed the street, noting a girl with a Tower Records bag moving a little way in front of him. *Still, I do have to feed. . . .*

"There!" Mariana stepped back from the screen, careful to save her document. "Finished!"

Acquiel rushed over. "Can I see it?"

Mariana smiled. "Sure." Her fingers ran over the keys. "Just as soon as I print it out."

The two turned to the big laser printer in the corner. It started to whir as things warmed up. Acquiel couldn't stop moving, bobbing up and down in excitement. Mariana smiled. *I feel the same way!* Paper began to roll through the machine. "Just a few seconds now," Mariana muttered.

"Will this one be good?"

Mariana gave the blonde a hug. "I hope so." She'd spent the last week on this painting—her first attempt to use her new medium in the way she had always used her old. Much of that time had been spent trying to pick the right subject matter until, finally, it had come to her.

The Holy Grail. *My favorite story!*

Paper appeared, rolling out, dropping into the hopper.

She had depicted the ultimate moment of the story. *The last good moment!* The cup of Christ, found, is held aloft by Sir Percival. *An odd character.* Mariana remembered that from the stories her father had told her so long ago. *Not the bravest of knights, or the purest . . .* She had tried to show that he was special, a driven man, touched by the Quest. *. . . Just the one who stayed at it until he succeeded.*

She had rendered Percival in full armor, his helmet at his feet, holding the Grail aloft, its golden promise shining in a ray of sunlight. *Just the way I've always pictured it!* Mariana sighed. *If it worked.*

Mariana put her arms around Acquiel as the last of the paper rolled off the printer with a faint *plop*. She needed the other girl's warmth. Needed her support.

Mariana heard the little blonde's heart speed up. *She's excited too!* Mariana detected the faint catch as Acquiel's breath stopped. *And just as anxious about this as I am*, Mariana thought, fingers trembling slightly as she reached out for the finished piece. *I hope it's all worth it.*

It was.

"Perfect!" Mariana couldn't believe it. "It's just the way I wanted it!"

"It's beautiful!" Acquiel was breathing again. "Who's that man?"

Mariana looked at the figure. "His name is Sir Percival. He's the Knight of the Round Table who finally found the Holy Grail."

"He must have been something very special." Acquiel pulled the paper closer, studying the tall figure. "Who was your model?"

"It was . . ." Mariana's looked down, and she remembered. "My God!" Light eyes suddenly flooded into her mind, filling her with memory. "Phillipe!"

"Who?"

"I forgot all about him!" Mariana let the piece of paper fall from her hands. "Kleist was supposed to—" She whirled around, eyes burning. "Bastard!"

Acquiel's eyes widened.

"Mariana! What's wrong!"

"I've been cheated!" Mariana headed for the door. "And so have you!"

Acquiel stood there, baffled, as the door slammed shut. "Cheated?"

Val spent hours roaming through the theater district, searching for some trace of Grimsdyke.

To no avail. The old Kindred knew too many people, had too many holes to disappear into. *I could spend years searching.* Val's frown was grim. *And still never find him.*

There has to be another way!

Then it hit him. The Blood Club! Most of the clans visited there at one time or another. *All I have to do is find a friendly Toreador—maybe one who's just sated himself on one of those druggie blood dolls!* Val grinned. *Someone happy enough to tell me what I need to know! Tell me who that damn sigil belongs to!* Val nodded, turned toward the nearest subway station. *I'll start right away!*

Val planned his campaign on the long ride down-town. *I'll make the Club my second haven. Become a regular!* He grinned. *Hell, maybe they'll put a seat aside for me!* It was a pleasurable thought. Val knew that the Club was always full of blood dolls, some of them quite striking, and all of them quite eager to share the warmth that raced through their veins.

It'll be fun!

"Mistress?"

Lady Ambrosia looked toward the darkened doorway. "This better be important."

"It is." The retainer shuffled into the room, carefully keeping his distance from the maze of figures lying on the cushions in the corner. "The girl and boy are both on their way to the Blood Club."

"So!" The Methuselah sat up, her attention fully directed at the cringing retainer.

"And in case they do *not* meet, I have arranged for Kleist to *again* get the information he needs."

Lady Ambrosia nodded. "Adequate." She made a languid gesture toward the door and the retainer backed out. "You will have a full report for me later."

"Yes, milady." The door closed.

*   *   *

Val got off the train at Astor Place, taking the steps to the surface two at a time, anxious to get out into the clean night. The Club was only a couple of blocks away, he'd be there in—

"Hey! Brujah bastard!"

Val turned to the echoing remnants of the yell. He had thought himself alone, the streets of Elysium clear and unthreatening.

"Think you're hot stuff, don't you!"

Val's eyes searched the street. There were three, no, *four*, dark figures moving there. Ambling through the shadows. Fast. *Too fast for cattle—they're Kindred*. Val went cold. Had the Sabbat finally decided to come out into the open? Were they ready to start their war?

Only one way to find out. Val decided to press the issue. "You do know that we're in Elysium?"

One of the shadows glided into the street. *Kindred, all right*. Tall, thin, dressed in the motley that was the street. But *definitely Kindred*.

"Who cares about Ee-leesium?" He pronounced it as two words.

Young, Val thought. *Uneducated. Could be Sabbat, could just be an anarch*.

The other shadows moved out into the street. *Four. No more back there*. Val had carefully shifted his position, gotten his back to a solid wall. It would have to do. "What do you want?"

Figures moved forward. "We want your head, pretty boy—and your nice leather coat."

Val showed his teeth in a hard smile. "Anything else?"

"All we need."

"Come and get them." Val's smile grew harder. "If you can."

The group of young Kindred moved as one. *They've*

done this before, Val thought. *Well, so have I!* He knew he'd have to be quick and sure. *Can't make any mistakes.*

Val prepared himself, folded his disciplines around him—and swept into action. He flowed into the midst of his opponents, hands and feet stabbing out, hardened claws sinking deep into soft flesh.

The world became a hell of blood and organs and displaced bones. Val moved through the little gang like a steel tornado, striking first to one side, then the other. Kindred fell, their bodies broken, their heads smashed. The fight went on for an eternity—and was over in a second.

Val found himself alone, blood racing through a body gone numb and cold. Around him were the remains of four opponents. They were in the midst of dying the final death, although too young for any really spectacular changes to take place.

Val watched as they died, watched as their flesh grew still, their minds stopped working.

Watched until they were dead.

Finally, he ran a bloody hand through his hair, inadvertently leaving a red streak. *Stupid. What could they possibly hope to get out of this?* His mind raced.

"You're pretty good."

Val whirled, his discipline still upon him. Fifty feet away a man—no, *a Kindred* stood. Short, barrel-chested and compact. *Didn't notice him before.* Val's face tightened as he realized why. *He was using Obfuscate!* He looked at the Kindred again, noting his power. *Not just a street tough. Somebody's enforcer!*

"You're wondering why they attacked you." The man nodded toward the fallen anarchs. "I made them do it." He smiled. "Made it easier to get close to you." The smile widened. "No way you were going to hear me while you were fighting them."

Val shook his head. "Why should you care about me?"

The stout man raised a long-draw Colt automatic. "I don't." The pistol drew level, laser sight projecting a pinpoint beam on the middle of Val's chest, right over the heart. "But I do care about the Sabbat." The man pulled the trigger.

Val tried to move, tried to dodge, but it was too late. The first round punched him hard in the chest, pushing him backward, off-balance and falling. He tried to turn the fall into a roll, but the second and third rounds hit him in the side and back, disrupting his balance, confusing him. His strength began to drain.

Val hit the ground, blood flowing from entry and exit wounds. He gave himself a split instant to find his center, trying desperately to marshal the energy for one final move, one last attack.

More bullets pounded into him, breaking his concentration, slowing his movements still more. *I'm losing it!* ran through his reeling mind.

Val lay on the ground, helpless, his system shutting down, falling into a torpor from which he knew he'd never wake. He tried to make one last attempt, tried to roll over, come to his feet. *Anything!*

It was no use.

Through dimming sight, Val saw the stout man standing over him, rolling his unfeeling body over as he jacked a new magazine into the pistol. "It's a shame, really." He popped the safety off, dropped the barrel of the gun until Val found himself looking straight down the bore. Red laser light blinded him. "Such a waste."

Val lost consciousness before the trigger was pulled.

*   *   *

Mariana was still angry as she reached the door of the
Club. *Imagine him taking advantage of me like that!* She was
just passing through the door when she heard the
shots down the street. *Gunshots? In Elysium?* She turned,
tempted to investigate, but the crowd around her
surged forward, pushing her inside before she could
move away.

Mariana sighed, forced to go with the flow. *It's not
really my job. . . .*

Inside, at the top of the stairs, Mariana quickly spotted Kleist, standing by the bar below. She rushed to the
stairs. *Don't go anywhere, Dieter!* she thought grimly. *I'll be
right down!*

A big human grinned and motioned to her as she
neared the bottom of the stairs, his breath stinking of
liquor and rotting meat. She tried to sidestep, move
past him, but he was blindly insistent, throwing a leg
across the steps to block her way. She sighed. *Why can't
he leave me alone!* Again, she tried to sidestep, but there
was no way to get around the buffoon.

She shook her head, then slammed the palm of her
hand down on his knee. She heard the cartilage shatter,
saw the pain fill his face. *Fool!* Before he could scream,
she rammed the flat of her hand into his diaphragm,
pushing the air out of him in one wordless *whoosh!* She
left him on the stairs and headed into the bar, signaling to the bartender that there was a problem behind
her. He nodded as she crossed the room and went into
the Treasure Room. *Now, if Kleist hasn't disappeared . . .*

He hadn't. He was holding court in the back of the
room, two women sitting with him, giggling as he fed

on their offered flesh. "Kleist!" Her voice cut through the stillness of the place. "We've got to talk."

She saw his eyebrows lift, then sat as he nodded. It took him a minute or two to disengage from his companions, then he sat down beside her.

"Is there a problem?"

She nodded grimly. "We had a bargain. . . . "

"And you fulfilled your side of it with great honor and dispatch!"

Mariana looked at him in surprise. His voice was a bit thick. She glanced at the two girls in the back of the room. *What the hell are they on?*

"Yes, Dieter, I did fulfill my end of the bargain."

He smiled and nodded again.

"Now, how about *your* side?"

"My side?" His voice was very thick now.

Fast stuff! Mariana was impressed. *Only a few minutes to go completely through his bloodstream!*

Mariana knew she had to be patient; Kleist was going to be a little slow for a while. "You were supposed to find a man for me—a Kindred."

"Right. Kindred."

Mariana leaned forward, eyes pinning Kleist to his seat. "When I loaned you Acquiel, you told me you had found him. . . . "

"Did find him."

"Who is he?"

Kleist looked down, thinking. "Kindred. Good-looking, intense—"

"I told you that!" Mariana's patience was beginning to unravel.

Kleist looked up, eyes widening as he remembered. "Right! Brujah."

"A Brujah!" Phillipe had been Toreador.

Kleist nodded. "Brujah. Couple of centuries old."

"An elder?"

Kleist shook his head. "Not that old. Wouldn't matter, doesn't like responsibility."

Mariana leaned forward. "His name, Dieter. Tell me his name!"

"Percival."

Mariana's eyes narrowed. *Is he making fun of me?* "Percival! What kind of name is that?"

"Good name. Knight of Round Table. Found Holy Grail."

Mariana snorted. "And where can I find this knight."

Kleist looked around, picked up his laptop. "Right here."

"Where?"

Kleist opened the lid. "Here. Got the location of his haven in my address file. Let me see . . ." His eyes glinted blue as the screen lit up. "That's right! Just the other side of the river."

"Brooklyn?"

Kleist nodded.

Mariana glared as Kleist touched keys. "You'd better be right about this, Kleist, because if you're not . . ."

"S'right. I'm always right."

"Milady." The retainer stood at the entrance to Lady Ambrosia's sanctum. He hesitated, fearful for his existence. "Our plan has failed."

"Failed!" The room seemed to shudder with the power of that one word. "Explain to me how we have failed."

He stepped gingerly forward, talking quickly to forestall his mistress's displeasure. "There may be another path available; I ran a new model through the computer and . . ."

"Damn the computer!" Twin eyes burned in the darkness. "Just tell me what has happened!"

The door slammed behind the retainer, trapping him. He swallowed once, playing for time. "It's the boy, milady. The Brujah."

The burning eyes smoldered. "What about him?"

"He's dead."

"We're all dead, idiot!"

The figure raised hands in supplication. "No. Really dead—the true death."

The smoldering became full flame, burning into the depths of the retainer's soul. Terrified, he lowered his head, waiting for his own final death.

No blow came.

"Who killed him?"

The question gave him room for hope. "We . . . I don't know."

Lady Ambrosia leaned back in her couch, eyes sharpening as she thought through various scenarios. "If you don't know who did the killing"—the fire burned brighter—"how can you be sure of the death?"

The retainer considered her question, hesitated, then blurted out, "Our intelligence—"

Fire touched the retainer, burning him, pinning him in place as he gasped. "*Intelligence!* That implies you're relying on someone else for information! Is that true?"

The retainer cringed away from Lady Ambrosia. He knew the door was mere inches away. *If I move quickly enough . . .* He sighed. *No. That's stupid.* He glanced at the waiting Methuselah. *She'd get me before I went ten feet.* There was only one way for him to survive this. *The truth.*

Lady Ambrosia stood, advanced a step. The retainer gasped. *This is the end!* But she stopped without touching him. "You haven't seen the body of the boy, have you?" The retainer shook his head, too terrified to speak.

"You don't know if Percival is alive or dead, in torpor or in Hell."

Another shake of the head.

The Methuselah glared at him. "You don't know anything, do you?"

A last shake of the head.

The ancient figure's face creased in what must have been intended as a smile. "And that's the only reason I'm going to let you live."

"Milady?"

The ancient one turned back into the darkened portion of the Sanctum. "If you possessed even a modicum of knowledge, I would have to treat you as a traitor. As it is"—the red eyes burned out again—"I merely think of you as a fool."

The retainer leaned against the wall for support. "Thank you, milady."

"Go."

He stared at those eyes, honestly puzzled. "Go where?"

"Find Percival's body—and when you do, tell me where it is."

"I'll bring it here!"

A huge hand came out of nowhere, smashing into the retainer's face, its unexpected force catapulting him into the far wall. "No, you fool!"

Red eyes burned into his from inches away. "Never bring *anything* here! Just find the body and report—do nothing else—*nothing*!"

"Y-yes, milady." The retainer struggled to hands and knees. "Nothing else."

The door opened. "Now get out!"

The retainer scrambled out. "And this time, do not fail me!"

Val drifted in a world of gray, unable to distinguish up from down, right from left. *Am I finally, truly dead?* The thought came from deep inside him, barely registering on the surface of his brain.

There was no possible answer.

He drifted for an eternity, lost in nothingness, then the world began to return. In snatches at first, and then, quite suddenly . . .

It was hot. Val looked up at the sun. Nearly noon. He took off his helmet, wiped sweat off his face with the sleeve of his uniform. *Bloody brilliant!* he thought. *Long sleeves in the friggin' desert!*

"Oy! You lot over there!" Val's mouth twisted. It wasn't enough to be broiling out here. No. Her Majesty had to send bloody Color Sergeant McChesney to make everything just perfect!

"Put your helmet back on!"

Val smiled sweetly at the man. *Damn, his face is red!* "Right away, Color Sergeant."

"Now, damn you!" Val kept the smile on while he pulled the sodden cork back onto his head. *Maybe we'll get lucky and he'll have a stroke!*

McChesney waited until the chin strap was fastened, then, giving Val his best glare, wandered down the line of marching men, looking for some other poor sod to harass. Val sneaked a peek at the sun. *A month on this march! Thirty bleedin' days!* He glanced ahead. *And who knows how much longer until we find the Frenchies?* Val watched as a drop of sweat rolled down his nose. *Old Boneypart ain't gonna quit and run away, that's for sure!* The column inched forward. *Am I?*

Val smiled inwardly at the question. Six months ago he would never have thought to ask. *I was such a child....*

He looked back at the sun. *At least it isn't dark.* He still had problems with the dark. Nightmares in which red-eyed figures grabbed him in iron grips and drained the life out of his helpless body. He shook his head thinking about it. *Nightmares every night.* His eyes followed McChesney. *Until the damned color sergeant beat them out of me!*

Val wiped off more sweat. *We'd better attack soon,* he thought. *Or we'll be in no shape to attack at all.* The remnants of the French army were more dangerous than anything Val and his comrades had ever faced, even though they'd been taught that merely being British made *their* army better than any other.

Did I really believe that?

Nelson had defeated the French fleet, leaving Napoleon and his Grand Army stranded in Egypt, their supply line cut. The British commanders had assumed it only a matter of time until the French surrendered—after all, what else could they do? *They can fight!* Val thought of the action he'd already seen. *Fight as well as we can.* Three of Val's mates had been shot in skirmishing actions—all had died. *Two of them after gettin' to the bleedin' field hospital!* Val shook his head. The battalion surgeon was a butcher, always quick to take the easy way out, amputate an arm or leg that might be saved— *then slow to stop the bleeding such surgery always caused.* Val and his mates had agreed that it was far better to die cleanly and suddenly at the hands of the French, than to linger in the care of Dr. Druitt.

The column came to a rolling hill line. Val groaned. Just what he needed. *Why can't we ride the bleedin' camels?*

We spent weeks learning how! The line trudged up the hill—and stopped at the top. *What the hell . . . ?* Val tried to see over the man in front of him, but he couldn't, the damn sod was too tall.

"What's goin' on?"

"Why'd we stop?"

McChesney appeared, moving fast. "All right, laddies." He pointed to right and left, motioning the line to spread out. "It's time to do our bit for king and country!" Val found himself moving to the side, heading to the top of the little hill.

He froze in place when he reached it.

"Oh my God!"

"Enough of that!" McChesney was right behind him. "We don't need to take the Almighty's name in vain for this lot!"

There were thousands of men in the valley ahead. The remnants of the French army. They were already drawn up into squares, their lines neatly trimmed, every man, every gun right where they were supposed to be. They were at rest, waiting for the British to approach. Val could hear them chattering among themselves, could smell the acrid smell of their tobacco. *We must be downwind.* He checked the powder in his lock, made sure it was dry and that there was enough to get a good flame. *Wouldn't want the damn thing to misfire now*! he thought numbly.

Off to the left, Val could see Colonel Martini and Colonel Parfitt talking. *They'll want to charge*, he thought, stomach going cold. *They always want to charge.*

They never had the chance to give the order. At that moment, moving as one, the French army pivoted and started to move—directly at Val's position.

Oh, God! I'm going to die!

*   *   *

Tessler had always considered himself more than a match for any member of the Kindred—until he found himself face-to-face with an angry Don Cruez.

"Tell me what you know of the destruction of Percival."

Tessler swallowed. "He was shot a number of times by an unknown assailant."

The Justicar's eyes pinned Tessler to his chair. "You saw this yourself?"

Tessler shook his head. "No, sir."

"Then how do you know?"

Tessler started to stand up—he thought better on his feet—but found he couldn't move. He glanced over his shoulder and saw Topper standing there, his slab of a hand casually draped on Tessler's shoulder.

Tessler ventured a smile, then turned to Don Cruez and began. "I had one or two friends keeping an eye on Val." He shrugged apologetically. "He was a little naive about some things."

"And your friends saw him killed?"

Again Tessler shook his head. "Not exactly. They saw him get out of the subway at Astor Place and knew he must be heading for the Blood Club." Tessler leaned forward. "The streets down there are pretty narrow. There was no way they could keep Val in sight without being seen themselves, so . . ."

"They waited at the Club."

Tessler shrugged. "What else could they do?"

The Justicar nodded. "Continue."

"A few minutes later, they heard gunshots."

Don Cruez's eyes flashed. "In Elysium!"

Tessler nodded. "My friends didn't think anything of it at first, after all, this city is controlled by the Sabbat. . . . "

Don Cruez's face twisted. "True."

"After a moment or so, they came to realize that Val would have been coming from the same direction as the shots, so they decided to take a look."

"And they found?"

Tessler glanced at Topper, still looming behind him. "They found the remains of five Kindred, already well into the final death."

"And one was Percival."

Tessler nodded. "At least, as far as we can tell." He picked up the package he had stowed under his seat. "This is definitely Val's jacket." He handed the leathers to Don Cruez. "As you can see, there are at least three bullet holes in it."

Don Cruez's fingers explored the surface of the coat. His long nails scraped at the blood crusted around the indicated holes. "Who did this?"

"I don't know." Tessler leaned forward in the chair, face suddenly angry. "But I want to find out."

Don Cruez stood up, eyes burning. "So do I." He held the jacket with surprising tenderness as he nodded to Tessler. "Look into this. Enlighten us both."

Mariana realized that it was too late to try to go to Brooklyn. She'd never make it there and back before the sun rose. *I'll go to the studio for a while, get some work done . . .* She headed for the door. *Then search for this "Percival" first thing tomorrow.* Her gaze crossed the shadowed opening of the Treasure Room. *Kleist's information had better be accurate!*

Outside, Mariana reconsidered her decision to go to

her studio. *I've spent a lot of time there the last few days.* She thought of Acquiel. *Maybe too much time.* A smile touched her face. *After all, I do owe the girl a bit of attention—I did promise. . . .*

Mariana strolled out of the Club planning how to please the little blonde blood doll. She noted three Brujah on the side of the street, but paid little attention to them. After all, this was Elysium. *Should I use the dressage whip tonight?* Her steps grew a bit faster. *Or the cat . . .* Mariana's tongue licked out, moistening her lips as she pictured Acquiel squirming under the leather's attentions. Yes, this *was* a good idea. They both needed the recreation. She turned the corner. *Not too far now.* Suddenly she realized that she was excited. She smiled—*most definitely the dressage*—and sped up.

Val learned the key lesson of war very quickly. It was *not* to die for your country. *You win by making the other poor bastard die for his country.* The British did that to perfection. Oh, the French fought hard enough, their experience and shooting skills put paid to many a British trooper, but, as the battle progressed, it became clear that the outnumbered French were also overmatched.

"Get your head down, you stupid nit!" Val grinned as McChesney flayed a trooper farther down the line. The big color sergeant knew his business.

Val peeked over his little barricade. The French were still there, but their formation had disappeared. They were fighting in squads now, making halfhearted charges at knots of British troops, firing, and then running back to the disorganized mass that was all that remained of their army. Val almost felt sorry for them.

Then he felt the heat from the sun, still hanging above, and was passed by a pair of scarlet-clad troops bearing a stretcher. *Napoleon started this.* Val's face set hard. *And now it's time for him to pay the piper.*

Val pulled the last prepared round out of his ammunition pouch. He motioned to the company runner and showed him the empty pouch. The boy raced away, moving at top speed to the commissary. *I hope to God the Commissariat is on top of this. If we run out of powder and ball now, we'll lose!* Val shook his head at the thought. *And that would be criminal.*

A sound of thunder interrupted his reverie. He peeked over the top again—and was shocked to see a full platoon of French troops charging right at him. Val dropped behind his scant cover, staring stupidly at his rifle. *One round.* He searched the back area for the runner. *Maybe he'll get back in time.* The thunder grew louder. *Then again . . .*

"Fix bayonets!" McChesney was right behind him now. "Here they come!" The big color sergeant crouched down behind Val, his huge Tower pistol at the ready. "Don't worry, m'lad. We'll stop 'em." The thunder stopped. "Now come on, get that sticker ready!"

Val pulled out his bayonet, jamming it onto the end of his rifle, turning it until it locked in place. *This is it!* he thought. *They're going to get me now!* McChesney picked that moment to stand up, firing his pistol. "All right, lads! Let's at 'em!"

Val scrambled to his feet, turning toward the oncoming blue jackets, his bayoneted rifle out in front as he'd been taught. He hadn't quite squared his feet when McChesney was hit, the blood splashing onto Val's shirt. *They got him!* Val was stunned. He'd thought the color sergeant invulnerable.

The world turned syrupy around Val. McChesney toppled in slow motion, face frozen in surprise and shock. Behind him, the French soldier who had fired the fatal shot was caught in the act of reloading.

Val brought his own rifle up, squeezed the trigger as he'd been taught, and watched the Frenchman go down, face gushing red. Val turned to his left, the world still frozen; there was another blue jacket there, his rifle up and trained on Val.

Val opened his mouth to yell, to plead. He tried to duck, to throw his body behind McChesney's, but there wasn't time. He saw the weapon fire. Saw the ball move toward him, the soft lead expanding slowly.

The world turned black and red.

Tessler had conducted the investigation personally. It had been swift and ruthless. He'd gathered everything that might shed some light on the events in Elysium two days before.

I still don't have enough of the answers. He shrugged internally. *Still, the Justicar wants to know what there is to know.* "I've gone as far as I can . . ."

Don Cruez's face was hard. "And what have you discovered?"

Tessler sat in his chair, acutely aware of Topper looming behind him. "There were a number of shots fired on that corner." He motioned toward a table. "At least six— we found that many expended casings."

Don Cruez nodded, silently urging Tessler to continue.

"The weapon was a .45 caliber automatic—probably the long-draw version, at least, that's what my expert says."

"How can he tell?"

"By the state of the bullets we found." Tessler motioned to another pile of metal on the table. "Five bullets, four of which show signs of having passed through flesh."

Don Cruez nodded again. "And the bodies?"

Tessler tensed. "There were five. All were Kindred."

"Five Kindred?"

Tessler nodded, a hard smile appearing on his mouth. "Four were quite young, and, judging by their dress, may have been anarchs."

"How did they die?"

"They were killed by Val."

The Justicar leaned forward. "What makes you say that?"

Tessler grinned. "I know Val's fighting style—he and I practiced together often enough—that was Val's work, all right."

Don Cruez nodded. "So Val was set upon by a group of assailants as he walked toward the Club . . . "

"At least five of them."

"How . . . oh, four dead, one to fire the shots."

Tessler nodded.

"Are you sure the fifth body is Val's?"

Tessler squirmed inwardly; this was the question he'd been dreading. "To be honest . . . "

Don Cruez's eyes pinned him to the seat. "You had better be!"

"No, I'm not sure." Tessler stood up, bypassing Topper's hand. "Oh, the other body is a Kindred, right enough. And old enough to be Val—it's not easy to judge after the dissolution, but I've seen enough"—he glanced at the Justicar—"final deaths to have some idea."

Tessler moved to the table, shifting through the other items there. "Val's jacket was there too, near enough the body. . . . "

"But you're still not sure."

Tessler turned, met Don Cruez's gaze squarely. "No. There's just not enough there." He took a deep breath. "I am sure of one thing, though."

"And that is?"

Tessler's face hardened. "Val was ambushed. In Elysium. By Kindred."

Don Cruez's face went thoughtful. "Yes, there does seem little doubt of that."

"What are you going to do about it?"

The Justicar stood. "I'm going to do whatever it takes to find out who is responsible."

Tessler licked his lips. "And then?"

Don Cruez's face was stone. "Then I'm going to call a Blood Hunt and destroy them—along with all their progeny."

Tessler nodded. "I want to help."

"Milady." The retainer had thought it best to make his report immediately after sundown. "The Justicar knows of the attack on his progeny."

Lady Ambrosia barely moved on her bed of pillows, just lifted her fangs from the throat of a thrall. Her voice was liquid. "His reaction."

"He is angry."

"As am I!" Lady Ambrosia pushed the thrall away, eyes turning their full force on her retainer. "Another day has passed." She glared. "Are you any closer to either the body or the killer?"

The retainer trembled, knowing he had to tell the truth, afraid not to lie. "Not yet, milady."

"I tire of hearing that."

The trembling grew more pronounced. "There is no trace, milady. Whoever is responsible is saying nothing."

"Find the weapon."

"Lady?"

Lady Ambrosia sighed. *Is he really such a fool?* She regarded the being before her. *He's served me well in the past, but perhaps it is time for a change.* She reached toward his mind, sensed the fear there—and the eagerness to please. *One more chance, then.*

She leaned forward. "Do I have to think for you? The weapon! It came from somewhere; find out where."

"But . . ."

Lady Ambrosia turned from her creature, pulling another of her thralls toward her growing appetite. "I want no more excuses." She bent, brushing hair out of the way.

"Find a way."

The retainer stood, unsure of what to do. Lady Ambrosia glared at him. "Now!"

She turned back to her feeding.

Val drifted in grayness. It all seemed somehow familiar. He moved without thought, without plan. *I'm in torpor,* he realized dimly. *Still alive.* He tried to open his eyes, tried to swim to consciousness, but he did not yet have the strength. *Soon . . .* He let himself fall back into the grayness. *I'll try again soon. . . .*

The light poured down in his face. It was late in the day now, the light slanting under the porch roof. Val's eyes opened a slit, then closed as he realized where he was. Druitt's hospital. *That Frenchie with the rifle! He must have . . .*

Val allowed his thoughts to wander around his body,

searching, exploring for the area that must be hurt. *Odd*, he thought. *I don't feel any pain, just tired.* . . . He tried to sit up—and the pain flooded in. Val gasped, eyes open and tearing. He looked down and saw the blood start to flow, soaking a white cloth tied to his chest. *I'm going to die*! Unwilled, a moan came to his throat.

"That'll be enough of that, laddie!"

That voice! Val's head turned to the side, the movement bringing more pain, more blood. This time, Val suppressed the groan that tried to force its way toward his lips. "Sergeant McChesney!" Val coughed the name out, though his lungs didn't seem to be working properly. "I thought you were dead."

McChesney, too, was lying on a stretcher, bandages swathing his chest and shoulders. Val could see that his bandages were also soaked through with red. "Not yet!"

The color sergeant tried to sit up, but didn't have the strength. "I'm going to tell you a secret, m'lad. A secret about death and the world beyond." His eyes went wide for a moment. "The world of darkness."

Val could see the pain the movement and the words cost the big man. He ignored his own hurts, determined to ease McChesney in whatever way he could. "I'm listening, Sergeant."

McChesney smiled. "That's Color Sergeant, boy!" He coughed as more blood flowed from his chest. "And don't you be forgetting that."

Val nodded. "I won't."

The big man nodded back, "I know it, son." He coughed again, blood spotting his mustache. "Now, remember this as well."

Val leaned forward, the pain forgotten. "Yes?"

"Remember that . . ." The cough came again. More pronounced now, more painful.

"Color Sergeant?"

McChesney's face was pale gray now, the color of the London sky. More blood flowed from his wounds as he fell back onto the stretcher. Val tried to move, tried to help, but his own pain returned, holding him, teeth clenched, on his own stretcher. His vision fluttered, blurred. . . .

The world went black.

Mariana smiled as she turned away from the sweat-slicked body of Acquiel. She was always amazed at the other girl's appetites. Mariana regarded the tip of the riding crop in her hand, then quickly licked a tiny spot of blood from its tip. *Waste not, want not!*

Her smile widened as she looked at the picture on the wall—the first portrait of Acquiel she had felt worth keeping. It showed the little blood doll, nude, regarding a variety of leather bindings. Her face seemed transfigured, and her body . . . Mariana tilted her head. It had taken days to get that body right. *Just the right measure of insolence and fear.* She turned to the real thing, struggling against her bonds on the big bed.

Yes, the picture is right. Mariana's smile widened. The first one she'd gotten right in how many decades? *Since Phillipe . . .*

Blue eyes flooded her mind. *Phillipe!* She'd forgotten him again!

She tried to think back. *I was in the Club. Kleist was drunk on tainted blood.* She could picture it now. Talking to Kleist, forcing the truth from him. *He told me a name.* A Brujah name . . . It was gone. Not a trace of it remained. *Am I going mad?* The thought frightened her. *Why can't I remem-*

ber? She tried to force her mind back. The Club, late at night. She'd left Kleist, gone into the bar. There was a disturbance. *Something about a shooting outside.* Mariana shook herself. She'd heard a gunshot. *Was it the same one?* She shook herself. No! *that's not what I want to think about!* Mariana forced herself to concentrate, pictured herself back in the club . . . *The bar. Late. Kleist drunk. He tells me to look for* . . .

There was a noise behind her. A muffled cry. *Acquiel!* Mariana turned. The blonde had managed to turn over, rolling her bound body on the big bed, fastening her wide, hungry eyes on Mariana's.

Mariana smiled, all thoughts of the Club forgotten. *I should blindfold her! That'd teach her a lesson.* Mariana raised the riding crop, still in her hands. *But first* . . .

"This is unbearable!"

The retainer held his position in the doorway. As far from Lady Ambrosia's seat as possible.

It was not far enough.

"First the boy disappears, apparently killed." Red eyes flared. "Now you tell me the gun used to kill him cannot be found!"

"I used the best technos available."

Lady Ambrosia got to her feet, robes swirling around her. "Apparently they're not good enough!"

The retainer flattened himself against the door. He did not wish to become the target of all that rage. "If there were a record of the weapon, they would have found it."

"What are you telling me?" Red eyes flashed fire, burning.

The retainer advanced a few wary steps into the sanctum. "The weapon is invisible—no record."

Lady Ambrosia growled, her arms and face swirling with conflicting energies. The retainer stumbled over his words, but continued. "They . . . did manage to backtrack the boy to some extent. He was searching for the creator of those knives used in the attack."

"As we planned!" Lady Ambrosia had regained control of her form.

The retainer nodded. "Apparently he went to Peter Grimsdyke for information."

"That one!"

The servitor nodded. "I tried to find Grimsdyke, discover what he and the boy had discussed." The retainer hesitated. "He, too, has vanished."

Lady Ambrosia returned to her seat. "Interesting."

"I also found that Kleist did, indeed, give the boy's name and the location of his haven to the girl."

"So?"

"Milady, she's made no move to find him. She seems more concerned with that pet of hers."

"The blond kine?"

The Kindred nodded. "Yes, but forget about her for a moment; think of the plan!"

Lady Ambrosia's face came up, eyes drilling into the retainer's. "You dare instruct me!"

The retainer let his head fall, bowing to his superior. "Never, milady. I want only to call your attention to the odd sequence of events."

Silence.

"You arranged," the retainer began, "for the boy and the girl to meet."

Silence.

"That meeting was to blossom into something more,

something that might reshape the power base of this city."

Silence.

"But things keep going wrong. The boy disappeared. The girl showed interest—then lost it. Things are used, then disappear . . . "

Silence.

"Kindred don't do what they should do."

Silence.

"Why?"

The silence continued. Thickened. Grew. Finally. "One of the others . . . "

"Milady?"

"One of the others has entered the game. Against me." Lady Ambrosia's eyes flashed. "Openly!"

The retainer held his breath and nodded. "That was my thought as well."

The darkness roiled. "We must find out who would be so bold."

The retainer headed for the door. "I will put all our people on it immediately."

Lady Ambrosia nodded. "Do that." She sank back into her seat. "I will pursue my own line of inquiries."

The retainer suppressed a smile as he closed the door. He might still be able to make this work to his benefit.

"As you say, milady!"

The universe swirled around Val, a gray place without landmark, featureless. He floated uneasily, caught between life and death, between darkness and light. . . . *Soon now.* The thought was deep in his mind, unheard, but felt. *Soon.*

Pain flooded through him, snapping his eyes open, flooding them with tears. There was a large, roughly hewn skylight over his head, the sun beating through it. Val tried to cover his eyes, found he didn't have the strength to move. *So tired* . . .

A man appeared, thin, bearded, clad in white, his shirt covered with blood. The man bent close to Val, a thin metal rod sparkling in his hand. The hand dipped, the rod moved to Val's side, touched . . .

Val's world exploded in red agony.

He screamed. The man turned toward him, surprised. "He's awake!" The rod withdrew. "Quickly! Hold him down!" Hands grabbed Val's arms and legs. Other hands held his head. Val's eyes moved wildly, trying to see faces, trying to find out what was happening.

Pain flooded through him again.

Val screamed, kept on screaming as the pain grew worse and worse and worse. . . .

The world went away.

Grayness flooded Val's universe. Swirling gray. He tried to think, tried to force himself out of the gray, into the real world. The dark world. He reached out, almost touched . . .

Not time yet . . . Grayness returned, pulling him down, drowning him.

Val opened his eyes. He could see darkness above, stars twinkling in the sky. *Night.* He turned his head and was blinded by the bright light of dozens of kerosene lanterns. *This must be the field hospital.* There was the scrape of metal on metal, followed by screams. They echoed through the big room, turned into gasping moans. *Druitt must be working on someone else.*

Val tried to sit up, but lacked the strength. Pain

flooded through him, agony so great that gray clouds filled his vision, almost blanking it out. He let himself fall back into the bed, lay as still as possible while he took great gulps of air. The gray slowly dissipated, dissolved entirely. Val lay there, letting his breathing slow. He worked to gain some control over his body, pushed the pain as far away from him as he could. He felt strength seep into him.

He looked around. His vision was clearer now, the pain somewhere deep inside. It was dark now, the kerosene lights extinguished. *Late.* He listened. *Quiet, too.* Val sat up, just a little, gritting his teeth against the return of the pain. He looked around, turning his head from side to side.

There was a man sitting next to him.

Druitt? No. The man wore no uniform. "Who . . ." Val's throat was dry, scratchy. *From the screaming.* The figure next to him produced a canteen of water, let some of it trickle onto Val's lips. Val swallowed, nodded his thanks. "Who . . . " *Better.* "Who are you?"

The figure smiled at Val, dim light glinting off sharp white teeth. "A friend." The smile grew wider. "The best friend you have."

Val shook his head, gritting his teeth at a stab of pain. "I've never seen you before."

The other laughed, keeping the sound low, controlled. "Perhaps not—but that doesn't change things."

"I don't understand."

The other moved closer. "Let me show you." A powerful arm went behind Val's shoulders, lifting him up. Val closed his eyes, fighting the pain. *I will not cry out in front of this odd stranger.* "Look at yourself."

Val stared down. A low moan escaped his lips.

"Yes, the musket ball punctured your lung."

Val's mind tried to run away, tried to pretend it had not seen what it had seen. *It can't be true!*

The big man eased Val back onto his bed. "Druitt can do nothing for this massive an infection."

"I'm going to die." Val's voice was barely a whisper.

The stranger smiled wider. "Yes and no."

Val looked at the man. "What does that mean?"

"It means I can give you a new life." The man's eyes seemed to glow. "A long life."

"How?"

"Like this." The stranger bent forward, lips brushing Val's neck. Val tried to fight the man off. *It's just like Piccadilly!* But he couldn't, he didn't have the strength. *I'm not ready to die!*

The stranger looked up, a drop of red blood just visible on his lip. "And you won't. You have my word." He held out his arm. "All you have to do"—he ran a razor-sharp fingernail over the arm and blood welled—"is drink."

Val lay there, mind whirling in circles. *He read my mind!* Val felt his strength receding; the gray returned to his vision. He dimly saw the stranger put the arm in front of him, the cut just inches from his face. "What—"

"Trust me."

Val's saw the slow trickle of blood, smelled the coppery sweetness. *This is wrong! Where's the doctor?*

The stranger pushed the cut against Val's dry lips. Val felt the red liquid touch him, felt it filter through his lips, touch his tongue.

He swallowed.

The stranger smiled, then bent forward, his own lips touching Val's throat. Val lay there, unable to speak, unable to move. The light slowly drained from the world, first becoming gray, then, finally, black.

He died.

* * *

Mariana dreamed of burning, animal eyes. *They're coming for me!* Fear filled her. Fear of the eyes, and what lay behind them. Only one person could help her. *Phillipe!* His image filled her mind. *Help me!*

Mariana awoke. *Phillipe!* She thought. *I was trying to find Phillipe!* A sound caught her ear. Whirring. *Sounds like my printer, but how* . . . She slipped out of the bed, taking a moment to give her companion a playful squeeze on bare flesh. She smiled as Acquiel glared at her from behind her gag. *I believe this one needs to use the necessary.* Mariana reached around Acquiel's tightly bound body, pinching a bit of flesh just below the waist. Her smile grew as the blonde gave a muffled squeal. "Do you need to use the bathroom, Acquiel?" Another squeal, louder. "I'll be with you in a minute." Mariana threw on a robe and headed for the studio. "Just as soon as I check out that noise." A third squeal, more insistent.

Mariana showed pointed teeth. "Now, don't do anything naughty or Mama punish!" The package on the bed shifted a bit, then sank back into the mattress. "There's a good girl." *I've got to think of something new today.* Mariana headed for the studio. *She's certain to do something to warrant another "punishment."*

In the studio, Mariana frowned as the whirring continued. It *was* the printer, turning out page after page of material. *I don't remember leaving it running.* Mariana scowled as she reached into the overflowing output tray. *Could Acquiel have activated it?* If the blonde had, Mariana *would* need to devise another punishment. *Something really painful.* Mariana picked up a page from the output tray, turning it over to see what was on it.

Odd. Eyes stared out at her. *Familiar eyes. Phillipe's eyes!* Mariana went through page after page of the printout. *They're all Phillipe's eyes! Now why . . .*

Then she remembered. *I've been searching for Phillipe—or rather, for that Brujah who looks so much like him. . . .*

Mariana remembered her discussion with Kleist, remembered loaning Acquiel to him for session after session. All in exchange for finding the man who belonged to these eyes. *He did find him! He told me his name! It was . . .*

A squeal came from the bedroom. Loud. Insistent. *Oh,* Mariana started to turn that way. *Acquiel needs to go to the bathroom. . . .*

She stopped, eyes staring at the picture in her hand. *Phillipe! I forgot about him! Just one noise and it was wiped from my mind!* Mariana shook her head, hard. *How many other times have I forgotten?* She looked down at the picture. *And why?*

Acquiel squealed again. *I've got to find out.* She headed for the bedroom, but kept the picture in her hand. *Soon.*

Val swam in gray shadows, hovering between worlds. He heard a voice deep in his mind telling him to wake up, to open his eyes, *it's almost time. . . .*

Val felt something touch his lips. His mouth opened automatically, and warmth rolled in. *Blood! It's blood!* Val's mind came to life. *I'm alive!* He remembered the night street, remembered the short man with the gun. Remembered the bullets. *But how . . .*

Val's eyes snapped open.

"Good day, young Percival." Peter Grimsdyke pulled the cup away from Val's mouth. "I knew you were almost ready to awaken." The actor smiled. "You're quite a powerful Kindred."

Val tried to move—and found that Grimsdyke was wrong. There wasn't an ounce of strength or power in him.

"I know you want to move." Grimsdyke moved away from his side. "But it's still too soon for that."

Val's eyes darted around, taking in the room around him, the night sky outside. *I must be in Grimsdyke's haven.*

Grimsdyke brought the cup forward again. "That you are." More warmth filled Val. "You're safe here with me." He smiled. "And soon, when you're strong enough . . ." The smile turned serious. "We'll see if we can answer all of your questions."

Tessler strolled down the street, fingers caressing the knife in his pocket. He was happy that Don Cruez had finally agreed to relax all restraints upon his investigation.

We're Brujah, damn it! Tessler grinned. *Rules are for the others!* Tessler was determined to find out what had really happened to Val—and who was responsible. The smile changed, became darker, angrier. *And then I'll show them who makes the rules!*

He sighed. *I can't do anything without more information.* He pulled the knife out, stared at the mysterious sigil. *This thing is the key.*

Val couldn't find out who made these . . . Tessler's smile turned predatory, sharp teeth shining in the night. *Maybe it'll be easier to find out who's using them.* Tessler nodded. *The anarchs. They have to be involved.* The four Kindred Val had killed in the street proved that. No one from the clans would violate Elysium. Even the Sabbat would hesitate at that. *But the anarchs* . . .

If the anarchs were involved in one attack, Tessler reasoned, they might well have been involved in all of them. Tessler nodded. Yeah, that's what I'll tell Don Cruez. He headed for the subway. If he ever asks. . . .

Twenty minutes later, Tessler was striding down Forty-third Street, wind from the nearby riverfront blowing his hair back, forming a dark halo around his head. I hate wind, he thought, looking around. Makes it hard to hear what's moving around you. He slowed, eyes darting from side to side, making sure he was ready. Gotta be more dangerous than they are!

He was in front of a bar called The Goth. Local hangout and headquarters of the anarchs. Tessler knew their leader, a youngling named, of all things, Christian.

Tessler settled his leathers more comfortably around him, smoothing his jacket for quick action. He ran his hands through his various pockets, checking to make sure his weapons were ready—just in case.

Yeah, everything's ready. He gathered himself. But I'll try talking first. . . . Carefully casual, Tessler slouched through the door.

The Goth had spent many years as a gay bar, supported by the hard trade that frequented the waterfront. It was devoid of overt decoration, projecting, instead, an air of painful simplicity. Tessler grinned at the weathered beams of the ceiling, the bare wood of the walls. They did look old, especially when compared with the modern sound system built onto racks behind the bar. Tessler shook his head at the volume and the music. Bauhaus! What a pitiful attempt at rebellion.

Tessler reached the bar, leaned against the dark wood, motioned to the huge bear of a human tending it. "I want to talk to Christian."

The kine looked him over, noting the well-worn

leathers, the thick belt, the attitude. . . . He shook his head and sneered. "Christian don't see outsiders."

Tessler smiled. He slowly brought his hand, fingers spread in a "peace" sign, above the level of the bar. His eyes never left those of the puzzled kine, even when he jammed the fingers into the man's nostrils, grunting as he lifted the man's bulk off the floor by that most tenuous of holds. *Hope the flesh doesn't rip. . . .*

The bartender's eyes glazed with pain and fear as he tried to pry Tessler's hands away. It was no use; he had no leverage—and his strength was no match for that of the Kindred. "I'm only going to say this once." Tessler lowered the man a little, allowing their eyes to come level. "I want to see Christian." Tessler moved, far too quickly for the bartender to follow. In a flash, Tessler's hand was back below the bar and the human was in a pile on the floor. "Now."

The human scrambled to his feet, holding his nose tightly, tears streaming down his face. "Y-y-yes, sir."

Tessler smiled and nodded as the man fled through a door at the rear. *Val was right,* he thought amusedly. *Sometimes it does pay to be polite.*

The man was back in seconds. Tessler was amused to see that his nose was already swelling. *Strong tissue!* he thought. "Christian?" he said, idly wiping his fingers on a bar napkin. A smile crossed his face as the big man quailed.

"He'll see you right away." The bartender motioned. "Through that door in back."

Tessler nodded and sauntered over to the door. He paused for a moment, tuning his hearing, working to sense anything through the din of the music.

There *was* movement in the room. Tessler concentrated. Three . . . no, four individuals. All Kindred.

Tessler smiled, carefully straightened his jacket, and opened the door.

"Hello, Tessler." Christian sat comfortably behind a desk placed in the middle of the room. He was a large, newly created vampire, hefty, with a balding head and florid face.

"Hi, Chris." Tessler strode into the room, noting the positions of the other three inhabitants. One behind him, the others flanking him. *Basic*. "How's it hanging?"

Christian shrugged. "Not bad." He motioned to two chairs facing the desk, lifted a carafe. "Care for a drink?"

Tessler pulled one of the chairs out, reversed it, sat. "Already fed."

Christian poured some of the red liquid into his own glass. "Change your mind? This is good stuff."

"I'll take your word for it." Tessler motioned to the other anarchs, stiffly waiting around him. "You might tell them to relax. I'm not here for trouble."

Christian smiled and took a sip. "What are you here for?"

Tessler rocked back, hands nonchalantly placed in pockets. "Information."

Christian sat back. "*You* want information from *me*?"

Tessler nodded. "It's a family matter."

Christian's face clouded. "A Brujah thing, eh?"

"That's right." Tessler let the chair fall to all four legs, leaning forward as he gathered his discipline around him like a cloak. *Might have to move fast . . .*

"Let's talk about a group of anarchs doing a little job." *Ready now.* "In Elysium."

The anarch grinned. "Elysium. Is that some place in Brooklyn?"

Tessler's smile hardened. "Don't try to bullshit me, Chris. You know what I'm talking about."

The anarch leader's grin widened. "Do I?"

Tessler *moved*. Lightning quick, he came to his feet, kicking his chair into the face of the anarch on the right. Simultaneously, Tessler's right hand came up and over, the knife in it driving deep into the wood of the table, pinning Christian's hand under it.

In a fraction of a heartbeat, Tessler twirled and threw a second knife with his left hand, the blade cutting through the chest and heart of the childe in the back of the room, pinning the dying body to the wall like some exotic butterfly.

That left only the fighter to his left.

Tessler ducked, allowed himself to hit the floor, rolling forward. There was a thunderclap of sound, and Tessler heard a bullet pass over him. *Guns!* He stopped his roll, came to his feet in one fluid motion. *Better be quick!* He kicked out, his iron-tipped boot shattering the knee of the gunman. Tessler flowed in behind the kick, snapping the Kindred's wrist, taking the gun away. He transferred the weapon to his own right hand, releasing the wounded childe, who dropped, falling into torpor. *Long-draw Colt!* he noted. *Interesting!*

He turned, eyes finding his first victim, still on the floor trying to untangle himself from Tessler's chair.

Tessler grinned. *Clumsy!* He put two quick rounds into the childe's head, watched brain splatter the wall, then, invested an eye-blink in putting one more weighted kick into the guard on the floor. The childe's skull collapsed with the force of the blow. Tessler watched as the anarch faded into final death.

He nodded. *Good enough.* Then stepped forward, bypassing the second body, and dropped himself into the still-upright second chair, right hand pointing to the hilt of the knife that still pinned Christian's hand to the table.

So fast had Tessler acted that the anarch leader had still not drawn a breath to cry out.

"Now, Chris"—Tessler's grin was steel—"let's talk about knives." He leaned forward. "And how they always seem to be attached to dead anarchs."

Lady Ambrosia came fully awake as the sun rolled beneath the smog-blurred horizon. She was not in a good mood.

She had spent the day thinking, analyzing, trying to understand what could possibly have gone wrong. *How could one of the others have learned enough about my plans to block them so effectively?*

She had reached no useful conclusions.

Her thralls were waiting for her to emerge from her dark seclusion, all of them offering themselves for her first feeding of the day. Lady Ambrosia smiled, assuaged for the moment. *This is the way the world should be.* She motioned her favorite to a nearby couch. *The way my world will always be!* She nodded and began to feed.

"Lady Ambrosia?" The retainer tapped gently on the door, afraid to enter without being invited. "Are you awake?"

The Methuselah drank her fill, taking distant notice of the thrall's brief struggles. She was unsurprised when the kine dropped into coma. *I believe I took a bit too much from this one.* She shrugged. *Ah well, there are many more where she came from.* Lady Ambrosia gestured for the other thralls to take the unconscious one away, then, sated and ready, she allowed the retainer entrance.

"Milady"—he bowed as he entered the room—"we have made some progress."

Lady Ambrosia sat back on her pillowed couch. "Excellent." This was shaping up as a much better night than the last. "Tell me all."

Mariana found Kleist sitting in his usual seat at the Club. The techno had his laptop open and running, his gaze, as usual, fixed on the tiny symbols scrolling across the screen.

"Kleist! I have to talk to you!"

"Mariana?" Kleist looked up in surprise, then, nodding, touched two keys on his machine and clicked the screen down. "I thought you were busy in your studio."

"I was—until I saw this."

She pulled the picture out of her pocket, handing it to Kleist. "It made me remember."

Kleist stared at the eyes, puzzlement clouding his face. "Is this supposed to mean something to me?"

"Think back." Mariana sat down, eyes intent on Kleist's face. "Our first deal." She leaned forward. "What was it about?"

Kleist frowned, thinking. "I wanted to use Acquiel . . ." He paused, looking around. "Where is she?"

Mariana shook her head. "Never mind her. The deal—what was it?"

Kleist's frown deepened. "I needed Acquiel for a series of pictures I was doing. You gave her to me in exchange for . . ." He shook his head. "In exchange for . . ."

He looked up, troubled. "You know, I can't remember what I was supposed to give you."

Mariana nodded. "I expected that. Look at the picture now."

Kleist stared down at the eyes. "They're eyes—so what."

"Whose eyes are they?"

Kleist shrugged. "Some Brujah that lives over in . . ." His expression changed. "That's what you were supposed to get!" He looked up at her. "The name and haven of this Kindred!"

Mariana nodded. "And did you give them to me?"

Kleist thought again. "Yeah." His face clouded. "At least, I think . . ." He opened his laptop, tapping in a code phrase. "Just a minute . . ."

Mariana looked down at the screen, watching the words scroll up at frightening speed. *It won't be there.* A grim smile touched her lips. *That would be too easy.*

"It's not here!" Kleist sounded shocked. "But it's gotta be! I logged it in myself." He gestured at the machine. "Saved it, too!"

"I'll bet you also deleted it."

Kleist hit more keys, scanning logs. "You're right! But why . . ." He looked up at her, eyes frightened. "What happened to me?"

"It happened to both of us." Mariana leaned back in her seat, face set. "I forgot all about Phillipe until those pictures appeared."

Kleist looked at the picture. "And I not only forgot, but erased my own records!"

Mariana caught the other's eyes. "Someone's been using us."

Kleist shuddered. "Someone extremely powerful." He looked at her. "Strong enough to get into both of our minds without our knowing it!"

Mariana nodded. "That's the way I see it, too." She leaned forward. "Now," she said, fixing Kleist with a questioning glance, "what do we do about it?"

He thought for a moment. "We could ask for help."

Mariana snorted. "From whom?"

"Anneke."

Mariana leaned back in her chair. "The Toreador Justicar? She's here?"

Kleist nodded. "That's what the staff here have been saying—and I've never known them to be wrong."

Mariana's mind raced. "What do you know about her?"

"Not much." The other shrugged. "But do you see another possibility?"

"No." Mariana sighed. "Where do we find her?"

Kleist tapped some more keys on his laptop. "I'll soon find out."

Val awoke in complete darkness. *This can't be the final death.* He shivered. *I know I'm alive. Grimsdyke told me so!* A light appeared, faint, coming from behind. *That must be him—I've got to get up.* He fought to move. *Can't stay helpless forever!* To his surprise, he found himself instantly on his feet, body moving easily, without strain.

"So, young Percival, you have recovered." Val whirled, saw the face of Peter Grimsdyke, then fell back, almost overcome by dizzy weakness. "Careful now." A hand steadied him. "Torpor leaves a body quite weakened."

"Why . . ." Val fought the dizziness down, brought his eyes up to hold Grimsdyke's gleaming gaze. "Why are you helping me?"

Grimsdyke helped Val to a chair. "But why shouldn't I help you, dear boy?" He settled in a seat of his own. "We are brothers in darkness, are we not?"

Val shook his head, confused. "But you're Toreador . . ."

Grimsdyke nodded. "I was reborn as such. Just as you were sired by a Brujah." The actor smiled. "So?"

"Our clans . . ."

Grimsdyke nodded. "Our clans have warred for these many centuries." The smile disappeared. "And whose fault is that? Are we so stupid that we cannot share a world of kine amongst our few selves?"

"I don't . . ." Val shook his head—and regretted it immediately. He fought the sickness down. "I don't understand."

"My dear boy, surely you know of the Eternal Struggle."

Val's eyes widened. "The Methuselahs." He breathed.

Grimsdyke nodded. "Yes, those ancient game players." The actor got to his feet. "They've picked you as the subject in one of their little plays for power."

"Me?" Val sat back, shocked. "What possible use could the Methuselahs have for me?"

Grimsdyke stopped at a refrigerator. "You are more important than you might think. Consider." He raised a finger. "You are the progeny of the Brujah Justicar. A Justicar who takes his job, and the Traditions, very seriously." Grimsdyke reached inside, pulled out a carafe of red liquid. "A Justicar who is arguably the most powerful being in New York City."

Val nodded. "But how could a Methuselah hope to get at Don Cruez through me?"

"He has something in mind. You can count on that!"

Val sat forward, brow wrinkled. "But, the shooting . . . ?"

Grimsdyke shook his head. "That was another player, his own move."

Val stood, fighting off the dizziness. "How can I end it?"

Grimsdyke returned to his chair, pouring the contents of the carafe into two glasses. "You can't." He handed one of the glasses to Val.

Val looked at the actor. "And how do I know you're not part of the plan?"

Grimsdyke smiled, raising his glass. "Well, I *did* save your life."

"That could have been part of the plan."

The older Kindred nodded. "So it could." He drained his glass. "You learn quickly."

"I wish I didn't." Val let his face drop into his hands. "How do I tell who I can trust and who I can't?"

Grimsdyke leaned forward. "You don't." He poured more blood into his glass. "For however long you exist, you'll never be sure of anyone again."

Val looked up. "What do I do?"

Grimsdyke smiled. "Drink up, then we'll discuss it."

"Tell me." Don Cruez leaned forward in his chair, fingers steepled.

"The anarchs were used by a Kindred elder." Tessler shook his head. "Dominated. Led like lambs to the slaughter."

Don Cruez nodded. "I suspected as much."

"Their leader thinks that the Kindred was Toreador— but he's not sure." Tessler looked up. "He's not sure of much."

"I know the type."

"I tried to trace the Kindred, used what little the anarch did know to try and reconnect with him." Tessler shook his head. "I got nowhere."

The Justicar leaned forward. "How many did you kill?"

"Does it matter? It was in the city. Sabbat territory."

Don Cruez sighed. "You're with *me*. I follow the Traditions—so will you."

Tessler nodded. "Yeah, I figured you'd look at it that way—but I believe that anarchs are outside the pale.

Not members of the Camarilla." He smiled, teeth gleaming. "Fair game."

The Justicar nodded. "Accepted. Do you have any other leads?"

"Maybe. I still have the knives and their sigils." Tessler shrugged. "I'm going to hit all the Toreador spots, see if I can find anybody who remembers such things."

"That's going to stir up trouble." Don Cruez frowned. "Don't kill any of them if you can avoid it."

Tessler grinned. "I'll try not to."

The Justicar nodded. "Do you need any help?"

The other shook his head. "Not at this stage. Maybe later."

"All right." The big Brujah stood up. "Keep me posted."

Tessler's grin hardened. "I will."

Anneke met Mariana and Kleist at the Blood Club. Elysium had been designed for safety, and the Club, with its substantially Toreador cast and staff, seemed the best choice in Elysium.

"I understand you have a problem." The Toreador Justicar took off her sunglasses. *Good*, Mariana thought. *I was wondering how she could see out of them.*

"I can see quite well, thank you." Anneke's smile was wintry. *I also hear much of what goes on around me.* That came directly to Mariana's mind.

Auspex! Mariana was shocked at the power of that mind in hers. *So strong!*

"If I had less strength, what kind of help could I bring to your problem?" Anneke's smile grew colder. "That is, if you'll tell me your problem at all."

Embarrassed, Mariana told the elder all, up to and including her certainty that someone was blocking certain of her thoughts.

"Interesting." Anneke's eyes turned inward as she considered what she'd been told. "It does seem that you've been used by some higher power."

"A Methuselah?" Kleist's voice was anxious.

Anneke chuckled. "Do such things really exist?" The elder leaned forward. "And are you sure there's no other possible explanation?" She turned her gaze to Mariana. "Perhaps a lover who doesn't want you to stray?"

Mariana shook her head decisively. "I don't have a Kindred lover."

Anneke allowed herself to fall back on her couch, eyes flowing over Mariana's form.

"Pity."

"Can you do anything to help us?" That was Kleist. Still anxious.

Anneke shrugged. "I don't know. If you are in the grasp of one of the"—she grimaced—"Methuselahs, I don't know what I *could* do."

Mariana felt fingers in her brain. *Although, for the proper reward . . .* "Anything," she whispered, then looked into the other woman's hungry eyes. "Anything at all."

Anneke nodded. "All right, then." She stood up, pulled sunglasses on. "I'll look into it. And if I find anything"— her eyes again devoured Mariana—"I'll look you up."

Mariana nodded, unable to meet those eyes.

"Right." Anneke headed for the entrance. "Until later, then."

Mariana shivered as she watched the Justicar leave. *Do I really need her sort of help?*

Her shivers intensified as the answer came. *You do, my dear. You most certainly do.*

*   *   *

"They have called in Anneke, milady." The retainer shifted nervously.

"Anneke?" Lady Ambrosia shifted in her couch. "The Toreador Justicar?"

The retainer nodded.

"Why her, I wonder." The Methuselah turned to her window, gazing out at the night-lit city. "And how did she come to be here, in a Sabbat stronghold?"

"I have not been able to find out, milady."

Lady Ambrosia nodded. "Another move by our rival." She allowed her mind to roam, searching for possibilities, new moves, combinations. "And an interesting one."

The retainer backed off a half step when Lady Ambrosia turned suddenly. "Find out where Anneke's haven is."

"Milady!"

Lady Ambrosia scowled. "I don't want to kill her! That would be too simple, too mundane." She turned back to her couch—and the thrall lying on it. "I just want to know whose protection she is under." She leaned down, mouth fastening on the thrall's neck.

"I'll put our best technos on it!" The retainer turned, anxious to be away.

"One other thing."

He stopped and turned. "The boy talked to Peter Grimsdyke before he 'died.'" Lady Ambrosia's tongue licked a drop of crimson from her lips. "Find Peter Grimsdyke and I think we'll find the boy as well."

The retainer bowed. "As you wish."

Lady Ambrosia turned back to the thrall. "Of course."

*   *   *

The night filled Val as he stepped out of Grimsdyke's haven. It was beautiful, air clear and cold, just the touch of a breeze to move the litter out of sight. *Perfect!* Val turned, looking at the night sky, reveling in life and freedom. *Even this life.* He smiled wryly.

Grimsdyke's haven was uptown, mere steps from Lincoln Center and its theater. Val pondered his next move. The information Grimsdyke had given him was interesting, especially if the actor's speculations were true. *A Methuselah, trying to kill me!* Val shook his head at the thought. *How do I avoid him? Do I hide? Go into torpor again?*

Val considered the city around him. *No. Not torpor.* He walked down the street, heading downtown, eyes darting around the street, watching the life of the city. *I want to live!* He smiled at the irony of that. *Well, I am alive—even if my life is different from the rest of theirs.*

Val caught a movement to his right. A girl peering at him from hooded eyes. He smiled. *Life!* The girl smiled back. Val slowed down, moved toward her open appraisal. *The other problems can wait.* He held out his hand, smiling as the girl took it. *First, I need to feed.* He looked down, smiled at what he saw. *Maybe I should pay more attention to Billy Joel's songs . . .*

Mariana spent a few more hours at the Blood Club before returning home. Her meeting with the Justicar had shaken her. *Are things really as dangerous as Anneke thinks?* she wondered. *And if they are, is there a way out?* She shook herself, trying to dispel the depression. *I've got to get out of here!* She looked around. Kleist was back in his corner, surrounded by women, working at his laptop. *Get back to Acquiel.* She smiled. *That would make them both feel better.*

The streets outside seemed cleaner than usual. Mariana glanced at the sky. *Stars!* She stopped to look. *We almost never see stars in the city.* She let the distant sunlight filter through her. *Odd that those suns don't affect us.* Again, she shook herself. *Don't think about that now.* She forced herself to start walking. *Don't think about anything except Acquiel.* Mariana smiled a tight smile. *Think about what you're going to do with her.* The smile brightened. *And to her.* Ideas flowed through Mariana's mind, new ways to use leather and rubber. *Yes.* Mariana's smile widened. *She'll like that.* . . . Mariana sped up her pace; it had been too long since she'd given the blood doll her full attention. . . .

She stopped. *Wait a minute* . . . Mariana searched her brain. *No. Everything is still there. Phillipe's eyes, the Brujah, the memory of the deal with Kleist.* She sighed with relief. *Have they stopped meddling with my mind?* Mariana hoped so. She was an artist, after all, and if she couldn't trust the images in her mind, what could she trust?

I can trust Acquiel. Mariana smiled. *And she can trust me to make her life* . . . *interesting.* Mariana went up the stairs, hurrying to her hidden haven. She'd left Acquiel in the bedroom, properly restrained, waiting for the return of her mistress.

"Acquiel?" No answer. "Acquiel, I'm home." She went through the door.

Acquiel was still on the bed, but she was spread-eagled now—tightly gagged.

And not alone.

"Hello." The man leaning on the bed gestured for her

to enter. "Why don't you close the door so we can talk in peace."

Mariana gathered her Discipline, ready to fight for the life of her companion.

"Oh." The man shook his head. "Don't try that." A knife appeared in his hand, tracing a thin strip of red across Acquiel's bared breast. "This one wouldn't survive."

"What do you want?" Mariana fought to maintain her calm.

The smile grew broader. "I want to ask you a few questions." He shifted the knife so that the point now touched the blonde's nipple. His hand opened, showing an inlaid hilt. "I believe this is your sigil?"

Mariana stared at the mark, confused. "Yes, of course it is, but—"

The man gestured. "Sit down." The knife moved again, drawing a moan from the tightly held kine. "I need some answers."

Mariana sat.

"Milady!"

Lady Ambrosia looked at the door in annoyance. It was almost dawn; she was tired. I *need to rest, to think* . . . She could feel the sun, just beyond the horizon, inching higher . . .

She shook the thought away. "This had better be important!"

"It is!" The retainer stopped on the threshold, bowing his head subserviently. "The girl has been attacked!"

"Attacked!" Lady Ambrosia came upright. "Who dared?"

The retainer cowered. "I am not sure, milady. I only

know that there is danger . . ." He looked up. "From another Kindred."

"Kindred . . ." Lady Ambrosia considered. "It could be an agent of our unseen competitor."

The retainer nodded.

Lady Ambrosia ignored him and turned to the window, staring out at the last lingering moments of night, feeling for an answer. "Or it could be one of Don Cruez's Archons, searching for the boy."

The retainer looked up, eyes puzzled. "How would they connect the girl with the boy?"

Lady Ambrosia glanced at him. "How was the boy *supposed* to find the girl?"

"The knives . . . "

"Exactly."

"What do we do?" The retainer glanced at the window. There wasn't much time.

Lady Ambrosia stretched. "We do nothing."

"Nothing?"

Lady Ambrosia glanced at the other as she moved toward the entrance to her inner sanctum. "What should we do?"

The retainer looked blank. "I don't know."

Lady Ambrosia reached the entrance, paused. *It's almost here. I could just stay here, watch the sun rise* . . . She pushed the thought back. "If we aid her, our competitor will know who we are." A dim hint of false dawn touched the horizon.

"But if we don't," the servant said, confused, "she might be destroyed."

Lady Ambrosia shrugged, entered her sanctum. "Then we start over, with another pair of puppets." She grasped the door, pulled it almost shut. "After all"—she smiled sadly—"we have all the time in the world."

The retainer stood, silent and confused, as the door locked.

Val spent more time than he had planned feeding. *First meal after the hospital*, he thought with a laugh, eyes on the girl beside him, *tastes extra special good!* He gave her a soft kiss on the neck. She moaned in pleasure. *I'm going to have to spend more time uptown!* Val gave her one last kiss, one last embrace, then he pulled on his coat and started back into the night. *It's late!* he noticed, checking his watch. But *I should have plenty of time to get to my haven before dawn.*

The subway didn't cooperate, though, running slow and late. He felt the sun touching the horizon just as he reached his stop. *This is bad!* he thought. It wouldn't do to be destroyed now, so near home.

He looked around for somewhere to hide out. He could sleep in the station easily enough, but he'd be helpless to stop the predators underground from doing what they would to his body.

No. He looked around. *There has to be another way.*

Val noted the tunnel running away from the station. He knew that it was a haven for the homeless, knew it harbored fugitives from the law, anarchs, and other, less inviting creatures. *It's probably full of Nosferatu!* He shrugged and grimaced. *Still, what choice do I have?*

He waited for the train to pull through, then jumped down between the tracks, careful to avoid the third rail. He padded into the darkness of the tunnels, looking for a deserted section, somewhere he could lie down and rest.

It took longer than he'd thought. He had to avoid the

boxes and rags that were shelters already in use. It wouldn't do to be caught there, asleep and helpless.

He moved deeper into the darkness, dodged a passing train, switched tracks. He felt cattle moving above him. Workers, preparing for their daily commute. His body was growing heavy, tired. *I've got to rest soon!* He kept moving, eyes searching for an unclaimed section. *There!* He moved to the right, where a gaping hole showed in the tiled walls of the tunnel.

Seems empty. He examined the hole, eyes and ears searching. *And it's been that way for a while.* He climbed in, found room to move on hands and knees. *I'll go in for a ways, get as far from the tunnel as I can, then I'll rest. . . .* He crawled.

The hole seemed to go on forever. Too far for Val to see the end. *I'll have to chance it,* he thought. *Sleep here.* He stopped, dug away at the wall, widening the tunnel enough so he could lie down. He yawned. *I'm just going to have to hope for the best.*

He felt the sun getting higher, felt his strength drain away. *I don't really have much choice.* He settled into the space he had cleared and, in an instant, fell into a deep sleep.

"She doesn't know anything." Tessler shook his head with disgust.

"Are you sure?" Don Cruez was pacing, unhappy with the situation.

Tessler nodded. "As sure as I can be." He grinned thinly. "She would have done anything to stop me from hurting her pet blonde." The smile grew. "Too bad, the kine would have been worth a little of my time."

The Justicar's face hardened. "This isn't a game, Tessler."

The smile disappeared. "Don't you think I know that?"

Don Cruez allowed himself to drop into a chair. "This is taking too long." He signaled Topper to bring him a drink. "Someone is blocking us."

Tessler leaned forward. "A Methuselah?"

Don Cruez shrugged. "Perhaps. But there are other possibilities."

Topper brought in a carafe, left it on the Justicar's desk.

"Did you know"—Don Cruez poured two glasses—"that another Justicar is in the area?"

"Who?"

Don Cruez took a sip. "Anneke."

"The Toreador!" Tessler's eyes widened. "She didn't present herself to you, did she?"

Cruez shook his head. "Rude, but not actually a violation of Tradition." He stroked his chin. "Perhaps you could learn what she is doing here?"

Tessler stormed to his feet. "Immediately!"

The Justicar smiled as the other stalked out of the room. *It must be nice to be young*, he thought, having another sip of his drink. *And to have so much energy.*

Val woke up to a whisper of sound. *What was that?* He tried to roll to his feet, but found himself unable to get any traction. *Where am I?* Then he remembered—he was still in the tunnels, lying in loose dirt. *What time is it?* He glanced at his watch. *After dusk. Time for me to . . .* The sound came again. *It sounds like footsteps.*

Val shook his head. *No time to investigate now.* He got his feet under him and started back toward the mouth of the tunnel. *I've got to get to Don Cruez, tell him what's going on.*

The sound came again. Louder now. Closer.

Val turned around, glaring back toward the inner darkness of the little tunnel.

He saw eyes. Hundreds, thousands of eyes. Red dots of light, all staring right at him.

"What in all the Hells . . . ?" The eyes moved and, in an instant, Val found himself inundated by rats. They burst out of the tunnel before him, racing for the open spaces of the subway. Thousands of rats. Small, large, black, white. Pets flushed down the toilets. Escaped lab rats. Wild riverfront rats. All the rats in the world. They ran over his feet, bunched up in the close confines of the tunnel, reached his knees, his waist.

Val fought, clawing at rat bodies, tearing into them, shredding skin from sinew and bone. He was covered with rat's blood.

They kept coming.

Val lost his footing, slipped in rat entrails. He fell; rats ran over his chest, his face.

Rats were suddenly in his mouth, clawing at his eyes. Everywhere.

Mariana stirred in her sleep. She moaned, sobbed. Tried to lash out—but didn't wake up. She was dreaming, lost in the past. Back in France, the war . . .

She was in her cell, surrounded by Germans. *Grinning. Always grinning.* They'd spread-eagled her on the floor, naked. There was a cage over her, lightweight, some sort of mesh. She didn't understand what it was there for.

Then the other German came in. The unsmiling one, the brown leather man. He had a bag in his hand, a heavy thing, sides expanding and contracting as if there were something alive inside.

He looked down at her, enjoying the fear in her eyes. He laughed and motioned one of the grinners. The guard opened a gate, set just over the juncture of her legs. The brown man laughed again, then upended his bag over the gate, dropping its burden into the cage.

The bag was full of rats.

Mariana screamed as the furry monsters touched her flesh. Screamed again when they began to bite her, ripping flesh off in great chunks. Pain engulfed her. . . .

Then the pain was gone. She was no longer the one writhing on the floor. Instead, she found herself standing, looking down, watching someone else scream in pain and terror. Someone she knew.

Phillipe! It's Phillipe!

Mariana woke then, screaming. "I've got to help him!"

Acquiel was next to her, stroking Mariana's soaked hair, hugging her hard, willing warmth into her chill bones. "Help who?"

Mariana turned wild eyes to the blood doll. "Phillipe. The rats have got Phillipe!"

"The rats?"

Mariana leaped to her feet, dragging clothes out of her cupboard. "We've got to help him."

Acquiel shrugged. It was no use arguing now. She pulled her own clothes on.

* * *

Lady Ambrosia was awake when she sensed the attack. *Rats!* She reached out, letting her mind's eye guide her. *Underground.* She dived into the earth, ignoring the fright of her unconscious, that part of her brain that didn't understand the changes the centuries had wrought upon her.

She dug deep, into the artificial tunnels the cattle had built. *Deeper.* The city was built on bedrock, but even rock cracked. Lady Ambrosia followed one of the cracks, finding the place it intersected with the cattle's holes.

The boy was there.

He was buried in rats, fighting grimly while thousands of the creatures tried to rip him apart, eat his flesh, drink his blood. *My opponent tries again.* Lady Ambrosia's mind assessed the situation. *With something strong enough to touch my own senses.* She ran the possibilities through her mind. *Who would use rats? The Nosferatu, perhaps?* Lady Ambrosia shook her head. No. *Too obvious.*

The Toreador! Lady Ambrosia's eyes lit. *Of course! The perfect choice—and so artistic a technique!* Lady Ambrosia's mind went grim. *I can't let her win. Not now. Not ever.*

Val fought grimly, without words. He fought as a Kindred, claws ripping at the beasts who would kill him if they could.

He'd tried, at first, to struggle back to his feet, tossing torn rat bodies to either side of him. But there was no room. His opponents were too numerous, too single-minded in their attack. Sheer weight of numbers kept driving him to his knees.

He had finally backed himself against the wall, using the dirt to guard his back, keep his hamstrings out of reach of gnashing teeth.

The tunnel began to fill with bodies. Hundreds of dead rats were scattered around, backs broken, heads shattered, bellies torn—killed however Val could kill them.

More kept coming.

Val husbanded his strength, holding himself back from full frenzy. He would use the Beast if he had to, but for the moment he fought with the skill and presence centuries of life had given him.

He knew it wouldn't be enough.

Val tore into the wall of teeth in front of him. If they would only slow down, give him a moment to think, to regroup. Then . . .

The wall of teeth receded.

Val kept fighting, too emotionally and physically charged to realize what had happened. He tore at the rats still in front of him, killing them in dozens, in hundreds. His claw shot out. . . .

And found no target.

Val's mind struggled back into full control. He looked out at the world—and saw that the rats had backed away. Their eyes still glared back at him, but from a distance.

Val showed his teeth in what might have been a grin. He leaned down to the river of blood in front of him, drinking deeply. He knew it was rats' blood, sour and filthy.

He also knew he needed the strength it would bring to survive.

The rats stayed back. Val didn't know what was holding them, but realized he had to take advantage of it now if he wished to live. He struggled to his feet, glaring at the eyes that still shone red in the tunnel. Careful not to break that eye contact, he began to back away, heading for the subway, where there was room to fight.

Room to run.

His feet, shoes and socks torn off in the fighting, kept slipping on the gore that lay ankle-deep on the tunnel floor. He knew that if he fell, he'd never get up again.

He kept backing up. The red eyes paced him, moving as he moved. Inch by inch, yard by yard, they kept their distance, always there. Always ready.

His foot slipped. He staggered for an instant, watched the wall of eyes waver; then he toppled backward, out of the side tunnel, into the main line.

The rats followed. A river of rats, flowing redly toward Val's supine position.

He didn't wait for them to reach him. He struggled to his feet, then, reaching deep inside himself, gathered his Disciplines and ran, speeding toward the station and the safety of numbers.

The rats followed.

Acquiel had never seen Mariana in such a state. She'd had to remind her mistress to put shoes on! Finally, though, the two had rushed out into the street, Mariana in the lead, racing toward the upper Village.

"Where are we going?"

"Underground." Mariana rubbed at her forehead. "We have to go under the ground."

"The subway?" Acquiel was even more confused.

"Yes!" Mariana's face lit up. "The subway!"

"The nearest station is over that way." Acquiel pointed to her right.

Mariana kept moving. "No. Not there. This way."

Acquiel shrugged. At least she didn't have a leash and collar on.

The two women rushed down Eighth Street, paused in front of the subway entrance there.

"Here?" Acquiel looked hopeful.

"No, not this one!" Mariana shook her head and started walking again, heading across Broadway. "Nearby . . ."

Astor Place was only a block away. Mariana plunged down the steps without pausing. "This is it!" Acquiel was only a step behind. "Come on!"

The station seemed peaceful enough. A handful of commuters were standing about, waiting to complete their daily commute. Others would come later, when the bulk of the city's workers finished for the day. Eyes turned as Mariana and Acquiel arrived, but the Toreador ignored them, pulling the blonde behind her as she plowed to the edge of the platform, eyes searching in both directions.

"What are we looking for?" Acquiel was puffing as she stepped to the side of her mistress. Running was not something she did a lot of.

"Phillipe." Mariana frowned, stroking her forehead. "Rats . . ."

"Hey!" Acquiel gestured at the men leering at them. "This place is full of rats!"

Mariana ignored her, focusing all possible attention on the darkness to one side. "Look!"

A man struggled out of the darkness, pulled himself up onto the edge of the platform. He was nearly nude; what few clothes he still wore were torn and tattered. Mariana noticed that his feet were bare, blood dripping off them. Hell! she thought, eyes wide. *There's blood all over him*!

"My God!" Acquiel was stunned by the sight, but still followed her mistress to the man's side. "Is he alive?"

Mariana reached the man just before he toppled onto his face. She raised his head and found herself looking into eyes the color of the morning sky. "It's you!" Her smile lit up the station. "At last!"

"Look!" Acquiel's scream pulled Mariana's gaze to the side. She saw eyes in the darkness. Red hungry eyes.

Rats' eyes.

Lady Ambrosia allowed herself to fall back into her cushions. She had done all she could. I *delayed the rats. Gave the boy time to escape the trap* . . .

She turned to her thralls. *If the boy survives, my plan may yet succeed.* She chose one, gesturing her to the bed. *If he dies* . . . Lady Ambrosia shrugged. That was a problem for later. For now, she had to feed, regain her strength. Her eyes hardened. She knew who was attempting to thwart her now. I *have to plan an appropriate revenge.* . . .

Val was almost drained when he reached the lights of Astor Place station. He could *feel* the rats following. *Not too far behind!* Val gathered himself and sprinted the last few yards to the station, running out of energy just as he reached the ladder to the platform. He took a moment to rest, risking a glance behind, into the darkness of the tunnel.

Red eyes peered back at him. Hundreds of them. *They're still following!* Val pulled himself up the ladder, staggered onto the platform, eyes locked on the predators behind him. *Got to feed, gain strength* . . . The lights dimmed, he felt himself falling. *No time. No time left.* . . .

He was caught, held. Soft arms circled his chest, supporting him.

Val's eyes opened, senses swirling as his vision brightened. He was inches from the face of a beautiful, dark-haired woman. *Got to feed!* Without conscious thought, Val grabbed the flesh in front of him, held it tight while he sliced into the white throat, exulting at the taste of the blood within. *I'm not going to die!*

Acquiel panicked when the blood-soaked man suddenly attacked her mistress. "Hey!" she yelled, throwing herself onto the other's back, trying to pry iron arms free. "Let her go!" She saw the teeth bite in, heard the blood move from throat to mouth. "You can't do that!" Helplessly, she beat at the man's head. "She's like you!"

The man shrugged her off, continued to feed. Acquiel looked wildly around, searching for any kind of help. There were other people in the station, surely they'd . . . but no. This *was*, after all, New York. People were already busily looking the other way.

Acquiel darted away, looked for something, anything, to save her mistress. There must be a fire ax, a piece of wood . . .

She raced to the edge of the platform, looked down.

And found herself face-to-face with a sea of rats.

Mariana relaxed into the embrace of the man she thought of as Phillipe. She felt his need and was perfectly willing to fill it. *Take it all!* she thought. *Anything!* She sighed.

For years she had dreamed of this embrace. *Oh, Phillipe! I've missed you so much!*

Mariana moaned as blood flowed from her veins into those of the bloody figure in front of her. She felt her strength waning with the exchange. Deep down, she knew this shouldn't be happening, knew it was wrong.

She didn't care.

For long moments she stood there, supporting her newly found lover as he drained her strength, regaining his. She began to think wild thoughts, dream impossible dreams. The two of them together, building a home, having children.

Impossible. And yet—

There was a scream. Long and impossibly shrill. *Acquiel?* Mariana's mind began to function once more. *That was Acquiel!* Thought replaced feeling. Mariana pushed away from the man before her, strength and sanity restored.

"Let me go!"

His eyes opened, reason suddenly flooding back into their blue depths. "Wh-who are you?"

She broke free. "Not now. There's some kind of trouble." Mariana turned to the edge of the platform, saw Acquiel standing there, looking down, mouth open in horror.

"Acquiel!"

The blonde screamed again, staggering. Mariana saw a dark shape on the edge of the platform, then another, and another. . . .

Dozens appeared. Rats, their red eyes locked onto Acquiel. The blood doll seemed fascinated by them, held in place by the glare of their tiny red eyes.

"We've got to save her!"

The man shook his head. "We can't. We've got to run. Get away."

Mariana turned, dark eyes searching sky blue. "I won't leave without her."

The man shook his head. "You're crazy."

"You don't have to help."

The man grinned. Mariana's knees turned to jelly. *My God, if he asks me to leave now* . . . She shook her head. *I don't know what I'd do!*

"I guess I'm crazy, too!" He turned toward the edge of the platform.

Val felt the life-giving vitae flow through his system. His strength returned, doubled. *Something's wrong!* His mind came back to life, rising above survival instinct. *There's too much strength.* . . . He stopped his hungry feeding. *She's Kindred!*

There was a scream.

Val's eyes snapped open, found themselves staring deep into eyes of darkest brown. "Wh-who are you?"

The other broke free of his hold, turned toward the station's edge. "Not now. There's some kind of trouble."

Val shook his head, trying to remember what he was doing here. He looked down at himself, shocked to discover his near-nakedness. *I'm covered in blood!* he thought. Then it all came back. *The rats!*

Val's eyes darted to the edge of the platform. A beautiful blonde stood there, staring down into the darkness below. Val knew that she was seeing the rats. *They've caught up!* He grabbed the arm of the other Kindred, determined to take her to safety.

"We've got to get out of here!"

She turned troubled eyes on him. "No." She pulled away, hair flying in the dim light of the tunnel. "We've got to save Acquiel!"

She's beautiful! Val sighed. *So beautiful.* . . . He caught himself. *I shouldn't be thinking like that!* He shook his head once, hard. Could it be a Blood Bond? He rubbed a hand across his face. *Already?*

Rats appeared on the edge of the platform. Just a few at first. They ran over the feet of the blond kine. One or two stopped to nibble. The girl screamed.

Val tried again to grab the dark-haired Kindred, ready to run out into the night. "No." She shook his hand away. "We've got to save her."

Val knew that there were too many rats to fight. Knew that it was too late to save the blonde. "We can't." He motioned to the exit. "We've got to run. Get away!"

The Kindred turned to him, her dark eyes burning into his brain. "I won't leave without her!"

He found himself thinking thoughts he'd never dreamed of before. Thoughts of home, family. Eternal life with those eyes, that face. No! He pushed the thought away. *That's impossible! We're Kindred!*

"You're crazy!"

He couldn't turn away from her eyes. *Much too soon* . . .

"You don't have to help!" She turned away, stalked toward the edge of the platform and certain death.

He realized that he'd do anything to make her happy.

"I guess I'm crazy, too."

He followed.

*   *   *

Acquiel screamed again as another of the rats nibbled at her toes. She knew that she should run, knew that she should do something to get away.

She couldn't move.

Those eyes, she thought, gaze locked on the thousands of red spots below. *They're holding me.*

Acquiel began to cry. She'd always known she would die young, had prepared for it, braced for it. But that death should have come from Mariana's embrace—a short death, opening her way to a larger world. The World of Darkness. *It's not time!* Acquiel's brain wailed. *I'm not ready!* She tried to tear her eyes from the hellish sight below, but didn't have the strength. Her cries grew louder, more hysterical. *I'm not supposed to die like this!*

Another rat bit her, hard; blood flowed. *Mariana!*

Mariana raced for Acquiel, calling up what discipline she possessed.

It wasn't enough.

The rats swarmed over the side of the platform before she could reach the blood doll.

Mariana watched in horror as hundreds of them swarmed over the blond form of Acquiel, covering her in gray and brown fur, forcing her, screaming, to her knees.

Mariana reached the rats, kicking and stomping as she tried to work closer to the inundated Acquiel. *I'm not going to make it!* Mariana realized. *She's going to die!* The thought made Mariana ill. For the first time, it occurred to her that she loved the blond girl. *She's like a daughter to me!* Mariana redoubled her efforts, tearing into the biting vermin, tearing at them with all the efficiency she could muster.

Suddenly she wasn't alone. A killing hurricane passed her, dead rats swirling off its surface like so many twigs.

Mariana stopped in her tracks, amazed as the other Kindred passed her. *He's doing it!* she realized. *He's going to reach Acquiel in time!* More rats bubbled up from the tracks, racing to intercept the blood-soaked Kindred. *I've got to help him!* she thought, moving again. *Got to keep a path clear for us to escape by!* She started killing again, artist's hands covered with blood as rats flew from her path.

Val passed Mariana as though she were standing still. *Never honed her disciplines*, he realized. *Too bad. I could use the help.* He focused his attention forward, locking everything he had on the struggling blonde. *Got to reach her before the rats do too much damage!* He increased his speed, claws arcing right and left, tossing the disemboweled remains of rats to the sides. *She's slipping!* He adjusted his course a hair. *Almost there . . .*

He reached Acquiel just as the blonde fell forward, precious throat mere inches from the voracious teeth of the rats. *No you don't!* Val grabbed the girl's body, pulled it to his side, clawing rats away from her, clearing her midsection, her legs. . . .

He saw eyes flutter, felt the beat of a heart. *She's still alive!* Val smiled grimly. *Now let's see if we can get her out of here!* He turned back, rats again flying away from his arcing claws.

And stopped.

There's a path!

And there was. A rough opening cut through living flesh was just in front of him. In the middle of the path stood the other Kindred, clothes nearly gone, blood covering every inch of her exposed flesh. She motioned to him, smiled—and returned to the slaughter.

We may make it yet! Val rushed forward, the blonde hanging over his shoulder.

And if we do . . . He would worry about that when the time came; for now, it would be enough to get out of this hellish underground. To see the sky, the stars . . .

He glanced forward where the other continued to kill silently, efficiently.

And to learn more about her. . . .

Tessler wandered down the street, head down, hands jammed deep in pockets. The night hadn't been kind to him. He'd searched all of the Toreador haunts, talked to all of his contacts—and hadn't found a trace of Anneke. *It's as if she's disappeared into thin air!* Tessler grinned sourly. *A good trick in this polluted hole!*

He shook his head. He'd promised an "instant" report to Don Cruez. Unless something happened soon, he was going to have to disappoint the Justicar. *And I really don't want to do that!*

Tessler headed down Eighth Street, heading for the Lower East Side and his haven. *If only something would happen!* It was almost a prayer. *Anything to give me a break.* He turned the corner, strolling toward the Victorian splendor of the restored Astor Place station—and came to a halt.

There was something happening at the station. Kine were bolting up the stairs, running into the night. Police cars were approaching, sirens wailing, lights flashing. *What's going on?* Tessler strolled closer.

Perhaps there was something here, something to take the Justicar's mind off Val and Anneke.

More cattle boiled out of the station. Tessler heard movement below. Feet. Hundreds, thousands of feet. *What the Hell?*

A figure streaked out of the station entrance, moving faster than any human could. *Kindred!* Another figure joined him, not as fast, but still moving with celerity. *Two! Something was wrong here.* Tessler glanced around. The area was full of humans, and yet these two Kindred were not even trying to hide their abilities. *The Justicar isn't going to like this!* Then Tessler heard the footsteps again. Thousands of feet, but wrong somehow, light . . .

The station entrance erupted into movement. Hundreds of figures appeared. *Rats!* Tessler could see them now, his vision passing over their hungry red eyes. *And so many!* He watched as the rats swarmed out of the station, heading straight as an arrow for the two Kindred, now stopped and waiting for them. *They must be exhausted!* Tessler's eyes fell on the two bloodstained figures—and widened in shock.

Val! He stumbled forward, heading for the figures across the street. *That's Val!*

Val and Mariana staggered out of the station, coming to a stop on the other side of the street, in the shelter of one of the old stores that littered the area. Val could feel his strength draining again. *Too much energy*, he thought. *Got to feed again*. He slipped the blonde off his shoulder, checking her for signs of life. *She's breathing*. He felt for a heartbeat. *Do I dare take vitae from her?* He moved his lips to her neck, mouth already tingling in expectation of the red flow to follow.

A hand closed on his arm, pulling him to the side. "Take it from me."

It was the dark-haired Kindred. She pulled the remnants of her dress away from her throat. "Go ahead." She smiled. "Do it."

Val nodded, let the blonde slip to the ground, gently, and touched his teeth to the side of the Kindred's neck. Rich, strengthening vitae flowed into his starved system.

That's twice, he thought, new energy filling him. *Have to avoid another time—Blood Bond. . . .* The world smashed into his senses.

Val turned, saw the cattle gathering around. *Uh-oh!* There were police cars pulling up, windows reflecting mad hues from the lights. It was only a matter of seconds before they found him, and then . . . *Don Cruez isn't going to like this.*

Val became aware of another sound. The pounding of tiny feet. *The rats!* He turned toward the station entrance. *They haven't given up!* Val saw the pack explode into the streets, red eyes searching for him in single-minded frenzy.

Val looked around, searching for a place to hide. There was nothing. Just some old buildings. *No good.* He looked for a weapon. *What'll kill rats?* His eyes lit up. *Fire! Fire will kill them!* He turned toward the police cars, a plan projecting itself in his mind. *Yes! That'll be perfect!* He strode forward, leaving the dark-haired Kindred and her blonde thrall hiding in shadow.

* * *

Tessler had almost reached Val when the other started moving. *Where is he going?* Tessler saw his friend head back into the street, moving purposefully toward the police cars. *Is he mad?* Tessler followed.

I need a fire, Val thought, racing toward the police cars. *Something big—hot.* One of the policemen turned toward him, eyes wide, unholstered pistol coming up. Val nodded. *Good!* He backhanded the cop, pulling the pistol from the suddenly limp hand as he sped by. The snap of the man's splintered index finger hardly registered. *I'll need this!*

Val looked toward the subway entrance. There were a couple of hundred rats there now, milling around, searching for their prey. Val could see more eyes on the stairs that led into the underworld. Red eyes.

Rat eyes.

Just wait there. Val grinned. Another cop appeared in his path. Val didn't slow down, just backhanded the man out of his way and kept moving. *I'll be along in a minute!* Val reached the first of the police cars parked at the side of the road—*this should do it*—and stepped in. The keys were still in the ignition. *Helpful.* Val turned the key—and whirled as the other door opened.

"Don't worry, cuz." Tessler grinned at him. "Just thought you might need a hand."

"Tessler!"

The Brujah pointed at the other cops, all pulling weapons out, ready to open fire. "You got something in mind?"

Val grinned, pressing down on the gas. "Yeah, you might say that." The police car roared forward, rear tires smoking. Val heard gunshots behind, one or two hitting the back of the car. "Anxious, aren't they?"

"New York cops are always a little trigger-happy."

"Yeah, I guess so." Val spun the wheel. "Hold on."

The car skidded as Val braked, turning on its own axis until it was pointing back toward the firing cops—and the station entrance. "Now!" Val floored the gas.

The car hesitated a moment, rear wheels smoking as they bit into the street—then they rocketed forward. Val held the wheel steady, pointing the hood ornament right at the Astor Place station entry. "Get ready to move."

Tessler grinned. "I was born ready!"

Val nodded, correcting his steering a hair as he sideswiped a stubborn cop. "Any second . . . "

The car plunged into the station kiosk, smashed through the cement wall. Val braked hard, felt the car skid on the mangled remains of hundreds of rats. "Go!" He rolled out of the door, watching as Tessler did the same on the other side. The car continued forward, lost momentum, stopped, teetering over the staircase.

Val came to his feet, pulled the cop's gun out of his pocket. "Take care of those other cattle, will you, cuz?"

Tessler's grin grew teeth. "Pleasure."

Val felt the air shift as Tessler moved off. He grinned. No one would bother him for a while. He gave the car one final kick, watching it plunge forward, turning over, crushing rats on the stairs below. *That takes care of some of them.* . . . Val peered down, watching for the telltale shininess of leaking gasoline. *Come on, these things always leak after a crash* . . . There it was! Val waited for the gas to spread. Just a little. He felt the rats moving toward him, sensed the first of them approaching his bare feet. The little puddle of gasoline grew, widened . . .

Now!

Val fired the pistol, aiming at the hard metal of the rear axle. One shot. Two. C'mon! I *only need one spark!* Three. Four.

Ka-Boom!

Val was thrown backward as the car disappeared inside a giant fireball. *That should do it!* He rolled to his feet, moving back far enough to keep his hair from charring. He could hear rats squealing, then screaming as they found themselves trapped inside the conflagration. Val nodded. *Yep.* He turned back toward the street.

Things were deserted now. Tessler had handled the police; Val could see their bodies neatly placed back into their cars. *I hope he's strong enough to Dominate that many; this might be too showy for Don Cruez to accept otherwise.* His cousin was on the other side of the road now, moving fast, working on the few spectators who hadn't shown enough New York sense to disappear on their own. Val grinned. *And people wonder why New Yorkers don't like to get involved!*

"Everything okay, cuz?"

Tessler grinned back. "No problems here. What do you call that, anyway?"

Val smiled. "Car bomb." He strolled away from the station, not at all bothered by the smell of burning rat. *I hope she's still here.*

She was. Right where he'd left her, leaning against the wall of a store, eyes filled with the carnage that had played itself out in front of her. "He's not going to kill them all, is he?"

Val shook his head. "That might be dangerous."

The other nodded. "To the Masquerade."

Val nodded and inclined his head toward the unconscious blonde. "Is she all right?"

The Kindred smiled. "She'll be fine. No serious

hurts." She raised a timid hand, touched his singed face. "You?"

Val grinned. "I'm okay." He raised his own hand, took hers. "Better than I've been in a long time."

Mariana smiled. "I'm glad."

"So am I."

Don Cruez frowned as Tessler finished his story. "And that's it, sir." The other Brujah shrugged his shoulders. "We made them all forget what really happened. They'll report some kind of mob fight, then a riot."

"And Val?"

"After he was sure all the kine had been properly instructed, he left." Tessler's face hardened. "With the Toreador."

"You *do* know who this person is?"

Tessler nodded. "I talked to her just the other day. She's the one who made those knives."

"And yet, you allowed Percival to go with her?!"

Tessler made a face. "I really didn't have much choice."

Don Cruez got to his feet, pacing. "And he told you nothing else."

"He promised to meet me tomorrow, tell me the whole story."

The Justicar turned toward Tessler. "You'll be there, of course."

"Naturally."

Don Cruez went to his sideboard, poured a drink. "It's important that we know why Percival is acting this way." He took a sip. "If he is under the control of one of the other factions . . ."

Tessler nodded. "We'll have to take steps."

The Justicar glared at him, eyes burning. "*We* have to do nothing—*I* will decide what is to be done."

"Of course."

"In the meantime . . ." Don Cruez returned to his chair, eyes vague as he let himself drop into thought. "Have you found Anneke?"

Tessler frowned. "Not a trace. Are you *sure* she's in town?"

Don Cruez leaned back in his seat. "At this point, I'm not sure of anything. However, I was given to understand that Anneke was, indeed, here."

"I'll keep searching."

The Justicar nodded. "Do that. And make sure Percival is all right."

Tessler nodded, coming to his feet. "I will." He headed for the door Topper held open. "You can be sure of that!"

The retainer smiled as he approached Lady Ambrosia's sanctum. *She'll be pleased tonight*, he thought. *Everything's finally going according to plan!* He tapped on the oaken door that secured the entrance. "Milady?" He could hear movement within.

"I have good news for you." The door remained closed. "Milady?"

More movement. *Am I wrong?* The retainer began to worry. *Is something wrong?* He shuddered. *Did someone manage to break in?* That would be the end for Lady Ambrosia—and him. *No!* He rallied. *Impossible!*

The door opened. "Well, don't just stand there." The retainer goggled at what he saw. "Come in."

The retainer whimpered as he entered the Lady's

sanctum. *She's going to kill me!* He looked around, wide eyes noting the thralls, each of them dead, each of them drained. *Just as she killed the rest of them!*

Lady Ambrosia was totally naked, her ancient body hairless and red in the dim light of the sanctum. The red was blood. The blood of her thralls.

But why?

"I needed the power." Lady Ambrosia smiled as she settled into her customary pile of cushions. She settled in, then sat up, her mouth showing a moue of annoyance. She reached behind her, extracted a limp arm, and tossed it aside. She settled back in, face reflecting serene comfort. "Come, sit." She smiled at the retainer, a smile full of long, sharp teeth. "Don't worry. I'm not going to kill *you*."

The teeth glittered in the dimness of the new night. "At least, not quite yet."

The retainer collapsed into the indicated chair. "I-I—"

"You came to tell me that the boy and the girl were finally together."

The retainer nodded.

"And that the Brujah Justicar was unsure of what to do next."

He nodded again.

Lady Ambrosia's smile widened. "I thought that might be the case." She glanced around. "Especially now that I have silenced my opponent."

"You found out who it was!" The retainer leaned forward, curious.

Lady Ambrosia nodded. A drop of blood flowed out of her hair, across her brow. "Yes, it was inevitable that I would."

"Who was it?"

"The Toreador."

"Lady Singhjul!"

Ambrosia nodded. "The rats gave her away."

The retainer was puzzled. "But . . . I would have thought rats meant Nosferatu."

"That's what we were supposed to think." Lady Ambrosia leaned back farther, eyes searching out the distant stars. "It was a clever ruse . . ." Her eyes sharpened. "But her threat is ended for now."

The retainer bowed. "A mighty victory!"

"Yes." Lady Ambrosia's eyes fixed on one star. "Now the girl and boy will grow attached."

"And the girl will paint her pictures!"

The Methuselah turned to the retainer, smiling. "And we will arrange for a gallery showing of those pictures."

"Nothing could be easier."

Lady Ambrosia's smile deepened. "Then the girl will die—and the boy will unleash his Beast."

"Many of the Kindred will die." The retainer's voice was stolid.

"Pawns." Lady Ambrosia leaned forward. "It is the king that I am interested in."

The retainer nodded. "Don Cruez."

"Exactly!" The Methuselah looked up, eyes locking with those of the retainer. "With him gone, war will certainly break out between the Sabbat and the Camarilla." Teeth glinted as she smiled. "The balance of power will shift."

"And the city will fall under your control."

The glint grew brighter. "Exactly."

The retainer looked nervous as his body started to move, slowly, unconsciously, toward the cushions. "Milady . . . ?"

"I've been a little hard on my thralls tonight." Lady Ambrosia's tone was dreamy, her eyes bright. "Yet I still need to feed. . . ."

The retainer's face went blank.

"Come to me."

His feet moved faster, uncontrollably. Without thought, the retainer found himself kneeling at the feet of the ancient one, watching as sharp teeth, still crusted with blood, descended toward his neck. He closed his eyes and mind just before the teeth touched.

It's funny. Val looked at the form beside him. *I've always thought it impossible for Kindred to fall in love, and yet . . .*

Mariana's haven had been closer to Astor Place than Val's. She had led him there while he carried the still-semiconscious Acquiel. Her concern toward the kine had troubled Val at first, but he had come to see it as an emotion he had never experienced—not even in his breathing life. *She loves the blonde!*

He had been even more surprised when he got inside the sanctum of her haven. The paintings were expected—Toreador always had paintings or sculpture or some such thing—it was the subject matter that caused Val's eyes to widen. Especially the portrait of Percival and the Holy Grail. *My portrait!*

There had been little time to get acquainted on that first night. Dawn was approaching fast, and both Val and Mariana (*pretty name*) were in desperate need of rest. Still, Mariana insisted on dressing the blond kine's (*Acquiel—got to remember that*) wounds before she would go to her bed. Val had helped, impressed by such loyalty.

They had all ended up in one big bed, the breather supplying needed warmth for the two Kindred. Val had fallen asleep before the sun crossed the horizon, feeling safe for the first time in weeks.

That had been three nights ago. Since then, Val had remained a guest at the Toreador's haven, not because he had to now, simply because he—and she—had discovered that they were happier together. At first, he had feared that his two feedings on Mariana had trapped them both in a Blood Bond, but, as time passed, Val came to realize that blood had nothing to do with what was happening. There was something special between them. Some feeling that came from deep inside.

They had taken to hunting together, feeding together, sleeping together—inseparable, as if they were two halves of a whole. *It's like being married.* Val marveled at the arrangement—and realized he would fight Don Cruez himself to keep things the way they were.

Happily, Acquiel also approved of the arrangement. She had quickly recovered her good spirits after the horrors of that night, and was quick to show Val why Mariana had picked her. *I've been living alone for too long!* he thought with a smile. *Much too long.*

Mariana had decided to do a new painting of Percival—one for which Val would model directly. Acquiel had tried to get into the act as well, but Mariana had told her in no uncertain terms that she needed only one model for this picture. The blonde had sulked for a full night, then had appeared at the studio, naked, trying her best to get Mariana to play with her during breaks.

Val had enjoyed the show, but was just as happy that Mariana paid the little blood doll no real attentions. He retained enough of his humanity to feel jealous. *And she knows it!*

That night, the two Kindred shared blood again—but this time, Mariana sipped from Val's veins. If there was to be a Blood Bond, it would be a mutual one, neither of the partners in thralldom to the other.

*   *   *

This time, Anneke found herself in a much nicer area. *Uptown.* She looked at the brownstone fronting of the houses, noted the bright decorations. *Lots of money here.* She checked her note. *Just another block or so.* She could see the Metropolitan Museum of Art down the street. *I should visit there.* She smiled. *Their Egyptian collection is supposed to be quite superb.* Not tonight, though. She had more important matters to attend to this evening.

She finally found the address on her note. A smallish building nestled between two high-rises. Anneke studied the heavily draped windows. *This place is old!* She climbed the short flight of front stairs, pressing the bell push at the top. *I can smell it!*

She heard a stirring inside. *I smell something else, too,* she thought. Then the door opened. "Come in." She hesitated a moment, staring at the huge hooded figure holding the door. *What the hell is that! None of my business.* She pushed by and entered a short entry hall.

"You're right on time," the hooded figure said from behind her.

"Is it ready?"

"Of course."

Anneke glanced around the little hall as the other closed and locked the door.

"Where?"

"I'll take you there." The figure turned toward her, face still invisible inside the hood.

"But first, there's a little matter my mistress wants to discuss with you." A covered arm motioned to a door opening off the hall. "If you'll come this way?"

Anneke nodded. *I've been expecting this.*

The door opened onto a simple, but elegant room. At one side was an exquisitely enameled Chinese cabinet. *Late eighth century*, Anneke noted. It was filled with beautifully carved jade and lapis lazuli figures. Anneke approached the display, impressed by the style and quality of the pieces. *Marvelous.* She noted one or two. *Incredible taste.*

"You like my collection?"

Anneke repressed the impulse to whirl. The voice was old. It could belong to only one being. "It's quite impressive." Anneke turned, slowly, the hint of a smile on her face as she looked at the figure behind the Chinese desk. "Lady Singhjul."

Ancient eyes set in a young face sparkled. "So. You know who I am?"

"I knew it had to be one of the . . . Old Ones."

The figure behind the desk chuckled. "You can call us Methuselahs. It won't offend."

Anneke bowed. "As you say. In any case, I knew the largesse I've been shown did not come from Don Cruez, and as this city is Sabbat controlled . . . "

Lady Singhjul nodded. "Astute. Very astute."

Anneke smiled. "A high honor coming from someone like you." The Justicar looked to the side, noted that the dark figure had withdrawn. "Now, I understand you want something from me."

The Methuselah smiled again, razor teeth touching red lips. "Call it a partial payment for your recent . . . gifts."

Anneke nodded. "I expected such."

"And there is another waiting for you here." Lady Singhjul inclined her head. "In a very tastefully decorated room below."

Anneke nodded again. "Tell me what you want."

The Methuselah leaned forward. "There's a young Brujah named Percival. . . . "

Anneke looked thoughtful. "I've heard the name."

"I know. A Toreador named Mariana has been searching for him."

Anneke nodded. "She asked my help."

Lady Singhjul made a gesture. "As it happens, she will not need assistance."

"And you would have preferred this Toreador had not been successful."

"Exactly."

"Now that she has . . . "

Lady Singhjul studied long nails. "I want her prize . . . removed."

"That should be easy enough."

The Methuselah sighed. "I hope you're right." She pushed a small folded piece of paper across the desk. "You can find them at this address."

Anneke took the paper, glanced at it, put it in a pocket. "I'll take care of it immediately." A smile crossed her face. "After I finish here."

The old eyes glittered again as Lady Singhjul nodded. "My servant will show you the way."

The door opened soundlessly. "Enjoy yourself, Justicar Anneke."

"I always do."

The dark figure of the retainer closed the door and led Anneke down the hall. She barely heard the whisper of the old Kindred that followed her.

"It could be the last time. . . . "

* * *

Mariana enjoyed showing Val the beauties of her world. *He's so open!* she thought in wonderment. *So willing to learn.* Mariana smiled. *Not to mention the fact that he's a terrific model.*

Mariana had done three studies of Percival—*I'll always call him Percival; it's such a romantic name!*—in the last week. All of them involving chivalry and the Holy Grail. *And each better than the last!* Mariana's smile grew wider. Last night, she and Percival had gone to the Club. Her Toreador friends had treated Val coldly, assuming he knew nothing about art or the important things in life—*that'll take time to fix*—but they'd all been excited about the work she was doing.

"You should exhibit these, Mariana," Andy had told her.

Dieter Kleist had agreed. "Yes, by all means." He studied the two printouts, carefully excluding Val, who was sitting next to him. "I know a little gallery that might be interested."

Mariana smiled. "It would *have* to be evening shows only."

"Of course." Kleist's grin was ironic.

She sensed a movement at her side, then blankness. Percival was gone. "Excuse me a moment." Mariana turned just in time to see Percival leave the Treasure Room. She made her excuses to the others, then followed, catching up to him just short of the staircase by the main bar.

"What's the matter?"

Percival smiled at her, then motioned at the action surrounding them. "I just don't like this place." He pulled her to one side, into the little cleared space behind the stairs.

"It's too loud here."

"That's the music."

His smile was wry. "You call this music?"

Mariana nodded, taking a second to identify the group. "Yes, that's 'The Cure' they're playing now."—another second—"I think the song's called 'Lullaby.'"

"It's all just noise to me." Percival shook his head, a gentle smile curling his lips. "I think of music as having an identifiable tune, words that mean something." He gestured at the speakers. "This . . ." He shook his head.

Mariana reached out, touched his cheek. "I don't think I understand."

Percival smiled at her. "I didn't think you would." He stroked her face. She tingled at the touch. "It's one of the differences between us." His smile grew sad. "One of many."

Mariana backed away a pace, giving herself room to stare him in the eye. "Don't say that!" She shook her head. "Don't even think it!"

Percival smiled and took her hand. "Whatever you say, milady."

Mariana hugged him. "That's more like it!"

He shrugged, motioning toward the big barroom. "What next? More meetings with your friends?"

Mariana shook her head. "No. I think we should go out and walk a little." She smiled. "Get away from all this noise."

He smiled. "Good idea."

Val grinned at the dusting of snow that carpeted the ground. *Looks like winter's finally here!* He liked snow. *It's clean!* And it made the city look better. *Almost livable.* He bent down, scooped up a handful of the stuff. *Too powdery to pack well*, he thought, letting it fall to the ground. *Too bad*.

Mariana didn't seem to have the same enthusiasm

that Val did. "Brrrr!" She grimaced at the ground. "I hate snow!" *Another difference between us.* Val shrugged—*getting to be a habit*—then moved quickly forward, scooping Mariana into his arms, pulling her, squealing, away from the Club's overhang into the middle of the street. "Come on!" He smiled into her laughing face. "I thought you wanted to get away from all that noise!"

Ten minutes later, they stopped at Washington Square Park. Val swept the snow off a bench, then bowed Mariana onto it. "Milady."

"I hope you know what you're doing." Mariana sat. "It's cold here!"

Val grinned. "Cold or not, we have to feed, don't we?"

"We could go back to Acquiel. . . . "

Val shook his head. "No. We depend on her too much. It's not fair."

Mariana nodded slowly. "I guess you're right. . . . "

"Besides"—Val grinned—"there's some good hunting right here."

"In the middle of all this snow?"

"Trust me." His grin broadened. "It'll only increase the quality of the kine."

He sat down next to her, gesturing outward. "You know that the university's right over there."

"Of course."

"And the dorms and frat houses are all around it."

Mariana was confused. "So?"

Val checked his watch. "So, around midnight, the last bunch of joggers will come out to do their laps for the day."

"Joggers?"

"Yes. They circle the park all day and half the night." Val's grin grew teeth. "Good-looking kine, healthy types. Might make good models."

"I don't need any more models." Mariana reached out for a quick hug. "Now that I have you."

Val's head fell. *I didn't realize she cared that much.* He hugged her back. *Almost as much as I care for her!*

There was a noise behind them.

"Goddamn, cuz!" Val whirled to find himself face-to-face with Tessler. The other Brujah grinned. "Aren't you embarrassed to do that in public?"

Val shook his head. "What do you want, Tessler?"

His cousin sat down on the edge of the bench, eyes dancing. "Just wanted to deliver a message from your sire."

"Don Cruez?" Val sat back, face suddenly serious. "What's wrong?"

Tessler gestured at Mariana. "Come on, man. You're not that dumb."

"He objects to Mariana?"

Tessler knitted his hands together and leaned back, using them to support his head. "He objects to a Brujah spending so much time with a Toreador." His eyes hardened. "Especially when it's the Toreador who made a certain set of knives."

Val's eyes widened. "She . . ." He turned to Mariana. "You made those inlaid knives?"

Mariana's eyes hooded. "Yes. I told your . . . friend there all about them."

Val turned again. "Does the Justicar think she had anything to do with those attacks?"

Tessler shrugged. "Who knows what Don Cruez really thinks?"

Val grabbed his cousin by the shoulders, holding him at arms' length, fingers sinking deep into the other's skin. "Tell me the truth!"

Tessler glared at Val, tried to shake his grip off,

failed. "I told Don Cruez that I did not believe the lady had anything to do with the attacks."

Tessler settled back onto the bench as Val released him, eyes level with his cousin's. "I still don't."

Val let himself fall back. "Good."

Tessler sat forward. "However, we still don't know who was behind those attacks." His face went sober. "And we don't know if they'll start again."

Val nodded. "You think I should be more careful."

Tessler's grin didn't reach his eyes. "I think you should find a hole and pull it in after you."

Val's own grin was rueful. "The last time I did that, I ended up hip-deep in rats."

"Could be worse."

Val looked at his cousin. "How?"

Tessler got up, looking down at the pair. "Next time, you might not have any help."

He strode off before Val could think of an answer.

The retainer shivered when he received the summons to Lady Ambrosia's chambers. He touched his neck, feeling for the nonexistent marks of his last visit. *Can't let her do that too often*, he thought. *If she ever learns of all the things I'm doing . . .* He closed his eyes, steeling himself, then hurried to her door. *Can't keep her waiting . . .*

He entered the sanctum to see Lady Ambrosia busily feeding. It hadn't taken long to replace her stable of thralls. "Ah!" Piercing eyes found his. "Sit down." The retainer took his usual seat by the door, watching as his mistress finished her meal.

"The boy and girl have had time to get acquainted." The retainer nodded, appalled to the depths of his

Toreador soul as the Methuselah rubbed her lips with a priceless bit of Irish linen. He winced as she discarded the stained result. "Now we use them to start the war."

The retainer leaned forward. "How do we do that?"

Lady Ambrosia smiled, motioning another thrall to join her. "We use a cat's-paw."

"We have no agent close enough—"

The Methuselah gestured angrily. "I need no agent for such a simple task!"

"Simple? But—"

"There are more than two people in their household, are there not?"

The retainer nodded. "Yes, the girl keeps a pet."

"A kine."

He nodded again.

Lady Ambrosia smiled, hands idly caressing the thrall lying next to her. "Well, that will be our entry." Her smile broadened. "And later, perhaps, our entrée." She chuckled at her cleverness. "Yes. I like that." Another gesture, this one of dismissal. "I will call you once I have made the proper . . . arrangements."

Acquiel struggled with her bonds. Mariana had put her in a leather "single-glove" and had been careful to run the connecting strap down between the blood doll's legs—right where she liked it. Acquiel could fight all she wanted—and immediately enjoy the fruits of her battle.

The blonde panted as she got herself off for the third—*or is it fourth*—time. She looked around for Mariana, expecting her mistress to be handy in case she needed a drink of water or a light caress.

She was alone in the room.

Acquiel cursed under her breath. Things had been so good before that man came. Now . . . She cursed again as a small movement restarted the fire within her. *She's always with him now!* Acquiel wriggled, testing the tightness of her bonds. *She never spends any time with me.* The heat spread between her legs, running up her back, flowing through her brain. Acquiel moaned. *Doesn't she love me anymore?* Her body was aflame. Acquiel began to move harder, rubbing the leather against her, tingling with its continued touch. *What can I do about it?* She moaned again. *Dieter!* The thought came from nowhere. *I can talk to Dieter Kleist!*

She came explosively. Yessssssss!

Far away, there came the sound of laughter.

Time passed quickly for Mariana. For the first time in her second life, she found herself completely happy. She had her work—*my light*—and she had Percival—*my life.* Only Acquiel spoiled the perfection. With more and more of Mariana's time taken up in work and play with Percival, the little blood doll had taken to sulking. Mariana hated that, and did her best to give the girl as much attention as she could. *The rest of the time I tie her as tightly as I can and give her mouth something to do besides bother me!* Mariana smiled. *That always pleases her!*

The idle talk in the Club about a showing of Mariana's work had turned out to be much more than that. Kleist showed some of Mariana's work to Ingrid Neilson, a gallery owner who frequented the club. The breather had been thrilled by the computer art and had offered to arrange a full-scale show.

Mariana, reluctantly, had agreed—after some argument with Percival: "It's not as if I'll tell them what I am."

Percival shook his head. "I'm not worried about that. They're just cattle."

"Kindred will go too!"

"How?"

Mariana sat next to Percival, taking his hand, smiling gently. "The gallery's in the Village. Inside Elysium."

He nodded. "So it's safe."

"More than that." Mariana smiled. "I got Ingrid to extend the hours. It'll be open until midnight!"

Percival smiled wryly. "Didn't she wonder about that?"

"Hey!" She tousled his hair. "This is *New York*. People always ask for strange things!"

He shrugged. "Maybe I am worrying about nothing. But"—a frown creased his forehead—"we do know there's still a Methuselah out there with something in mind."

She mirrored his frown. "I don't see how that could have anything to do with my art."

"She made you forget about me, didn't she?"

"Only because I hadn't met you yet." Mariana hugged Percival to her. "I could never forget you now."

He hugged her back. "I feel the same way."

She pulled back. "Good, because I need your help."

He looked at her. "My help? For what?"

She laughed, pulling him to his feet. "I've got to do a bunch of new things—and I'm going to need a model!"

He followed her. "What about Acquiel?" He nodded toward the blonde, tightly spread-eagled on the bed.

"Later." Mariana looked at the other girl, noting how fast the blood doll's breathing was. "For the moment, though . . ." Mariana walked over to the dresser beside the bed, pulled out a thick rubber device. She moved to Acquiel's side, hand idly caressing the girl's breast. "Just to keep her out of trouble . . ." She inserted the rubber device into the bound girl's ready orifice, touching a tiny switch as she slipped the thing in. "This should do the trick."

Acquiel moaned as the little motor started up, pleasure vibrating through her body. Mariana gave her one last caress, then headed for Percival and the studio.

Demetrious Slater was sitting in an uptown bar, eyeing the cattle in a languid hunt, when Peter Grimsdyke found him. "So, Demetrious." The little actor smiled. "May I join you?"

Slater looked up, surprised at being addressed. "Oh. Grimsdyke, isn't it?"

The thespian smiled. *Interesting. He's going to play dumb!* "My fame precedes me!"

Slater shrugged, indicated a chair. "What can I do for you?"

Grimsdyke sat, motioning to the waiter for a glass of beer. "I'm curious, dear boy." He smiled as the brew was put in front of him. "What did Masika say about my little problem?"

"Masika?" Slater was puzzled for a moment, then remembered. "Oh! That Brujah thing."

Grimsdyke nodded. *How stupid does he think I am?*

"Didn't he contact you?"

"He did not." The thespian shook his head. "And it has now been several weeks."

"Odd," Slater said, eyes searching for an exit.

"Yes." Grimsdyke noted the motions. *He's worried now, must not have talked to the Archon at all.* The thespian smiled. *Good.* "Did he give you any reason why he might ignore the matter?"

"No." Slater sat back. *Determined to brazen it out.* "He didn't discuss it with me at all."

"Ah well." Grimsdyke stood up, the beer still untouched. "I guess it doesn't matter. As you requested, I made sure the boy could not contact me again."

Slater relaxed. *Ah! That made him feel better!* "Good. I knew I . . . we could count on you."

"Always, dear boy." The thespian dropped a bill on the table. "Good hunting to you."

"And you, sir."

Grimsdyke strolled out of the little bar, a tiny grin on his face. *He didn't tell Masika, yet the boy was attacked again.* He nodded. *Definitely someone's agent.* The actor turned a corner, then pressed himself into the darkness. *I think I'll wait here for the dear boy.* Long teeth gleamed in the dim light. *Perhaps we can have a more productive chat in private.*

Val watched Mariana's preparations for the gallery show with decidedly mixed emotions. He'd always been taught that the Masquerade was the foremost of the Traditions. He couldn't help but think that a display of Mariana's work might lead to publicity—and any notoriety could compromise the Masquerade. *I'd like to talk to someone about this,* he thought. *But who would I go to?* Val shook his head. *I can't go to Don Cruez, not with his feelings about my liaison with Mariana.* Val glanced to his side, where Mariana was preparing Acquiel for a modeling session. *Acquiel is no good.* He shook his head again. *She's still kine.* He sat back, thinking. *There must be somebody. . . .* Then it came to him. *Of course!*

Val jumped to his feet, snatched his leather jacket out of the closet. "I'm going out for a while."

Mariana turned to him, curious. "Hunting again?" She smiled. "Want me to go along?"

He shook his head. "Not this time." He walked to her side, noted the look of disappointment on her face. "I've got to think a few things out."

She looked into his face. "Still worried about this opening?"

He nodded.

"You're being foolish."

He shrugged. "Perhaps."

She pushed him away. "Okay. Take your walk. Get it out of your system." She turned back to Acquiel. "I've got work to do anyway."

He nodded. "I know."

Ten minutes later, he walked down the stairs at the Eighth Street Station. *Astor Place'd be easier*, he thought. *But they haven't reopened it yet. Something about the smell.* He smiled. Nobody had been able to figure out where all the rats had come from. *Not even the Kindred.* The smile faded. *Somebody tried to kill me the last time I was down here.* He looked around, eyes scanning the faces on the dim platform. *And I still don't know who it was.* He touched the knife in his pocket as the train thundered into the station. *And Mariana wonders why I worry.*

The train ride went smoothly this time, getting Val uptown in good time. *Now, if I can just remember where it was* . . . He walked past Lincoln Center. It was snowing again. A heavier fall this time, the snow coating the plaza, painting it a bright, pristine white. Val smiled. *It'll turn gray soon enough.* He noted the theater, turned the corner. *It's down here, a half block or so.* . . .

Val strolled along, feet sinking into the new-fallen snow. *Looks like about two inches* . . . His mind rolled back, thinking of snowfalls at home, of sleighs and mulled rum and . . .

A dark figure stepped out of the alley, blocking Val's path.

Tessler had given up keeping an eye on Val. There was no challenge to it. His cousin spent all his time at the haven he shared with Mariana, only coming out to hunt or socialize at the Club. Tessler sneered. *Always with that Toreador bitch!* He shook off the thought. *That's his decision. She's not my problem!*

Tessler's real problem was more immediate. He still hadn't been able to find Anneke, despite having half the Brujah in the city looking for her. *She's got to be getting some really high-class help!* Worse, he couldn't even find Anneke's Archon, Masika. *Hell, I can't even find Slater, Masika's "friend."* Tessler snarled. The whole city had turned upside down. Before this all started, the Brujah could do anything, find anybody. Now . . . *Someone's screwing around with us.* Tessler's teeth shone as he bared them. *And when I find out who that somebody is . . .*

Mariana shook her head in disgust. *This isn't working.* "All right." She clicked the computer off, not bothering to save what was on the screen. "I guess that's enough for tonight."

"Can I see it?" Acquiel bounced down off the little stage they'd built, smiling despite the hours of posing.

"There's nothing to see." Mariana shrugged her shoulders. "My heart just wasn't in it tonight."

Acquiel pouted. "That's because he wasn't here."

Mariana frowned. "Percival?"

"Who else?"

Mariana reached out, grabbed the other girl's shoulders, turned her around, face-to-face, eye to eye. "Are you jealous of him?"

Acquiel let her head fall, unwilling to meet her mistress's eyes.

Mariana shook her. "Look at me! Are you jealous?"

The blonde's eyes slowly, reluctantly, came up. "Yes."

Mariana hugged the girl to her. "Why, Acquiel? Tell me why?"

Acquiel began crying. "You never have any time for me now. Never do anything with me."

"I'm with you now."

The blond girl turned away. "It's not the same."

Mariana let her go, her own eyes falling. "No. It's not." She stood up. "I love him, Acquiel." Mariana paced to the other side of the room. "And I can't be happy without him."

Acquiel's sobbing filled the room, masking the sound of the door closing.

Val stopped in place, knife appearing as if by magic.

"Oh my, dear boy." A familiar voice laughed. "I don't think you'll need that!"

"Grimsdyke!"

"In person!" The actor grinned, moving into the light. "Forgive me for startling you. I never could resist a dramatic entrance."

Val stepped forward, grinning. "I'm glad you're here. I need to talk to you."

"And I to you, dear boy." The thespian motioned toward a nearby door. "Shall we do it inside? Out of the snow."

Val smiled. "I like the snow. It's clean."

"So it is." Grimsdyke held out a hand, watching as white flakes filled it. "It's also damned cold."

Val nodded. "I won't argue that."

Grimsdyke's haven was exactly as Val remembered it. It looked small, but was actually quite large, the dimensions of the place masked by the clutter that stood everywhere. Piles of books, scripts, costumes, mementos—and, stacked everywhere, posters. Film posters. Theater posters. The souvenirs of several long lifetimes in the arts.

"I've seen this one before." Val pointed at a colorful theatrical poster pinned to a barely visible wall. "Don Cruez has one in his office."

The thespian nodded. "Yes. One of his finest performances."

Val's eyes widened. "You mean that old rumor is true?"

Grimsdyke nodded. "Yes indeed. Don Cruez walked the boards in the old days." He smiled. "Right alongside me."

"But Don Cruez is Brujah!"

"So?" Grimsdyke looked quizzically at Val.

Val's brow furrowed. "Well, I mean . . . "

Grimsdyke filled two glasses from a carafe of red liquid in his refrigerator. "You mean that only Toreador become involved with the arts." He offered a glass to Val. "Not so, my boy. Any Kindred can be touched by the Muses." He took a sip from his own glass. "It just requires the courage to admit it."

Val nodded. "I see."

"But that's not what I wanted to talk to you about

this night." Grimsdyke settled into an overstuffed chair, pushing several books out of his way. "At least, not directly."

Val leaned forward in his own chair. "Can I ask you a question first?"

"Of course. My business is not urgent." Grimsdyke sank back into his seat.

"You follow the Traditions." It was a statement, not a question.

Grimsdyke nodded, smiling. "You know that I do."

Val turned his head, trying to formulate his question. "That's my problem. Mariana . . . "

"The girl who was trying to find you."

Val's head whirled back. "How did you know that?"

Grimsdyke made a soothing gesture. "Later. Ask your question first."

Val nodded, thought for a second. "Well, Mariana has been asked to give a display of her art."

"How wonderful!"

Val shook his head. "No. You don't understand. This is a gallery display—open to everyone—Kindred and kine."

Grimsdyke shrugged. "How can that make a difference?"

Val gestured. "Don't you see? There's danger there. Danger to the Masquerade!"

Grimsdyke stood, indicating a pile of playbills stacked against the wall. "My dear boy, I go in front of the footlights nearly every night!" He kicked them over, letting them spread out. "I've done so thousands"—he considered—"perhaps tens of thousands of times."

He returned to his seat, took a sip of his drink. "Don't you think I would have stopped if there were any chance of compromising the Masquerade?" He pointed to the poster Val had noticed earlier. "Don't you think your good sire would have stopped?"

"This is different."

Grimsdyke's brows rose. "How?"

Val paused to think. *It's not, is it?* "I-I guess I don't know."

"If you don't know, don't worry about it." Grimsdyke smiled. "It will make things easier between you and your lady."

Val nodded, relaxing back in his chair. "It sure will."

The actor stood, refreshing his drink, bringing the carafe to refill Val's. "Now, as to *my* business . . . "

Val nodded.

"You may not know this, but I killed a Kindred to save your life."

The one with the gun! Val's eyes widened. "You were the one!"

Grimsdyke nodded. "His name was Alfonso. He was Toreador."

"You broke the Tradition." Val eyed the other Kindred, waiting.

"So I did." The thespian took another sip of his drink. "Should I have stood back and allowed you to die?"

Val slowly shook his head, still studying his companion. *He wants something.* There was nothing on the actor's face. *I wonder what?*

"I see you understand."

Val nodded.

"And you're wondering what I want." Grimsdyke leaned forward and smiled. "It may surprise you."

It was nearly dawn when Lady Ambrosia signaled for the retainer. *Late! This must be important!* He hurried to the sanctum, the thought of being caught in the sun spurring his steps. "You sent for me, milady?"

Lady Ambrosia was already standing at the door to her inner sanctum, eyes hooded. "Yes. I am uneasy at several things that have happened."

The retainer frowned. "What might those be?"

Lady Ambrosia glared at him. "Again you are ignorant!" She reached out, held him in place with her mind. "I should leave you here for the sun." His eyes moved, without conscious thought, to the big window. There was gray light on the horizon. Dawn was close. "But—"

She released him, sighing. "I know, you lack the discipline to touch minds." She shook her head. "If you don't develop it soon . . . "

He shivered.

She opened the inner door. "Slater is dead."

The retainer nodded slowly, absorbing the news. "Wasn't he Masika's friend?"

"And one of my opponent's cat's-paws."

"What happened to him?"

"I believe Grimsdyke killed him."

"The actor?" The retainer's face showed his puzzlement. "Why?"

"That's not important at the moment." She glanced back, saw the light on the horizon. "What is important is that with him gone, Masika will have to deal directly with Anneke."

"So?"

"Anneke is also working with my opponent," Lady Ambrosia snarled. "And, unlike you, has substantial Auspex!"

The retainer's mouth opened in shock. "Anneke will be able to gain knowledge of your plans!"

"Only if she manages to contact Masika."

"I see." The retainer took another nervous look at the window. "I'll handle this personally, make sure that

Masika disappears for a time." He thought for a moment. "And perhaps I can do something about Anneke."

"That would be nice." The door shut, leaving the retainer just enough time to rush to his own haven before the glare of first light touched the horizon.

"You're Inconnu!" Val was shocked at Grimsdyke's statement.

"Is there something wrong with that?"

Val stood, started to pace. "It's just that . . . "

"My dear boy, being Inconnu is no different from being Toreador." He smiled at Val. "Or Brujah. The difference is that we have grown tired of the endless struggle."

Val stopped, looking back at the actor. "Okay. I understand what you're saying." Grimsdyke's nod encouraged him. "What I don't understand is what you want from me."

"Dear boy . . . "

Val shook his head. "The truth."

Grimsdyke's smile faded. "As you will." He stood up, placing his glass in the little sink on one side of the apartment. "Despite what the Camarilla says, we of the Inconnu do not consider ourselves a separate sect."

"What are you, then."

Grimsdyke looked at him, eyes clear. "Think of us as an audience. We watch. Stay out of the affairs of the Methuselahs. Avoid their fights."

"But you helped me."

Grimsdyke nodded. "Yes, I did."

"Why?"

"Because I want you to join us, dear boy." Grimsdyke's

eyes fastened on those of Val. "You have great potential, you could be as great as your sire." He smiled. "Don Cruez and I are old friends. One day his *ideals* will force him to turn his back on the Camarilla and join the Inconnu."

Val stood up, mind swirling. "I can't believe that!"

Grimsdyke's smile widened. "Yes, you can." He laughed as Val headed for the door. "You already do."

Val didn't come back to the haven that night. Mariana waited until the last possible moment, keeping the door open even as the sun touched the horizon. *I hope he's all right.* She sighed. *I wish we hadn't quarreled.* She shut the door, locking out the light. She could feel the inevitable malaise flowing through her body. *I've got to get to sleep.*

Acquiel was already in the bed, rolled up in a near-fetal position, thumb in mouth. Mariana smiled. *At least I can spend a little time with her now.* She lay down beside the blood doll, pulling the lithe body tight against her, reveling in the warmth that flowed through her as the kine snuggled into the embrace. *When I wake up, I'll make her happy.* Mariana smiled. *It's been too long.*

Anneke woke to the sound of a scream. *The sun's down!* She rolled off the edge of her bed. *Could that be Masika finally arriving?* There was a harsh bark of noise in the room next to hers. *That was a gunshot!* Something was seriously wrong. Anneke calmed herself, questing out for a sense of the situation.

Anarchs. She could feel their minds. *Undisciplined. Raw* . . . Another gunshot.

They're killing the staff! Anneke stiffened. If they found the hidden door to her sanctum . . .

Why give them the chance? Anneke smiled, the expression never reaching her eyes. *After all, they're only anarchs.*

She nodded to herself. Yes, this was the right action to take. *Just make it quick. No mistakes.* She moved to the doorway, her hand on the catch. *Follow the door, then play the situation by ear.* She pressed down.

The other room was a charnel house. Three of the staff were down, each shot through the head with a high-velocity handgun. A fourth was still alive, grappling hand to hand with three of the attackers.

There was no sign of the hooded retainer.

Anneke sprang into action as soon as the door opened. She carried no weapons, preferring to use her skill and speed against any opponent. Now, with four armed adversaries, she burst into Discipline-assisted speed and crashed into the three anarchs surrounding the surviving staff member. *Can't give them room to operate!*

The first of the anarchs died immediately, heart crushed by an upthrust hand. Anneke was on the second before the first dropped. *This one is big!* A bear of a Kindred, bulking some three hundred pounds on his six-foot-plus frame. Anneke smiled as she snapped his elbow, the smile widening as she turned the screaming Kindred toward the doorway, letting his body take the bullets meant for her. *Fool!* She accelerated forward, pulling the twitching body with her, flinging it into the path of the last anarch. His gun clicked on an empty chamber. *Out of bullets.*

It was just cleanup from there. The surviving staff member crushed the life out of his final opponent, grunting in satisfaction as he pulled the anarch's still-beating heart out of his helpless chest. "Bastard!"

Anneke was more careful. She disabled the last of the anarchs, studiously breaking all the bones necessary for movement before setting the remains of the creature down on a table. "Tell me who sent you."

The anarch looked at her, pursed his lips, then spit in her face.

Anneke smiled. "Good try." She reached out, twisted the broken bones of his forefinger, snapping it off. "But maybe you ought to think about this." She dropped the finger in his screaming mouth. "I'll be back."

She searched the house as quickly as possible. The doors were unlocked, not broken. The alarm system was disarmed. *An inside job.*

There was no sign of either the Methuselah or her hooded retainer.

Anneke thought about that as she returned to her disabled anarch. Had the Methuselah set up the attack? She shook her head. No. That made no sense. *If Lady Singhjul was doing this, they would have known where to find me.* Anneke smiled. *Besides, that one wouldn't have needed anarchs!* Someone else, then. But who?

Anneke gently lifted the anarch's thumb. *Maybe this one will be able to tell me.* She smiled at his pleas. *Too bad he's not a bit older. I could use the vitae.* She shrugged. *Ah well, to business.*

Another finger snapped off.

✦

Tessler strode into Don Cruez's office without knocking. "I found Anneke."

The Justicar glared at him, then, still frowning, pointed him to a seat. "Try to show a little respect."

Tessler nodded. "I'm sorry, it's just been so frustrating."

"I understand. Now—Anneke?"

Tessler nodded, sat back in his chair "She's been staying in a house near the edge of Elysium." He grimaced. "The place is one of Masika's havens. I checked it out days ago, but there was a secret room."

"Forget that." Don Cruez leaned forward. "Tell me the rest."

"The house was attacked last night."

"Attacked!"

Tessler nodded. "Anarchs again." He scratched his head, careful not to muss his hair. "Funny, though, they didn't break in. The door was unlocked."

Don Cruez nodded. "A setup."

"That's what I figured. Especially since the house also had an alarm system." Tessler grinned. "Not that those mean much with the technos in everything."

The Justicar nodded. "So there was a break-in."

Tessler settled back. "Yeah. They sneaked in just after sunset, while the four Kindred in the household were still rising."

"Interesting. They braved the sun?"

"Must have. Too close otherwise."

"*Anarchs* did that?"

Tessler shrugged. "That's what I'm told—and the evidence certainly seems to support the interpretation."

Don Cruez leaned back. "Tell me the rest."

"There's not much else to tell." The Brujah leaned back again, letting the chair go to two legs. "The anarchs had guns—heavy stuff, .44 Magnums. They shot three of the staff members before they could react."

"The fourth?"

Tessler started to put his feet up on Don Cruez's desk, but froze when he saw the Justicar's glare. "They tried to take him alive. I figure they were looking for Anneke, and when they didn't find her . . ."

Don Cruez nodded. "They thought they'd find her through the last servant."

"Right." Tessler nodded. "Only thing is, that last servant was stronger than all of them combined. He held them at bay until Anneke came out of her little hidey-hole."

"What happened then?"

Tessler grinned. "She killed two of them right off. The servant took a third."

"And the other."

Tessler's grin hardened. "He stayed alive a bit longer. I figure Anneke spent a little time talking to him."

"What could she have been after?"

"I don't know." Tessler let his chair fall to the floor. "I can tell you that Masika wasn't among the dead." He looked up. "And he didn't come out of the house."

"Could he have been in on it?"

Tessler shrugged. "Maybe. Or maybe he was just set up. The point is, Anneke surfaced, and I've got some of our people keeping an eye on her."

"Good." Don Cruez shifted his seat, turning it to look out into the night. "Let's see if we can finally get this all resolved." He sighed. "Talk to the anarchs for me. Tell them that if they keep trying to kill other Kindred . . ."

"You'll call a Blood Hunt?" Tessler's eyes shone. "Can you do that? I mean, this is still a Sabbat city."

Don Cruez glared at him, eyes hard. "I'm Justicar of the Brujah. I do what I want!"

Val came back to the haven the next morning. He didn't tell Mariana where he'd been or what he'd been doing. *He's troubled,* she realized. *Something happened to him.*

Mariana decided not to press the issue. She had too much to do getting ready for the gallery show in any case.

"Could you pose for me today?" She smiled at the sour expression on his face. "Just one more time, I promise."

He nodded. "What's this one for?"

She took him into the studio, led him up onto the stage she and Acquiel had built. "I want to do an Anne Rice suite." She smiled. "And you'll make a marvelous Lestat."

"I thought Tom Cruise did that."

"Well . . ." Her smile grew wider. "Not very well."

He smiled back. "I would have thought that you and Acquiel would prefer her other stuff. Those *Sleeping Beauty* books, for example." He stopped, looked around. "Where is Acquiel, anyway?"

"She wants to go out."

"And you're going to let her!"

Mariana shrugged. "She's just going to the Club." She started to show him the pose she wanted. "Andy and Dieter will keep an eye on her." She finally got him into position. "She'll be all right."

Val shook his head. "I hope I will."

Mariana reached the keyboard. "Don't move now. This will take a little while."

"*Now* she tells me!"

"Quiet!"

"Are we going to hunt after we finish here? Seems like a nice night."

Mariana glanced out the window. "It's snowing out there!"

He grinned. "Like I said, it's a nice night."

She shook her head. "Where do you want to go tonight? Back to the park? Health food?"

His grin widened. "I thought we'd hit Chinatown. I haven't had a little chink in a long time."

She threw a book at him. "Beast!"

He nodded. "You got that right!"

They both laughed as she went to work.

Acquiel had dressed very carefully for this trip to the Club. She'd pulled out her best—and briefest—dress, been extra careful in applying makeup. *I've got to look my best!* she thought. *Can't let Mariana be disappointed in me!*

Mariana. Acquiel sighed. Yesterday had been wonderful. Like the old days. The two of them, playing the old games. Acquiel tied up, tortured—brought to a slow, wonderfully sexual boil! *I just love it when Mariana plays mistress!*

But now *he* was back again. Taking up all of Mariana's time, pushing Acquiel out of her bed, getting the attention that should have been the little blood doll's. *It's not fair!* Acquiel had decided *she* was the one who was going to get all the attention tonight. She looked at her reflection in the mirror outside the Club's staircase, wriggling, just a little, to see how the dress moved. *Yes, I think this will work.* She walked away from the mirror, let herself undulate down the stairs. *They'll watch me now!*

They did, of course. Male jaws hit the floor all over the bar. Organs leaped to attention. Acquiel grinned as men pushed toward her. *This is going to be fun!*

But it wasn't. Acquiel enjoyed the stares, enjoyed frustrating the human males who approached her. Somehow, though, she never got the high she expected. *I'm not used to being alone,* she realized. *And there's nobody here* I *care about*. She finally wandered into the Treasure Room, trailing an entourage of failed suitors. Kleist was sitting in his usual corner, surrounded, also as usual, by a group of blood dolls, any of whom, by their glares, would gladly have killed the blonde on the threshold.

Acquiel didn't care. She dismissed the men behind her, and dropped, sighing, onto the floor at the techno's feet.

"Huh?" Kleist was startled by the thump. He looked down. "Acquiel?" He let his laptop snap shut, eyes searching the dimness of the Club. "Where's Mariana?"

"Home." Acquiel stared at the floor. "With him."

"Val?" The blonde nodded. "I thought you guys were real happy together."

Acquiel looked up at him and suddenly, unexpectedly, the light in the room changed. Things grew misty, foggy. Acquiel tried to speak, but her voice would not work. Her mouth moved, sure enough, but not at *her* command.

Trapped in her own mind, Acquiel tried to control her own suddenly foreign body—and was shocked when she heard her own voice say: "I'm worried about her, Dieter." I *didn't say that*! She fought with all her force to regain control of herself, but it was no use. There was nothing she could do except listen and watch.

Soon, even that was taken from her. The mists in her mind grew deeper, darker. *This is wrong!*

Acquiel went to sleep.

The shell of Acquiel stayed awake, looking up at Kleist with liquid eyes, telling him things he wanted to hear: "He keeps making her do things, crazy things. She never has any time left to paint."

Kleist leaned forward. "What about her show?"

Acquiel shook her head. "I'm not sure if she'll make it."

"That'd be a shame. Her new work is quite remarkable."

"He doesn't want her to get any attention." Acquiel looked up, eyes fiery. "Dieter, isn't there anything you can do?"

"I don't know what."

The blonde's arms came up, wrapped around Kleist's legs. She put her cheek against his thigh. "Please. You're so smart. Can't you think of something?"

"Well . . ."

She smiled up at him, increasing the temperature in the room noticeably. "I knew you'd help." She wriggled, pressing her lips against his legs. "Could you do one other thing?" Her eyes lifted, promising. "Take me home tonight." She kissed him again.

"Be my master!"

"You failed." Lady Ambrosia sat in her chair of state, eyes fixed on the wretched form before her. "Why are you still alive?"

The retainer sat miserably, eyes roaming the room, unwilling to focus on the form before him. "I sent what I considered a significant force—"

"Four anarchs!" Red eyes glowed with suddenly malevolent light. "Four!"

"They should have been enough!" He looked at her beseechingly. "I arranged for them to be in her sanctum before the sun set! All they had to do was kill the retainers."

She grunted. "They didn't even manage that!"

He shook his head. "I don't understand it." He looked up—and was shaken by her glare. "Milady?"

"Why weren't you there?"

His hands groped toward her.

"You promised me you'd handle it *personally*."

He shook his head. "I did. Every step."

"But you weren't there." Her voice was dangerously low.

The retainer shivered. "I didn't think . . . "

Teeth shone. "I do the thinking!"

The retainer crumpled into a frightened mass.

Lady Ambrosia *moved* off her chair, disappearing from his sight, reappearing next to him, clawed fingers touching his throat, caressing his frigid skin. "I should kill you for your repeated failures."

The retainer shrank from her touch, but she stayed with him, nails biting into his skin, drawing tiny droplets of blood. She smiled a hard smile, allowed her tongue to touch one of the red drops. "As I should kill you for your . . . secret dealings with the anarchs."

The retainer looked at her, eyes wide with fear. "You know about that?"

"You fool!" She laughed, a harsh sound with no humor in it. Her spittle flew into his face, mixed with droplets of his own blood. "I know *everything*!"

He slumped into his chair, all hope gone.

"I *should* kill you . . ." Her hands pushed his chin up, forcing him to look into hell-bright eyes. "But I'm not going to." She *moved* away, instantly reappearing in her chair of state. "Instead, I'm going to give you one last task—one last chance to prove yourself worthy of being my servant."

He leaned forward, hope reborn in his heart. "Anything!"

"I know." She laughed again, a harsh, sibilant sound. It filled the room, freezing any optimism in the retainer's heart.

*   *   *

Val stood up and stretched, commanding each muscle to tense and relax, forcing blood into his extremities. *This posing is hard work!* he thought. *I wonder how kine put up with it.*

Across the room, Mariana hit a few keys on her console and sat back. "Want to see?" The box that was her laser printer began to whir. "It'll be ready in a few minutes."

Val crossed to her side, giving her a quick caress. "And then we can hunt?"

She smiled and nodded. "Then we can hunt."

He nodded. "Okay. Let's see what you've made of me."

They both watched as the paper rolled through the printer, finally dropping into the output bin. "Pick it up," she told him.

"Oh no." He smiled, gesturing toward the machine. "It's your creation."

Mariana shrugged. "All right." She reached out, picked up the paper. "Whatever you say."

Val turned his head to the side, trying to peek over her shoulder, but she hid the picture from him, deliberately blocking his view. "Hey!"

She turned to him, holding the paper so he couldn't see it. "You wanted me to go first." She smiled. "You've got to wait your turn."

He nodded. "Just don't take all night!"

The Toreador grinned, studying the print in front of her. "I don't know about this." She shook her head critically. "Maybe I should have tried something else." She peeked at him over the top of the print. "Yes, it's the eyes . . ." Mariana shook her head again, changed her grip on the paper. "Have to try again tomorrow." She started to rip the paper in half.

"Hey!" Val sprang forward, grabbed the print out of her hands. "Let me see it!" He turned the picture around, guarding it from her reaching hands. "What's wrong with the eyes?"

She laughed. "Nothing."

He turned toward her, puzzled. "Nothing? Then why . . . ?"

She smiled. "I just wanted to see if I could get some sort of response out of you." She put her arms around him, gave him a quick hug. "See if you really cared about my work."

"Of course I care." *I care about everything you do.*

She relaxed her hug, held him at arm's length. "Then why are you so worried about this exhibition?"

"I'm not worried about it."

Mariana looked at him, puzzled. "But yesterday . . ."

He shrugged. "That was yesterday. I've had a chance to think about it some more since then."

She leaned forward, looking into his eyes. "Do you really mean that?"

"Of course I mean it."

Mariana hugged him again, harder, eyes bright. "That's wonderful!"

He nodded. "I hope so." He put his arms around her, gave her a hug back. "We'd better go hunting now." He glanced at the night. "Before it gets too late."

She stepped away from him, smile radiant. "Whatever you say."

*　　*　　*

"What do *you* want?" Topper's blunt features creased as he saw the face of the Kindred at the door.

"Don't worry, dear boy." Peter Grimsdyke smiled as he pushed past the hulking Brujah. "I just want to see the Justicar for a few minutes." He took off his coat, tossing it to the other man. "Just hold this for me." His smile widened. "That's a good fellow."

"Don't push him." Grimsdyke turned in time to see Don Cruez come out of his office. "He'd just as soon kill you as talk to you."

The actor looked the big guard/retainer over, eyes sizing up the larger Kindred. "Do you think he could?"

Topper growled at the question. "Little man, I'd tear you to pieces!"

Grimsdyke smiled. "I wasn't talking to *you*."

Topper turned to his master—and was shocked when he saw the Justicar considering the question. "Don Cruez!" Huge arms thrust out in supplication. "Surely you can't believe . . . "

Don Cruez raised his hand to silence his servant. "Never underestimate Kindred strengths, Topper." He motioned to Grimsdyke, who strode serenely past the big Justicar, heading into the other's office. "Peter here is much older than you." Don Cruez shrugged. "He may be older than I!" He stepped back into the other room, pulling the door behind him. "Consider that before you get yourself in trouble." The door shut with a loud *click*.

Topper snorted at the closed office, then glared down at the overcoat still in his hand. He started to throw it on the floor, then stopped, thinking about what Don Cruez had said. At last, somewhat self-consciously, he placed it carefully on a chair to the side of the room. Sometimes it was better to be careful.

Inside the office, Don Cruez returned to his desk and sighed. "It's hard to get good help."

Grimsdyke levered himself into a seat and nodded. "Especially in a clan full of rebels."

The Justicar glared at him. "Damn it, Peter! I told you, I'm not ready to make that choice just yet."

Grimsdyke leaned forward. "Come on, Cruez. You know you're sick of all this infighting. Sick of being a pawn in the damned Methuselahs' games."

Don Cruez came to his feet, pacing around the desk. "At least I can fight back this way." He glared at Grimsdyke. "Rather than just *observing*."

The actor's smile widened. "Sometimes we observers can do some good of our own." Grimsdyke stood, walked to the sideboard. "I just happened to be around Elysium one night a few weeks ago." He selected a glass, nodding at the heft of the crystal. "I happened to *observe*," he said, smiling, "a Toreador named Alfonso as he shot a helpless Kindred in the streets."

"Percival!"

Grimsdyke nodded. "The same." He picked up a carafe, poured a little red liquid into the glass. "I was in time to save your childe." He took a sip. "And take him to a place of safety."

Don Cruez looked at the other. "That was *your* doing!"

"Only Alfonso." Grimsdyke grinned. "Your Percival took care of the others quite by himself." He returned to his seat. "Quite a powerful being."

"What do you want, Peter?"

Grimsdyke smiled, raised his glass in a silent toast. "You do know that Percival is in the middle of some Methuselah's plan."

Don Cruez sighed. "I suspected it."

"It is more than a suspicion to me." The actor glanced

at the Justicar. "I had a little talk with a Kindred named Slater." Grimsdyke's smile turned grim. "He had quite a lot to say about the plan—and you—before he . . . went away."

Don Cruez looked puzzled. "Me?"

Grimsdyke gave the Justicar a withering look. "Don't give me that innocent crap, Cruez."

The other smiled. "Sorry. You'd be surprised how often it works."

"You should have stayed on the stage."

"Too public." Don Cruez looked down at the actor. "And we were discussing something else—a plan." The Justicar smiled wryly. "If a simple observer can discuss it."

Grimsdyke nodded. "Imagine a situation in which a Brujah went renegade—started killing Toreador all over the city."

"I'd have to stop him." Don Cruez shrugged. "I can't see how that would create any problems."

"What if that Brujah were someone close to you?"

The Justicar's face grew thoughtful. "Percival?"

Grimsdyke poured another glass from the carafe as he nodded. "Exactly."

Don Cruez leaned forward, stared at the actor. "But Percival has far too much common sense to do such a thing."

"As things stand now, I would agree with you." He smacked his lips. "Good stuff." He turned to Don Cruez. "But there have already been three attempts on his life, all involving Toreador and their quite-identifiable weapons. If there were more . . ."

Don Cruez stood, began pacing. "You're saying that some Methuselah is planning to use Percival, to force *me* to take action." He sat, face set. "What if I do nothing?"

"Than a Conclave will be called, and someone else will take action for you."

Don Cruez sighed. "What do *you* think I should do?"

Grimsdyke shrugged. "Call a Conclave of your own Now." The actor smiled. "Name a prince for the city." The smile broadened. "A Brujah prince. Stop the plan before it starts."

"I can't do that!" Don Cruez banged on his desk. "What would I use as my justification?"

"Ah, Cruez, always the Idealist." Grimsdyke shook his head. "You're well named." The actor brought a finger up. "Couldn't you use the anarch attacks as an excuse?"

Don Cruez shook his head. "Not serious enough."

Grimsdyke shrugged and got to his feet. "Well then, I guess you're going to have to wait for the damned Methuselah's plan to play out and do what you can to blunt it." The actor headed for the door. "I wish you good luck, you're going to need it." He stopped at the door, smiled back toward the desk. "Unless, of course, you decide to join us. Become Inconnu."

Don Cruez stood up, pressing the button that signaled Topper to come to the door. "I will consider it—after this is done."

Topper appeared, Grimsdyke's coat held gingerly in his hand. The actor took his property and chuckled. "Do make sure you survive." He looked back at the Justicar. "I still have dreams of our costarring in a proper comedy."

Percival took Mariana uptown for their hunt, but made a detour, leading the Toreador to the Metropolitan Museum of Art, a place she knew well. *He wants to show me some of the art he understands.* She realized it was a sign of his trust—and whatever problem he was trying to deal with. *I'll let him do the talking,* she decided. *Maybe he'll finally tell me what's bothering him.*

They walked past the guard, who warned them that the museum would be closing soon. Mariana couldn't help but smile at that. *As if they could find us if we didn't want to be found!* She looked at the man. *Not bad-looking.* Mariana licked her lips. *Maybe we'll dine here tonight.*

Val took her to the right as they entered, down the long hall, into the Egyptian section. They passed through the tomb displays, brushing past all the gold and sculpture, into the big glasshouse that the museum had erected in the seventies. "This is what I wanted you to see."

The temple! Mariana smiled. "I've been in here before." She stepped up onto the first platform, studying the stone edifice perched on top of the second. "They moved this here because of the Aswan Dam, didn't they?"

Val nodded. "I saw it before they moved it." He looked out through the glass, into his past. "In the desert."

Mariana took his hands, led him to the long stone bench. "When you were alive?"

He nodded. "Just before I died, actually." He turned, looked her in the eye. "Mariana." He hesitated.

Come on! she thought. *Tell me! Get it out of your system!*

She watched him gather his strength. "Mariana, did you know your sire?"

What?

"I met mine right here, in front of this very temple." He looked at her, his eyes far away. "A long time ago . . . "

"I thought your sire was Don Cruez." She shook her head. "The Justicar."

Val nodded. "He is. And I thought I knew him. . . . "

Again he stared at the temple, eyes boring into the past. . . .

Val had awakened in total darkness. He'd been terrified, unable to breathe, unable to speak. He'd tried to move, but found himself unable to do even that. *Am I paralyzed?* he'd thought, mind racing. *Did that butcher Druitt cut my backbone?* But that wasn't the answer. Val could feel his limbs, he just couldn't move them.

Then he heard the sound.

Somebody's digging! He tried to pinpoint the scratching. *It's . . .* His mind reeled.

It's right above me! Val struggled for movement. *I've been buried alive!* He felt his finger move, just a little. *I've got to get out! Got to tell them!* The shoveling sounds grew louder, closer. *I'm here!* Val screamed in his mind. *Here!*

I know, the thought came back, stunning Val into mental silence. *Just wait. I'm coming.*

It was Don Cruez who dug Val up that night. Freeing him from the shallow grave of a British military casualty.

Val came back to himself, back to the present. Mariana was holding him tightly, eyes worried as she watched his come back into focus. "Are you all right?" She stared at him. "You went so limp."

He nodded, putting his own arms around her. "I'm fine." He looked at the temple in front of them. "Just a little lost."

"No need to be." She smiled at him. "Whatever else is going on, we have each other."

His own spirits lifted at the thought. "Yes." He turned away from the temple, turned away from his past. "And we always will!"

*   *   *

Acquiel woke in a strange place. *Where am I?* She tried to move—and found she was tied down, held in place by leather and steel. *This isn't Mariana's work! Who . . .* She tried to think back, tried to remember what might have happened the night before. *I went to the Club,* she recalled. *But I didn't have any fun.* The faces of those insipid men came to her. Her face twisted with disgust. *Ugh!* She continued to run through the events of the night before. *I decided to go home,* she frowned, *but first, I wanted to say hello to Dieter Kleist.*

Dieter Kleist! Acquiel glanced at her wrists, noted the irons holding them in place. *This is his house!* She frowned. *I don't remember going home with him!* She shook her head—as far as it would go. *I don't remember anything after I went into the Treasure Room.* She shifted position and felt the pain in her back and her buttocks. *Feels like he really went to work on me.* A grin came to her face. *Mariana will kill him.* The grin widened. *Or Val will.* The thought of the big Brujah tearing Kleist a new a-hole comforted Acquiel. *All I have to do is wait until dark.* She saw the sun outside. *A couple of hours. Kleist will wake then, and set me loose.* She frowned as another thought came into her mind. *At least, I hope he will.*

She began to worry.

Tessler followed Anneke uptown, to a large brownstone on the East Side. *Swanky neighborhood,* he thought, looking around. *She has rich friends.* He smiled. Rich or poor, they weren't going to do her any good if she tried to pull anything off on the Brujah. He checked his pockets, making sure his weapons were handy. *As if they'll do any good against . . . a Justicar!*

Tessler shook his head at the thought. *I'm amazed she*

hasn't noticed me—Don Cruez *would* have. Is she *so sure of herself she doesn't worry about such things?* Tessler glanced around, checking his surroundings. *Or is Don Cruez covering me somehow.* He shrugged. *Kinda late to worry about it now!*

Tessler had, after all, spent most of the night following Anneke. First to a succession of dives on the Lower West Side, then, working steadily uptown, to some of the nicer places in Midtown. *She's met a lot of Kindred tonight.* Tessler had kept a careful list. Anneke *had* talked to a lot of the Camarilla last night, but had yet to have a single word with the Brujah. *Or the Toreador, now that I think of it.* Puzzling. But in keeping with what Don Cruez had told him. *She's planning to call a Conclave, all right.* Tessler grinned. *Only it's not time yet.* He had gotten close enough to overhear several of her conversations. *Soon, though.*

Tessler wondered what it was all about. Don Cruez hadn't told him everything. *He never does.* Tessler's grin widened. *He's afraid I'll do something against the rules.* The Brujah shook his head. *As if rules meant anything to me!* The door to the brownstone stayed closed. Tessler glanced at the sky, noted the fringing of gray at the horizon. *Kind of late for another visit.* He nodded. This was her new haven, then. *Got you, sweetie!*

Tessler headed away from the door, running a map through his own mind. *Let's see now . . .* He knew he had a haven nearby, in the cellar of one of the local churches. *Kind of a downer,* he thought. *But it'll have to do.*

The Brujah hurried to cover, aware of the sun just over the horizon. *I'll be back, though.* He looked back at the brownstone. *Back to find out what you're up to!*

* * *

"Are we ready?" The retainer shuddered at Lady Ambrosia's softly spoken words. *She's just waiting for me to make a mistake,* he thought. *Then she'll finish me.*

"You're wrong about that." The Methuselah smiled as the retainer whirled in amazement. "It surprises you that I can read your thoughts?" The smile turned ugly. "Do not compare my powers to your miserable abilities." The retainer cringed. "Still"—Lady Ambrosia settled back in her chair, the smile gone—"I may not kill you yet." She regarded one of her fingernails. "That is"—she turned toward him—"if you do not fail me again."

The retainer nodded. "No . . . I mean, yes, milady." He struggled to regain control of his shattered thoughts.

The fool! Lady Ambrosia thought. *This one is a waste of the vitae that keeps him alive.* She watched as his mind clarified. *Even now he tries to hide trivialities. From me.* She shook her head. *Yes, I will replace him—after the plan is complete.* She motioned him to continue. *Then . . .*

"We are ready with every detail of the plan." He looked up, catching the Lady's eye. "Also, we have reestablished surveillance on Anneke."

"It's about time."

The retainer started to sit down, but thought better of it when he saw the Methuselah's eyes. "I have several of our cat's-paws watching her."

"Don't lose her again."

He bowed. "I don't intend to."

The Methuselah leaned forward. "What has she been up to?"

The retainer nervously consulted some notes in his hand. "It seems as if she has spent the last few days conferring with a variety of Kindred." He looked at her, some of his self-possession regained. "Rather powerful Kindred. Elders. Primogen."

"And?"

"I believe that she is planning to call a Conclave."

Lady Ambrosia sank back into her seat. "To what end?"

The retainer looked down. "That, I do not know as yet."

"Find out. And in the meantime"—she leaned back in her chair, eyes going to the night outside—"let the plan go forward." She looked down at him. "On the night of the gallery opening."

He bowed again. "As you command."

Her eyes flashed at him. "So it had better be done!"

Mariana began to worry when Acquiel did not return the next night. "I don't understand it." She shook her head as Percival tried to calm her. "She's never stayed away this long before."

"Are you sure nothing's happened to her?" Percival frowned. He liked the little blood doll too, but she was, after all, only a kine.

Mariana broke away, paced the floor. "She's still alive." Her brow furrowed. "I would know if she were dead."

"Any idea where she could be?"

Mariana shook her head.

Percival grabbed his leathers. "Well, we know she went to the Blood Club last night." He checked his knife, put it in his pocket. "I guess we should start there."

The Club was full when Mariana and Percival arrived. The main bar a writhing mass of kine and Kindred, all playing their games, all after something. "We should check with Kleist first," Mariana said as she pulled Percival down the stairs. "If anyone knows anything, he will."

Mariana pushed her way through the crowd, slapping away the occasional hand that attempted to grope her. There weren't many of those; Percival's glowering form saw to that. The Treasure Room was right in front of her, also packed with the Club's clientele.

Kleist wasn't there.

"He's not in his usual space."

Percival looked around. "You know anyone else here?"

"Well"—she glanced to the balcony above—"there's always Andy."

"Who's he?"

"He plays Graves, the butler."

Percival shook his head. "I didn't see any butler when we came in tonight."

Mariana sighed. "Neither did I." She plunged back into the crowd.

Acquiel squealed as the whip touched her. *I hate this!* She tried to plead with the man wielding the leather, but the gag he had placed in her mouth made communication impossible. The whip came back, touching her buttocks with another line of fire. *It's only fun when someone I love does it!* She shivered as Kleist's hand touched her right under the latest welt, knowing that she was wet, knowing that he would misinterpret that fact. *And I don't love him at all!*

Kleist lacked Auspex; the whip crack that followed proved that conclusively. *Why is he doing this?* Acquiel's brain was spinning now, distracted by the potent combination of pain and pleasure. *Why?*

The whip fell again, and again. Acquiel's world narrowed, focused down to the white-hot pain, the growing need for something more. *He's got to stop!*

He did.

"What the Hell is going on here!" Mariana pulled the

whip out of Kleist's shocked hand. "What do you think you're doing?"

"She wanted it." The Toreador stared over Mariana's shoulder. "She said you were neglecting her." Kleist pinned Percival with a withering glare. "Spending all your time with him!"

"Is that true, Acquiel?" Mariana turned to the helpless blonde. "Did you ask him to whip you?"

Acquiel shook her head as hard as she could, yelling into her gag.

Mariana rushed to undo the harness around the girl's neck, pulling the oversize ball gag free. "Now answer me, did you ask him to do this?"

Acquiel gulped in air, tried her best not to drool spittle all over herself. *I hate that!* She licked her lips, moistened her tongue. "N . . ." She swallowed again. "No! I never even talked to him!"

Kleist's face whitened. "She's lying. She came to me in the Club. Asked me to be her master."

Acquiel shook her head as hard as she could. "No! I didn't! I wouldn't!"

Mariana watched them both. "There's something wrong here, but one thing's for certain." She glared at Kleist. "You're going to release her." The glare hardened. "Right now."

"But—"

"Do it." Percival's hand was heavy on the Toreador's shoulder. "Or I'll do it." The Brujah grinned. "After I finish with you."

Kleist pushed the hand away, but he didn't challenge the bigger man, just walked to the St. Andrew's cross he had the blood doll on and concentrated on removing her bonds.

"Mariana, I have no reason to lie to you." He looked

at her, sincerity in his eyes. "I tell you, this girl asked me to do this."

Mariana nodded. "I believe you."

"Hey! I told you that—" Acquiel started to protest.

"I believe you, too." Mariana held out her arms, gathered Acquiel into them. "Even though I think I ought to punish you anyway." The blonde looked up, surprised. "After all,"—Mariana's smile grew—"you did think you weren't getting enough attention."

Val grinned as he watched Mariana *punish* Acquiel. He could see the feelings passing between the two. *They're family*, he realized. *Even when Mariana whips her*. He watched as Mariana caressed the blond girl. Watched Acquiel moan and writhe. He smiled. *Maybe I should try to give them both more attention*.

He slipped into the suddenly just-big-enough bed.

Weeks passed. Happy weeks in which Percival, Mariana, and Acquiel became a family. Each evening, right after the sun set, Mariana would go to work, using one or the other of her lovers as a model. Later, after the work of the night was done, Mariana and Percival, together, would tie and torment Acquiel, leaving the little blonde suspended in an ecstasy of sensation when they went to hunt. Later, after feeding, all three would share the big bed, exchanging warmth and togetherness.

It was a wonderful time for all of them. A little Eden of belonging and being wanted. It had to end.

Finally, it did.

Mariana's gallery opening had become the talk of the Toreador community. After all, it wasn't every day that one of their own showed enough talent for a public showing. Oh, there were always the artistes, the Toreador capable of producing art of some fashion, but there was something about the Kindred state that prevented them from ever doing anything both Kindred and human could enjoy.

At least, such was the case before Mariana discovered the art of computers. Now . . .

The gallery was not a big one. Just a little hole-in-the-wall lost in the depths of Greenwich Village. But that wasn't important. What mattered was that this was a true opening, and, as such, an excuse for a Kindred festival.

"Look!" Mariana pointed at the door for the fifth time in the last ten minutes. "Isn't that Andreas?"

Val shrugged. "How should I know?"

Mariana turned, snorting through her widening smile. "Brute! Don't you keep track of the elders?"

"Why should I?"

She slapped him in the chest. "Because we're supposed to respect our elders."

He shook his head. "I'm Brujah." He smiled. "They should respect me!"

She stuck out her tongue at him. "Beast! I think I'll circulate a bit."

He kissed her hand. "Do that." He smiled. "See what they think of your pictures." He saw her hesitate. "Don't worry." He squeezed her hand before releasing it. "They'll love them." Mariana smiled and moved away.

"Do you really believe that?" Val turned to find Acquiel behind him, worry lining her face.

"Of course I do."

Acquiel moved closer, her dress shifting to show interesting bits of creamy flesh. "I hope you're right." She sighed. "I worry about what rejection would do to Mariana."

Val took the blood doll's hand in his, felt her warmth run through him. "Don't worry." He gave her a quick kiss. "It'll be all right." Val caught a motion at the door. "My God!"

Acquiel turned, eyes going wide as she saw the tall, leather-clad man there. "Who's that?"

"That's Don Cruez." Val shifted his feet. "My sire."

"Percival!" The Justicar caught sight of the other Brujah, instantly striding toward him. "It's good to see you!"

Val bowed. "Good to see you, sir."

"Why have you stayed away from my house?" Don Cruez stopped, eyes devouring Acquiel. "And who is this magnificent creature?"

"This is Acquiel, sir." Val motioned to the blood doll. "Mariana's"—he hesitated, then looked the big Justicar in the face—"and my friend."

Don Cruez nodded. "Good for you." He took Acquiel's hand, gave it a long Continental kiss. "And where is this Mariana Tessler's told me so much about?"

"Over here, sir." *Maybe this will be all right.* Val prayed. *At least, it's not as bad as it could be.* He looked around, eyes suspicious. *Tessler doesn't seem to be here.*

Tessler stood outside, watching as the elders of the Toreador clan walked into the tiny gallery. *What an opportunity*, he thought. I *could clean out the Camarilla elite with one little firebomb*. He shrugged. Don Cruez had forbidden any such attempt. *Ah well*. He knew he should go in. Knew he should say hello to Val, make an attempt to see the woman's "art."

But *it's not my way*. Tessler's eyes glinted. *It's not the Brujah way!* It was bad enough that Don Cruez had gone inside. *He had to do it*, Tessler realized. *He owed it to Val*.

Tessler didn't owe anybody anything, so he waited outside, where, he told himself, he could keep an eye on things. *After all, with so many Kindred around, there's no telling what might . . .*

Anneke! Tessler watched as the Toreador Justicar stopped in front of the gallery, looking around, eyes searching for watchers. *She can't see me!* he realized. *The streetlight is masking me from her*. Tessler froze in place. *I'm invisible if I don't move.*

He watched as Anneke checked the street, then went up the stairs into the little gallery. *Anneke too!* He snorted. *Who next?*

He never got an answer. As he stood there, watching the doorway of the gallery, he realized that the night was darkening. *Strange*, he thought, checking the streetlight over his head. *It shouldn't be . . .*

Ebon night stole over him, too quickly to react, too completely to fight. In an instant, the essence that was Tessler was gone. In its place, standing in the husk by the streetlight, was someone else. Someone old and powerful.

Tessler's body moved forward, heading for the gallery and the object hidden deep beneath it.

* * *

Lady Ambrosia smiled as she looked at the world through the eyes of her cat's-paw. *It's working just as I planned!* She chuckled, filling the darkened room with the sound. *Better!* She hadn't planned on Anneke actually being *in* the gallery when things came to fruition. *Her presence will make things so much more interesting.* Violence would become certain, followed by more violence, and more . . .

Teeth shone in the darkness. *Within a week, final death will stalk this city.* Lady Ambrosia nodded. *Just as I planned.* The cat's-paw reached the building, walked around the side, headed for a barely visible staircase. *Then will come the Conclave.*

The Assembly would end the reign of the Sabbat, Lady Ambrosia was sure of that. *And then my minions will take charge. The city will fall into my hands like a ripe apple!*

She guided her cat's-paw down the stairs. The doorway at the bottom was unlocked. *My retainer got that much right!* She smiled. *Should I reward him or punish him?*

Later!

Down the hallway now, to the right. She came to the furnace, a huge, ancient affair that heated water, then pumped it through rusting pipes that honeycombed the building's structure. *A primitive device, but a perfect landmark!* She made her borrowed eyes look around. *It should be somewhere nearby.*

There! Her thrall hurried to one side of the furnace, nearly crawling to get under the pipes. Hands reached out, picking up the neatly painted toolbox sitting alongside the boiler. *Now, let's see if that imbecile got the rest right!*

She caused the lid of the toolbox to be raised, found herself looking down into a maze of wires, all connected to a tightly packed cylinder of some grayish material. She accessed a portion of her thrall's mind, let his eyes look down on the package in his hands. *Yes. He recognizes it.* She clamped down on his consciousness, crammed it back into oblivion. *Now to put it in the proper place.*

She pulled the box out from behind the furnace, let her eyes search the ceiling, looking for the point directly under the gallery. *I believe . . . yes, right there!* Mentally, she marked the spot. *Now . . .*

Ten minutes later, everything was in place. She pulled the little clock out of the now-empty toolbox. Set the alarm. *I'll give it twenty minutes.* She pushed the little plunger in, then carefully plugged the clock's wiring into the device attached to the ceiling.

She nodded to herself, then walked her cat's-paw out of the cellar, up the stairs, back across the street.

Right where he started from.

Forget, she told his still-imprisoned mind. *Forget everything that happened since Anneke walked into the gallery.* New pictures appeared in Tessler's mind. *Remember this instead. . . .*

Mariana had been amazed at how much everyone seemed to like her new art style.

She'd expected the Toreador to praise it. *After all, I'm one of them!* But the human visitors seemed to like it too.

"These tell wonderful stories!" she heard one woman say, staring at her portrait of Percival and the Grail. "Look at Sir Percival. You can actually see the triumph lighting up his face."

The lady's companion said nothing, but Mariana noted that his eyes kept drifting to another picture. One of her nudes of Acquiel.

Men! She laughed to herself. *They're all animals!* That

reminded her. *Where is Percival?* She glanced around. *He should listen to what these people think of him.* She laughed. *Or, at least, what they think of his portrait.*

There he is. She squinted. Percival was one of the tallest men she'd ever seen, but he was standing alongside someone who dwarfed him. *Who . . .* Then realization struck her. *My God!* Her eyes widened. *That must be Don Cruez!* She shook her head in wonder. *The most powerful Kindred in the area—and he's come to see my work!*

I hope he likes it. Mariana headed for the pair, straightening her hair and dress as she went. *I hope he likes me!*

Anneke paced slowly through the gallery, studying Mariana's work. *These are good!* she realized. *Incredible use of color, it's almost as if . . .* Anneke shook her head. *No.* It was impossible for any Kindred to see the sun, difficult even to picture it. *Especially as we get older.*

She bent forward, examining the landscape in front of her more closely. *And yet . . .* She shook her head. *This does look the way I remember sunlight looking.* Anneke stood up. *An amazing talent!* She looked around, saw Mariana in the corner, talking to two tall Kindred. *A pity I couldn't solve her problem.* She shook her head. *My reward might have been quite . . . rewarding.* She chuckled. *No matter.* She started toward the little group at the back of the room. *I have other work to do.* She pushed aside a few kine, ignoring their glares of protest.

"Mariana." The Justicar took off her glasses and smiled. "Wonderful show."

"Anneke?" Mariana was surprised to see the Toreador Justicar. She looked at Don Cruez, noted the slight tightening of the muscles around his eyes.

Anneke smiled at her expression. "Why so shocked, my dear?" She gestured around her, taking in the walls of pictures. "Surely no self-respecting Toreador could ignore such a display."

"Apparently, though, a self-respecting Toreador can ignore the Traditions." Don Cruez's tone was mild, but his eyes were angry.

Anneke turned to him. "Are you referring to the Fifth Tradition?"

Don Cruez nodded. *You know I am!*

Anneke's brows rose with the strength of that thought. *Auspex in a Brujah!* She sent back. *Unusual.*

"You haven't answered my question." Don Cruez's tone continued to be mild. "And I think we might continue this conversation orally." He motioned to the others. "I'd hate to be rude."

"Rude!" Anneke laughed. "This from a Brujah!"

"From a Justicar."

Anneke nodded. "So." She turned away for a second, accepting a glass from a passing waiter. "I *will* answer your question then." She took a sip. "Ugh! Wine!" She tossed the glass back onto the tray, not caring that it splashed onto the white-clad servant. "You'd think there'd be something for *us* to drink." She glanced questioningly at Mariana. "Ah well, where was I?"

The mildness was slipping from Don Cruez's voice. "Answering my question."

"Yes!" Anneke smiled at the big Brujah. An insolent smile. "Hospitality." She gestured. "As there is no prince here, I felt no need to present myself to a"—she looked at Don Cruez—"lesser personage."

Don Cruez nodded, deliberately ignoring the implied insult. "And yet, I believe the wording actually specifies: ' . . . the one who ruleth there.'" The big Brujah looked down at the Toreador. "While I am here, I rule New York."

"Really?" Anneke's tone was breezy. "I thought the Sabbat ruled here." She smiled. "Certainly the killings in Elysium bear that out." Her smile grew harder. "I believe something should be done about that. That is why I have asked for a Conclave."

"You've called a Conclave?"

"Yes. I think this city needs a prince. Someone with the power and the will"—her smile turned into a sneer—"to control the anarchs."

"So, that's your game!" Don Cruez leaned forward, anger showing in his face now. "Well, let me tell you . . . "

"There you are!"

Everyone whirled at the new voice. It was Dieter Kleist, stalking up to them, anger showing in every line of his body. "First you steal my technique." He reached out, grabbed Acquiel by the arm. "Then you try to steal my property."

"Hey!" Acquiel squealed as he pulled her away. "Let go!"

Val moved quickly, his own hand closing on Kleist's like a vise. "Do what the lady says."

Anneke smiled, her own hands disappearing into pockets. "I don't think you should hurt my friend."

"And I don't think you should move." Don Cruez's voice wasn't mild anymore. "Not even a little."

Mariana stood there, eyes on the standoff, unable to think of a single thing to say.

Then the world exploded underneath her.

"Too soon!" Lady Ambrosia pulled back in rage, severing all outside contacts. "The explosive went off too soon!"

The retainer sat by her side, eyes wide as his own tenuous contact with their assorted cat's-paws dissolved. "I don't understand. The incendiary device was very carefully constructed!"

A clawed fist shot out, backhanding the retainer on the side of the head, catapulting him into the wall. "Fool!" The claw reversed direction, ripping across the retainer's face, cutting deep into flesh, smashing the nose. "Lady Singhjul found a way to interfere with one of your contacts!"

The injured Kindred rolled up into a ball, cringed away from the mad eyes of the Methuselah. "No, milady!" It was almost a sob. "Impossible!"

Lady Ambrosia towered over the cowering retainer. "It just happened!" Furious, she turned from him, paced back across the room. "How can we know who was destroyed? It could have been the boy, the girl." She snarled. "Even the Justicar himself!"

"Go!" She whirled, eyes dissecting the still-supine retainer. "Get me answers." She gnashed gleaming teeth as she pushed the quaking Kindred away. "Find out who lives, and who has died the final death!"

The ancient creature settled back into her cushions, eyes still radiating death. "And then find who betrayed me to Lady Singhjul." The eyes turned to him, glowing gates into Hell. "I want whoever it was." The gates opened. "And I want them still alive."

Val was thrown backward by the blast. *What the Hell was that?* He scrambled to his feet, shoved away several kine who were milling around, blocking his way. *Something in the basement must have exploded!* He looked at the huge hole in the floor. *Boiler, maybe.* He turned to look for Mariana—and discovered the rest of the problem. *Fire!*

Fires were not unusual in any big city—but for Kindred, flames produced a special fear—one that often triggered uncontrolled frenzies. Val found he had to use all his willpower to keep control of his Beast—to stop himself from racing mindlessly away from the flames. *Not yet!*

All around him, other Kindred *were* going into frenzy. They fought their way through burning dividers, tore at fabric, clawed at brick walls, anything to get away from the blaze.

Val angled through them, searching for the one person that meant the world to him. *Mariana!* The whole gallery was ablaze now, the fire fed by Mariana's pictures and the fabric-covered dividers on which they were hung. Val searched through the flames and swiftly growing smoke. *Those dividers are giving off some kind of fumes,* Val realized, watching the gray smoke fill the room. *It probably won't hurt us.* He looked around, saw Toreador fighting their way to the door. *But it might slow us down.*

Val could see at a glance that the door was useless, despite the continuing rush for it.

It's blocked, he realized. *The metal is probably bent from the explosion.* He looked around. *Don Cruez might be able to open it.* He turned his head. *Or Anneke.* Neither was in sight. *I don't know who else.* He continued to look around. *Where the hell is Mariana?*

"Mariana!" Val's head snapped around. *That was Acquiel!* But where . . . Then he saw her. The little blood doll was with Kleist, hoisted over his shoulder like a sack of flour. *He's heading for the door.* Val saw the ceiling catch fire, flames leaping around the room. *He'll never get her out that way!*

"Kleist!" Val ran toward the Toreador and his soft burden. "Not that way!"

The techno turned as Val approached, snarling like some animal at bay. "Leave me alone, Brujah!" He pulled a gun out of his pocket, the muzzle pointed at Val. "I'm getting out of here." His free hand patted Acquiel's struggling rump. "And she's going with me."

Val shook his head. "I don't think so." He moved, using his Discipline to weave toward and around his prey. Kleist fired his pistol once, twice. I *didn't think he had the nerve*! Val saw the bullets go wide, one of them hitting a kine screaming in the corner, the second putting a neat hole in one of Mariana's pictures. Then Val was on him, right hand sweeping down, taking the gun, snapping off the tip of the trigger finger. Before Kleist could react, Val's left hand grabbed him by the collar and locked tight, holding the Toreador in place.

Kleist screamed and tried to turn, desperate to flee from this suddenly savage adversary.

He couldn't move.

"Let the girl down." Val's tone left no room for argument. "Now."

Kleist released his grip on Acquiel. The blonde slid down, landing on the floor in a heap, breath whooshing from her body.

"Acquiel?"

The girl scrambled to her feet, put herself behind Val, coughing a little as the smoke grew worse. "I'm here, Val."

He nodded at her. "Stay with me." He turned back to Kleist, shook his head at the fear in the Kindred's face. "Get out of here." He released the Toreador, who immediately broke for the door. "Not that way!" But it was too late, the techno was gone, disappeared into fire and smoke.

Val turned back to Acquiel. "Do you know where Mariana is?"

The blonde shook her head, the coughing getting worse. "No. That bastard Kleist"—a toss of her head—"pulled me away just as the whole place went up." She coughed again. "What happened?"

"I don't know yet." Val started toward the far wall. There were windows in the bathrooms; he remembered seeing them. "Let's get you out of here first, then we'll figure it out."

"I won't go without Mariana!" The blood doll drew herself to her full height, glaring at Val.

"You'll do what you're told." He grabbed her hand, dragging her after him. "Don't worry, I'll make sure Mariana gets out."

Tessler was knocked off his feet when the gallery exploded. *What in the Hell?* He pulled himself up, watched in shock as flames roared through the gallery, spread to neighboring buildings. *So fast!* He wanted to run, get away from the growing heat, but he pushed the instinct down. *Got to stay. Don Cruez is in there!* He shielded his eyes as flames blasted through the upstairs windows. *That can't be natural.* He moved toward the door. *Somebody set this up.* He shielded his eyes as glass rained down. *And I know who it was!*

Snow on the windowsills in front of him melted instantly, creating tiny clouds of steam that floated before his eyes. Tessler clamped down on his Beast, held his ground, stepped forward. He sniffed the air, trying to make out any smells. *Could be gasoline, but there's no smell . . . Gelignite, maybe.* His face set hard. *Or plastique.*

He rubbed his eyes, forcing cinders out. *Don Cruez is in there.* Tessler made a second try for the door, throwing an arm up to avoid the worst of the flames. *And Val. . . .*

Tessler reached the door, pulled at the knob. It came off in his hand. *Damn!* He drove his fingers into the crack at the side, working to get some leverage. *Got to pull this open . . .* The door was hot, and Tessler could see his hands starting to blister. *Can't think about that.* He set his feet, bent forward. *One good heave . . .* Tessler could feel vibrations on the inside. *They're pushing from in there too.* He mustered up all his strength—and pulled with everything he had.

The door held firm. Tessler let go, buried his hands in the snow, trying to save what muscle he could. *I need some kind of tool.* His eyes scanned the street, the alleys.

A crowbar, tire iron, anything.

There was nothing.

Mariana shook her head, dazed from the force of the explosion. She came to hands and knees, found herself in a corner, a wall behind her.

There were flames everywhere.

Fire! Her eyes widened at the heat. *So hot . . .* She got her feet under her, tried to find a way around the flames. *Nothing. There's no path. . . .* She looked at the fire in front of her, considered jumping through . . . *No. It's too wide, all over the rug and floor . . .* Her eyes grew wide as the realization struck her. *I'm trapped! Surrounded!* She tried to peer over the fire, see if Val was nearby. The smoke was too thick. She backed up, flattening herself against the wall as the flames moved closer, higher. *Just like the last time . . .*

Mariana had awakened in the dark. *So*, she thought. *It was all a dream after all*. Her eyes filled with tears. *They'll come back. Hurt me again*. She'd been hurt so much. *I can't take the pain anymore*. Her mind began to scream. *I'll die!*

You can't die. Mariana looked around wildly. Someone was talking to her—in her head! She began to laugh. *It's finally happened. I've gone crazy!* The laughter filled her, began to leak out, turned to sobs. *Crazy . . .*

Then she wasn't alone. There was someone with her, hugging her to him, holding her tight. "It's all right, Mariana." The voice was familiar, soothing. "They can't touch you now. Never again." The laughter began to go away. "I promise." She knew that voice. . . .

"Phillipe?"

There was a hint of a chuckle. "Yes, child. It is Phillipe." The hug grew tighter. "I'll stay with you from now on." She could feel his smile. "Stop anyone from ever hurting you again."

He did, too. Mariana and Phillipe had lived in the burned-out ruins of farmhouses and barns, living off the vitae of Nazi soldiers in the nearby camps. Mariana enjoyed feeding on the Germans; it gave her a sense of revenge, even though, at Phillipe's insistence, she seldom killed her prey. "If we kill too many of them, they will start murdering the villagers," he told her. "And we don't want their deaths on our heads, do we?"

Mariana shook her head. She didn't want to kill anyone—except the Nazis.

Weeks passed. Mariana and Phillipe moved up and down the coast of France, feeding early in the night, then finding a secure place to sleep. There, Phillipe would teach Mariana the traditions of the Kindred, making sure she understood each of them. Impressing on her the importance of the Masquerade. "They're cattle, Mariana." He gestured at the thousands of Germans in the fields. "Nothing compared to us, and yet, if they were sure of our existence, they'd band together, hunt us down."

"Kill *us*?" Mariana was still young, completely secure in her newfound power.

"Yes." Phillipe nodded sadly. "Whatever it took, they would find a way." He gestured with Gallic simplicity. "They would destroy each of us."

Mariana learned her lessons, learned the importance of the Masquerade. She also learned to love Phillipe. He was more than her sire. He was her world.

Until, one night in 1944 . . .

"Look at them all!" Mariana never tired of watching the bombers fly overhead. She knew they were heading for Berlin, ready to give the hated Nazis some of their own medicine. "Must be a thousand of them!"

Phillipe nodded. "More every night." He motioned her to follow him. "The war is going badly for the Germans."

"Good."

Phillipe had smiled at her ferocity. "Perhaps." He motioned her to follow him. "But if the Germans lose, we must begin to feed on the others—the innocents you want to avoid harming."

Mariana shrugged. She had learned much over the months. There were no "innocents." All humans were kine—cattle for feeding. She turned to ask Phillipe if that was right when a sudden noise split the sky. A high-pitched, screaming sound.

Phillipe whirled. "Get down!" He pushed her to one side, whirling her away as . . .

The ground exploded with terrible force.

She'd regained her feet in seconds, but had been unable to reach Phillipe. He was trapped inside a ring of fire, his body torn by the force of the explosion. Mariana stood just clear of the flames, trying to reach him. She took one step into the flames, watched the flesh of her feet blister and peel off the bones. She'd cried out then, backed away.

There was nothing I could do.

She came back to the present. Found herself unbroken, but surrounded by flames, their heat burning the hair from her head. *Just as there's nothing I can do now.* She felt her eyebrows crisp, the tiny hairs blow away. She couldn't cry; there was no moisture left in her body. She sank to the ground, naked now, her dress gone. *This isn't fair!*

She wailed once, letting her spirit voice its pain.

The flames closed in, touching her body, burning, always burning.

Val carried Acquiel to the back of the room, away from the thickest of the flames. He kicked several of the dividers out of his way, wincing as he saw Mariana's work fall into the flames. *She'll do more*, he promised himself. *We have all the time in the world.* As he moved, he looked for the girl, but the smoke kept thickening. At times, he couldn't even see the wall he was heading for. *Got to get Acquiel out first*, he decided. *Fumes are too thick.* He looked at the blood doll in his arms. *She'll die if I don't get her outside.* His lips quirked. *Mariana would never forgive me if that happened.*

Finally, after ducking around a fresh outbreak of flames, Val found the back wall of the gallery. He followed the naked bricks, and found himself in the little passage that he knew led to the bathrooms. *Just a little farther*. The air was clearer here, the heat less intense. *Got to find a window*. Finally, in front of him, he saw the glow of the outside world.

He sped up, racing down the corridor, then, at the last second, he threw his body against the window, closing his eyes and sheltering Acquiel as the frame gave, catapulting him out into the snow. *We made it!*

He took a minute to roll in the snow, letting the cold wetness bathe his skin, extinguishing any cinders that might have lodged in his hair or clothing. That done, he checked on Acquiel. *She's still breathing!* He picked up a handful of snow, rubbed it over her blistered cheeks and forehead. "C'mon, girl!" He rubbed a little more over her breasts, tearing open the sheer straps that held her dress closed. "Talk to me!"

The blonde's eyelids fluttered. "Mariana?"

"No." He used his fingers to clear sooty water away from her eyes. "It's me, Val."

"Val!" She tried to sit up, fighting against his hands. "You've got to get Mariana out. Got to . . ." She fainted.

Val let her head fall to the snow, pulled off his leather jacket, spreading it around her, tucking the ends under her body. He stood, turned back to the gallery. The flames were worse now, visible through the broken window. *She's right*. He jumped up, caught the edge of the frame. *I've got to find Mariana*.

Val leaped into the burning building just in time to hear a long, ululating wail. *Mariana!* He raced forward, throwing himself through the wall of flame that marked the end of the corridor—and found himself in the middle of the burning Hell that was the gallery.

*　　*　　*

Outside, Tessler finally found a tool. *The fence!* He leaped to the wrought-iron fencing that surrounded the gallery's entrance, grabbed one of the spiked posts with the tattered remains of his hands, and, with a grunt of effort, ripped it loose. *This should work!* He jumped back to the front door, drove the tip of the post into the frame, and, using every iota of his remaining strength, ripped the door open.

Flame rushed out; Tessler's eyelashes disappeared, instantly turned to ash. He tossed his head, closed his eyes, stumbled forward. *Got to find Don Cruez . . .*

A figure pushed by him, dashing out the door. Tessler turned, got a glimpse of the face—*Kleist*—and headed deeper into the flames.

There were bodies everywhere. Kine and Kindred. Some had succumbed to the fumes, some to the flames. Tessler ignored them all, narrowing his senses as he searched for one figure.

"Don Cruez!" Tessler found the Justicar lying in the middle of the room, next to a huge hole in the floor. There were thirty-foot flames shooting out of the hole, starting new fires in the city, gutting the rooms above. Tessler struggled to the Justicar's side, rolled the big man over, looking for signs of life. *He's pretty badly burned.* An understatement. The flesh on Don Cruez's chest had melted off like wax, baring huge areas of rib and lung. *He's in torpor.* Tessler grabbed the Brujah under the arms, careful not to rip off more blistered flesh. *Got to get him out!*

With a tremendous effort, Tessler lifted the Justicar off the floor, cradled the limp body in his arms, and started to run for the door. Under his feet, Tessler felt the floor shift, individual boards warping in the immense heat. *It's going to collapse!* He redoubled his speed, felt his feet slip as he stepped in someone's ruined remains. *Shit!* The floor shifted again. Tessler stumbled back to his feet, moved forward. *Almost there!* He tripped, banged his shoulder against the doorframe—and was outside, falling into the wonderful coolness of snow.

He let his battered body rest a moment, then, with the sound of sirens getting steadily closer, he pushed the pain back, picked up the still body of Don Cruez, and ran into the street. *I've got to get him to one of our havens.* Tessler turned the corner, avoiding an approaching police car. *Make sure he gets some vitae.* He picked up his pace. *Then I'm going to find out who was behind all this.* His mouth went grim. *So I can kill him.* He felt his teeth grind into one another. *Slowly.*

Val fought his way into the middle of the blazing room. He could feel his hair burning, his eyes boiling in their own liquid. *Can't think about that.* He looked around, shielding his face as much as he could. *Got to find Mariana.* He stumbled forward. *We were standing about . . .* He skidded to a stop. *There!*

The floor was gone. In front of Val was a huge hole, filled with raging flames that leaped from below the floor to beyond the ceiling. *No.* Val took another step forward. *NO.* The heat grew more intense. "NOOOOOOOOOO!" He staggered away, hands in front of his face, the Beast fighting him for control every step of the way. He fled the fire, racing through curtains of flame until he reached the safety of the hallway. Val hesitated there, leaned against the wall as he tried to make sense of what was happening. The floor shifted between his feet, board edges lifting, belling against the wall. *The building's going to collapse*! Val broke into a run—and the Beast seized control. *Got to survive!* He could just make out the window at the end of the hallway, flames already touching its frame. Behind him, walls started to crumple, falling inward, toward the great hole in the floor. The building shuddered.

Val stumbled, then dived for the window just in front of him, bursting free and rolling onto the snow just as the gallery collapsed into itself.

He finally stopped, flat in the snow, lying alongside the still-unconscious Acquiel. He crawled to the blonde, checked to make sure she was still alive, still breathing. Then he rolled onto his back, stared at the icy stars above. *You took her from me*, the Beast howled, raging inside him as he cursed the stars. *You killed her!*

"They had nothing to do with it, you know."

Val whirled, but found himself unable to get to his feet. *Soles are burned*, he realized. *Worse than I thought*.

"Not afraid of me?" A familiar laugh came to his ears as a figure appeared. "Are you, dear boy?"

"Grimsdyke." Val croaked the name, his throat dry, the tissues seared.

"In the flesh." The actor looked at the fire burning scant feet away. "Although I must say I had planned to arrive a little bit earlier." He turned to Val, reached out to help the Brujah rise. "Mariana?"

Val's eyes misted. "In there."

Grimsdyke sighed. "I feared as much." He made sure Val could stand on his own, then leaned forward to pick Acquiel up. "We have to go."

"Go?"

Grimsdyke nodded. "Hear the sirens? We wouldn't want the firefighters to put you in the hospital, now would we."

Val shook his head. "Would it matter?"

"My dear boy." Grimsdyke started forward, Acquiel held tenderly across his chest. "I would think you'd want to find the beings responsible for this."

"Responsible?" The Beast stirred again, ears prickling.

Grimsdyke turned. "Surely you don't think this was an accident?"

Val's eyes widened. "Somebody set this fire?"

The actor nodded.

"Do you know who?"

"Perhaps." Grimsdyke turned and started away. "At least, I have some suspicions."

Val followed, mouth set, Beast raging frighteningly near the surface. "Tell me."

"As soon as we get to safety."

"No." Val's voice was mild, but the madness was in his eyes. "Tell me now!"

The kine work quickly. Tessler stared at the little pile of rubble that had been an art gallery. *They've got most of it cleared away already.* The Brujah stared into the ashes and debris. *Val's in there.* His thoughts turned dark. *Along with that Toreador friend of his . . .*

"You're half-right, cousin."

Tessler turned, hand darting under his coat for a weapon—then he froze. "Val?" He squinted into the darkness before him. "Is that you?" *Can't be. Nobody could survive. . . .*

"Wrong again." A figure stepped out of the night, light glinted on white, even teeth. "I survived."

"Val!" Tessler moved forward, eyes playing over the figure in front of him. *He's different.* Tessler forced a smile. *Not just the burns.* He stepped forward, arms lifted in welcome. *Something else. Something deeper.* "It is you!" The other Brujah stepped into the light, and Tessler noted the degree of damage his cousin had taken. *My God!* Tessler thought. *Why didn't he go into torpor?* Val's face was badly burned, eyebrows gone, hair singed and uneven. He limped as he approached Tessler, one hand firmly held in his jacket pocket.

Tessler glanced at his own right hand, carefully bandaged while the skin grew back over naked bones. *His must be worse,* Tessler realized, noting how shallowly the pocket was filled. The other figure reached him. "How are you?"

"Alive." No smile crossed the tight skin of that face. "And angry."

Tessler nodded. "You're not the only one. Don Cruez . . ."

Concern flickered across Val's face. "How is he?"

"All right." Tessler hesitated. "Well, as much as can be expected."

Val nodded. "Tell me all of it."

"He was burned pretty badly." Tessler licked his lips. "And the explosion did a little damage."

"Why isn't he in torpor?"

"He is." Tessler attempted a nonchalant shrug. "Not too deeply, and Topper and I make sure he gets vitae."

"I see."

"Look, Val," Tessler said as he leaned forward, putting his hand on his cousin's shoulder. *Burned there, too.* "Why don't you come back with me?" Tessler smiled. "Don Cruez would be overjoyed to see you." The smile disappeared. "And then there's the Conclave coming up. . . ."

"The one Anneke asked for."

Tessler nodded.

Val's lips formed a smile. "I wouldn't worry about that too much."

"What do you mean?"

Val turned away from Tessler, stalking onto the lot that was once an art gallery. "The last time I saw Mariana, she was standing right about here."

"Val?"

The Brujah turned to his cousin. "The fire that killed her and injured Don Cruez so badly was no accident."

Tessler nodded. "We know that."

"Anneke was involved."

Another nod. "Along with Kleist and some anarchs."

Val shook his head. "Not Kleist. He was inside, next to me." Val's eyes narrowed as he remembered. "As surprised as all the others."

"But I saw him!" Tessler's surprise was genuine. "Right before the explosion, coming out of the basement."

Val turned to his cousin, eyes hard. "You didn't see anything." His eyes softened in understanding. "That's a false memory."

Tessler stiffened. "Ridiculous!"

Val turned away, looking back at the ashes of the gallery. "I wish it was." He turned back to his cousin. "You've been used. Dominated."

Tessler snorted. "No Kindred can Dominate me!"

Val's smile was sad. "A Methuselah could—and did." He turned away. "It's too bad." He started limping away. "I had hoped you were strong enough to break the Domination, tell me what really happened." He looked back at the stricken Tessler. "I guess I'll have to find out on my own."

Tessler stood in the ashes, unable to move, unable to speak. *What if he's right?* It was an impossible thought. It *has to be impossible!*

* * *

"He didn't know."

"I'm not surprised." Grimsdyke settled back in his chair, a glass of red liquid in his hand. "They seldom do."

Val paced the floor. "But he's my cousin!"

"My dear boy." Grimsdyke sipped his vitae. "Brujah or Toreador, Ventrue or Gangrel, all are the same to the Methuselahs." Grimsdyke sighed. "Pawns in their damn games."

"I'm not a pawn anymore!"

"There's no way to be sure of that," the actor said, turning sad eyes on the troubled Val. "Their plan may be more convoluted than we can know."

Val's eyes went flat. He pulled his left hand out of his pocket, stared down at the newly grown muscle covering the now-unbroken bones. "This itches."

Grimsdyke smiled. "It's healing."

Val nodded. "And as soon as it's healed . . . "

"I know." Grimsdyke sighed. "You're going to get your revenge." He looked at the angry Brujah. "Do you know how many others have tried?"

"They weren't me."

Another sigh. "I wish you'd reconsider."

Val's voice was grim. "Never."

Grimsdyke rose, walked to the side of the haven. "What about the girl?"

Val stared at him.

"Don't be dense." The actor refilled his glass. "The blond blood doll." He held up the carafe, offering some to Val. "The one you pulled out of the fire."

"Acquiel."

"Lovely name." Grimsdyke replaced the carafe, picked up his glass. "What do you plan to do about her?"

Val looked down, scratched at the healing flesh of his nose. "I hadn't thought . . . "

Grimsdyke reached Val, looked him right in the eye. "She's the last link with your Mariana; are you willing to just throw that away?"

"No."

Grimsdyke smiled. "You see," he said as he returned to his seat, "she is your responsibility. You must take care of her."

Val scowled. "You should be ashamed of yourself!"

Grimsdyke's smile disappeared. "Dear boy—"

"No!" Val's face was grim, his voice hard. "You know the Methuselahs, know the games they play." He stalked past Grimsdyke, headed for the sanctum. "You have power." He opened the door. "But you don't use it." He stepped inside. "Don't you dare talk to me about responsibility."

The door slammed.

Acquiel couldn't sleep. Her burns hurt, yes, but it was her heart that really kept her awake. *Why did Mariana have to die?* She couldn't keep the tears back. *She should have had centuries!* The blonde twisted on the big bed, found herself looking at Percival. *Look at him*, she thought. *Look at his face.* She hadn't seen a genuine smile from him since . . .

Since Mariana died. She shook her head. *Face it. He loved her as much as I did.* She wanted to go to him, ached to cuddle him to her, feel the blessed coolness of his body.

But I can't. She twisted again, found herself staring at

the ceiling. *Not without Mariana* . . . She noted a tiny crack at one edge of the room. *No*, she realized, *it's not a crack*. She squinted, saw movement. *It's a spiderweb!* Suddenly, she saw the spider, scurrying out of the web, rushing down the side of the wall. *I wonder where he's going*, she thought, letting her eyes close. *I wonder where we're all going.* . . .

Acquiel . . .

The blonde sat up in the bed, eyes flying open. "Mariana," she muttered. "Is that you, Mariana?"

It's me, little one.

"You're alive!" Acquiel's heart filled, began to beat so hard she was afraid it would burst.

Yes, little one. I'm alive.

"But Val . . ." She glanced at the Brujah, still sleeping. "Val said you were gone."

Val is wrong.

Acquiel felt tears flowing down her face. "Where are you, Mariana? Why can't I see you?"

You will, child. Soon enough.

"How did you escape?" Acquiel crawled to the edge of the bed, searching for the source of the voice. "Where did you go?"

Later, Acquiel. First I need you to do something for me.

"Anything."

First, find a knife. Val usually keeps one in his pocket. . . .

Acquiel crawled out of the bed, padded to Val's side, looked through his pants. "I don't see . . ." Her hands brushed something hard. "Oh! Here it is!"

Does it have a mark on the side?

Acquiel ran her hands over the blade. "No."

On the hilt—the handle.

"Oh!" Her hands shifted their grasp. "Yes, there's something there."

Good. Now take the knife back to the bed.

Acquiel held the knife carefully, not wanting to cut her hands. *Not now!* She smiled. *Mariana will be wanting to do other things with those hands.* It wouldn't do to have an open wound. *Not at all . . .*

Back in the bed, Acquiel crawled up to the top, sat up, the headboard supporting her back while she cradled the little blade. "I'm there."

Good. Now, hold the blade by the hilt.

"The handle." She shifted her grip. "I've got it."

Hold it out in front of you.

Acquiel complied.

Push it down, really fast, into your stomach.

Acquiel frowned. "But Mariana—"

Do it!

Acquiel's muscles clenched, then the knife flashed down, right toward her naked belly.

"That should finish it." Lady Ambrosia settled back into her cushions.

"How?" The retainer shook his head. "The girl is only mortal, why should that change the Brujah's actions?"

"It will." The Methuselah turned to the window, staring out at the eternal stars. "He is very close to the edge now; the death of the kine will push him over."

The retainer was puzzled. "And then what?"

"He will let his Beast take over." Lady Ambrosia smiled. "Many will die, and at the end, the Conclave will force the Sabbat—and the Brujah Justicar—out of the city."

"And you will take control."

The Methuselah nodded. "Just as I planned."

The retainer hesitated, sidled toward the door. "Is it not odd that Anneke should be the one to call the Conclave?"

Lady Ambrosia turned to him, eyes glinting dangerously. "What do you mean?"

The retainer backed away, stopped only when his back hit the door. "What could the Toreador possibly hope to gain?"

"The anarchs, fool!" The Methuselah's contempt was slicing. "She was going to use the anarchs' actions in Elysium as a lever to gain control of the city."

The retainer shook his head. "But aren't the anarchs working for Lady Singhjul?"

Lady Ambrosia nodded once.

"And isn't Anneke also working for Lady Singhjul?"

Another nod.

"Then surely it would be possible for Don Cruez to make the connection—and use it to gain, not lose, power at the Conclave."

"But he won't."

The retainer looked thoughtful. "Anneke couldn't know that."

Lady Ambrosia erupted from her cushions, grabbing the retainer in steel claws. "Fool! Are you saying I've been outsmarted? Do you think that Lady Singhjul has beaten me?"

"No, milady, it's just . . . "

Blood flowed. The retainer's blood. He looked down at his chest, saw his own rib cage. Lady Ambrosia glared at him, claws dripping his blood. "I've taken enough from you!" Her hand dipped again, pulling out the retainer's heart. He saw her close her hand around it, then his vision went dark.

Forever.

Percival!

As Val's eyes flashed open, he saw a streak of silver to his left. *What in the* . . . He *moved*, rolling to one side, catching the slim hand before the knife could touch flesh. "Acquiel!" He pulled the knife out of her hand, throwing it to one side. "What are you doing?"

She stared at him, eyes fixed. "Mariana *told* me to do it."

"Mariana!" He looked around, willing the blood doll to be right.

There was nothing. He took the blonde into his arms, hugging her to him. "Mariana's not here, Acquiel. She's gone."

"She talked to me." Acquiel's voice was low, sincere. "She said you were wrong." The blonde looked up, caught Val's eye. "She said she wasn't dead."

"I wish it were so." Val sighed. "But she is dead." He looked down at the blood doll. "And someone is try-ing to use you." His eyes hardened. "Use you to get to me." He gave the girl a hug. "Just as they used you to start a fight between Mariana and Dieter Kleist. Remember?"

Acquiel nodded.

Val laid her down in the bed, let her curl up next to him. "We've got to make sure they can't hurt you." He looked down at the blonde. "Would you like to be one of us?"

Acquiel's heart skipped a beat. "A Kindred."

Val nodded.

"Mariana always said that she would give me the Embrace."

"I'll do it for her."

Acquiel nodded. "Yes." She looked at him. "I think that would be a good idea." She smiled. "Sire."

Val smiled, then bent over the blood doll. "All right, don't be afraid." His teeth punctured the skin of her neck.

Afraid! Acquiel smiled as she felt the blood rush out of her veins. *What do I have to be afraid of?*

Val drank deeply from the blonde's body. He knew he was breaking the Traditions—and he didn't care. *She has to be protected!* he thought. *And this is the best way to do it. Mariana would have done the same thing if she were still . . .* He stopped. *Mariana.* It was her voice that had awakened him! *Was the girl right?* His eyes roamed over the room, looking into corners, searching all the dark spots. *No. She's gone.* He continued to work on Acquiel. *The voice was in my imagination.* He felt the girl's heart slow. *This is all the Methuselah's doing.* It slowed again. Skipped a beat. Acquiel gasped. *It's the only thing that makes sense.*

He cut his own skin, felt blood rise, pushed it to Acquiel's mouth. *Live, Acquiel. Live forever.* He watched as the change began. *Live for Mariana.* He smiled grimly. *Live for me.*

"We have one week." Don Cruez's voice was a whisper of what it used to be. "One week until the Conclave."

Tessler looked at the big Justicar, saw the signs the fire had left. *He's healing too slowly,* he thought. *He should have stayed in torpor longer.*

"No time for that, Tessler." Don Cruez smiled. "We have to make sure that Anneke and her minions don't take over this city!"

"Why should we care?"

"Because it's my responsibility to stop a war from breaking out between the Camarilla and the Sabbat." The big Brujah shifted in his seat, hesitating just a trifle when some of the burned flesh moved. "And because I don't give up."

"Okay." Tessler nodded. "I can deal with that."

"Good." Don Cruez pulled some paper out of his desk. "Now, you say that Dieter Kleist set the firebomb in the gallery."

Tessler nodded. "I saw him go into the basement just before the explosion."

"But Val told you he couldn't have done it."

"Val said a lot of things to me." Tessler sprang from his chair, started pacing. "Crazy things."

"Are you sure they were crazy?"

Tessler whirled on the Justicar. "Are you saying I shouldn't believe my own eyes!"

Don Cruez spread his hands. "I'm not saying anything." His eyes hardened. "I'm asking if Val could be right."

Tessler rubbed at his forehead. "I honestly don't know." His eyes lifted, haunted by questions. "I hope not."

"All right." Don Cruez signaled to Topper. "We'll assume that Kleist, Anneke, and the anarchs were all working together." He nodded at Tessler. "I want you to find Kleist." He smiled. "And the truth."

Tessler headed for the door. "It'll be a pleasure."

I'll start with the anarchs, Val thought as he started for the waterfront. *Tessler mentioned a bar*. He checked the street signs. *The Goth*.

The interior of The Goth had changed little. The music was still loud—*God, how can they stand that!*—the interior still simple, unaffected.

Val strode up to one of the things that *had* changed. "I'm looking for someone named Christian."

The new bartender, a wry ferret of a man, shook his head and smiled, showing brown, stained teeth. "Ain't no Christians here."

Val shook his head. *No time for this.* The music blared in his ears, waking the Beast within. *Always so close to the surface.* Val fought it down. "One more time. I want to talk to whoever is in charge here."

The ferret grinned, hands dipping under the long, stained mahogany of the bar. "Oh! That's different!" He stood up, exposing a sawed-off twelve-gauge. "You want to speak to whoever's in charge." His face hardened. "Well, that'll be my friend, Shotgun!"

Val shook his head and *moved*, right hand jerking the weapon out of the human's grip, left hand lifting the man by his shirtfront, pulling him over the top of the bar. "You just can't do it the easy way, can you!"

Val threw the little man to one side, aiming him so that his head hit a beam right under the bar's CD player. "Gotta make it hard." Val turned the shotgun in his hands, aimed it toward the barkeep, who put his hands up in fear.

"Hey! No!"

Val fired. The load of double-O buck tore the player to pieces. Bits of plastic, transformed into shrapnel, pelted the wooden walls, creating a new art form. *Mariana might have approved.*

"One more time, who . . . "

"I'm in charge, man."

Val turned slowly, facing the five young Kindred who

filtered out of the side room. "About time you came out here."

The anarch leader gestured at the smashed CD. "We were kind of enjoying the music."

"You call that music?"

The anarch grinned. "'Sisters of Mercy' are very musical." His face hardened. "And we don't like anyone busting our stuff!"

Val nodded. "That's good." He looked down at the shotgun in his hand, broke it in half, tossed it aside. "Because if you tell me what I want to know, nothing else will get busted."

The anarch's smile turned nasty. "What makes you think we'll tell you anything?"

"Oh"—Val's smile was nastier still—"I don't *think* you'll talk." It disappeared. "I *know* it!"

Anneke was angry as she approached the brownstone. *Fool!* She climbed the stairs, eyes scanning the street around her. *Was that fire part of her plan?* She touched her forehead, felt the slowly growing eyelashes. *Or is there more to this than I've been told?* She touched the doorbell. *Knowing the Methuselah, that's going to be an understatement!* The door opened. "I have to talk to the mistress."

The dark figure nodded. "She's expecting you."

Anneke followed the figure (*man, ghoul, something else?*) down a dimly lit hallway. *Some nice paintings here,* she thought, turning her head to study one. *Have to take a better look when there's more time.*

The hooded figure opened a door, bowed the Justicar into the same room she'd met the Methuselah in earlier. "Please have a seat." He indicated a sideboard, stocked with glasses and a carafe of vitae. "The mistress will see you shortly."

Anneke entered the room, not turning as she heard the door close behind her. She looked around, eyes drawn once again to the Chinese cabinet that dominated one wall. She paced across the room, aware that she was being watched. *Damn Methuselahs! Can't do anything without sneaking around.*

A faint chuckle reverberated through her brain. *Damn!* Anneke resisted the urge to run. *What good would it do?* Instead, she walked to the cabinet, gazed into its depths.

Her reflection looked back at her, caught in the mirrored backing of the furniture. Anneke stared at herself for a moment, then, pursing her lips, took her glasses off.

Worse than I thought. She shook her head, studying the pale pink line above her eyes. *The hairline's wrong, too.* She put the glasses back on. *I need more vitae to finish healing.*

"And you shall have it, my dear."

Anneke caught herself. *Damn! She did it again!*

"Of course I did." The voice was clearly amused. "That's why I am who I am."

Anneke bit her lip, turned slowly. "Lady Singhjul."

The Methuselah, dressed in colorful silks, was sitting behind the Chinese desk. "Yes, my dear?" She chuckled. "Is there something I can do for you?"

The Justicar shook her head. "You've already done quite a bit." She pushed her glasses up, indicated the burned skin of her brow. "This is not a good look for me."

"No, my dear, it isn't." Lady Singhjul smiled, eyes glittering. "Nor will anger toward me improve it." The smile disappeared. "Not at all!"

Anneke recoiled internally. *Don't do anything stupid!*

"My apologies, Lady Singhjul." The figure behind the desk inclined her head gracefully. "Be assured that I do not, in any way, blame you for my injuries."

"I would hope not!"

"However,"—Anneke steeled herself—"I *did* receive them while moving your plan forward."

"So you did." The smile reappeared on Lady Singhjul's face. "A fine job!"

"I'm glad you see it that way." Anneke took a step forward. "You'll understand, then, why I ask for an extra . . . payment."

Lady Singhjul nodded. "Yes. In fact, I anticipated your request." She reached down, touched a button on the edge of her desk. "You'll find that which you require below."

That was too easy! Anneke braced herself for the kicker that was bound to follow. "And?"

"There is no 'and.'" The Methuselah smiled again. "I consider this no more than an obligation to a loyal servitor."

The door opened, the hooded figure standing ready. "Please, accept my hospitality." Lady Singhjul's smile grew wider. "And remember, you still have one more responsibility to me."

Anneke nodded. "The Conclave."

"Exactly."

The Justicar walked toward the door. "I'll be there." She stopped at the threshold, looked back at the Methuselah. "I consider that *my* obligation to you."

"Good." Lady Singhjul nodded as the door closed. "Very good."

*   *   *

Tessler's hunting went slowly. He had a lot on his mind. *Don't need all this!* He tried to push the thoughts away, bury them in the back of his mind. *I'm Brujah! We don't worry about anything!*

"Now, you know that isn't true!"

Tessler whirled, knife out. And froze. "Val?"

The other nodded. "Who else?"

The knife disappeared. "What are you doing here?"

"Hunting." Val glanced at the busy streets of the East Side. "Same as you."

"Want to join me?" Tessler grinned. "Be like old times."

Val nodded. "Sure."

The two Kindred strode down the street, eyes perpetually in motion, looking for just the right walk, just the right sway of hip and hair. "There's one." Val nodded to the right.

"Looks good." Tessler's brows rose. "Real good."

"How do you want to do this?"

Tessler chuckled. "Hey, you're the good-looking one." He made a motion. "Be my guest."

Val nodded and lengthened his stride, pacing the redhead he had noticed. It didn't take long for him to strike up a conversation, and, ten minutes later, he and the girl were turning into Gramercy Park. Tessler grinned. *He always did have the gift.*

Time passed. Tessler settled in at the entrance to the park, leaning against a gate, making sure that nobody happened along at an embarrassing moment.

Finally, Val came out, face slightly flushed with the flow of new blood. "She's still in there." He motioned. "Just waiting for you."

Tessler grinned. "Hey, I don't take sloppy seconds." He turned away from the gate, strode down the street. "Let's find another one."

"Whatever you say." He followed his friend, throwing an arm around his shoulder. "But you're wrong—this isn't like old times."

Tessler stopped, turned to his friend. "Why do you say that?"

"I'm not the same as I was."

Tessler looked at him. "I don't know. Everything seems to be healed."

"Not that." Val pointed to his chest. "Inside."

Tessler shrugged. "Can't help you with that."

"Yes, you can." Val's eyes went sharp, the animal close to the surface. "You can tell me what I need to know."

Tessler was adrift. "What's that?"

"I'm looking for Anneke." Val's voice went low. "She's the next link in the chain."

"What chain is that?"

Val's eyes burned. "The chain that leads to the Methuselah that murdered Mariana."

Tessler turned away. "You're crazy, man!"

"Maybe." Val grabbed him by the arm, pulled him back. "But I want that address."

Tessler tried to pull away, was shocked when he couldn't.

"Don't make me angry, Tessler." Val's voice was earnest, his eyes dead level. "Please."

"You think you can beat me?" Tessler's head went up. "Me!"

Val nodded. "Don't make me prove it."

Tessler moved, twisting his body away from Val's grip, pulling his knife. Fool! *Doesn't he know that I'm the best!*

"Not anymore." Tessler was stunned to find Val behind him, knife-edged hand smashing at his wrist.

The Brujah watched in amazement as his knife fell into the gritty snow. "Now, tell me what I want to know."

Tessler's world went red. He couldn't be beaten. Wouldn't be beaten. His Beast roared into his mind, struggling for freedom. Tessler loosed it. I'm the best!

Tessler's Beast lunged for Val, but Val was gone, replaced by his own Beast. Bigger, stronger, more powerful than anything Tessler had to offer. Tessler's Beast saw that it could not win, started to draw back.

And in that moment, the thing that had been Val sprang, teeth bared.

"Nooooooo!" Tessler's scream was that of a soul that had lost all hope.

"Is he dead?"

Topper bent forward, examining the broken body before him. "No, Don Cruez." He shook his head. "He's alive. In torpor, but alive."

Don Cruez turned away, headed for his desk. "Who could have done this?"

"I don't know." Topper shrugged. "The body was dumped outside, almost on our doorstep." He indicated the broken heap before him. "In just this condition."

Don Cruez sighed. "The city has gone crazy." He sat down. "Only an elder could have beaten Tessler so completely." He turned his seat, stared out at the lights of the metropolis across the river. "But why do it at all?" He sighed again, turning back to his retainer. "Take him to the sanctum, see that he gets all the vitae he needs to recover."

"As you say, sir." The big man nodded, leaning forward to lift the body. "I'll . . . wait!" His hand darted out, pulling a slip of paper from Tessler's pocket. "Look at this!"

"What is it?" Don Cruez was out of his chair, striding to his retainer's side.

"A note of some kind." Topper glanced at the paper. "Addressed to you."

"To me." Don Cruez took the offered document. "Interesting." He unfolded the sheet and read:

> Sire:
>
> I am sorry to deliver news in this way, but my time is very short. Mariana is dead, and I am determined to destroy those who murdered her. I must do this alone; you will understand why.
>
> I know that a Methuselah is involved, and she has Dominated several others, including Tessler.

Don Cruez looked at the body on the sofa. So . . . He went back to the note.

> Tessler doesn't know that he was the one who planted the bomb in the gallery. I do not blame him for that. But there are others who _must_ pay. The anarchs who were willing cat's-paws; Anneke, who betrays her trust in exchange for elder blood.

"Diablerie!" Don Cruez nodded. He had long suspected it.

> All must die, including the one who planned it all. Please do not try to stop me—because I will not be stopped. As your childe, I can do no less for the one I loved.
>
> Percival

"He's loosed his Beast."

"Sir?"

"Percival." Don Cruez indicated the slip of paper in his hands. "He's gone rogue."

Topper looked down at the broken body of Tessler. "Percival did this?"

The Justicar nodded. "And he'll do more." The big Brujah returned to his desk, set the note down. "Percival is more powerful than most think." He shook his head. "And now, he is also more ruthless."

Have to take care of the rest of the anarchs first. Val nodded. He had to cut off his enemies from their reinforcements. He snorted. *Reinforcements. More like cannon fodder.* Still, he knew this wasn't going to be easy. The city was full of anarchs, few of whom were allied to anyone, Camarilla, Sabbat, or Methuselah. *I don't have to worry about the loners.* Val reminded himself. *Just the groups. The ones who stick together.* He smiled without humor. *Making themselves a bigger target.*

His visit to The Goth had been quite rewarding. *Lots of stuff there, just the kinds of equalizers I'm going to need.* He glanced at the satchel he was carrying. *Just about everything I might need.* Val walked crosstown, heading for the string of biker bars and hangouts that studded the waterfront. *Lots of anarch havens there.* He nodded. *Good place to start.*

Reaching the crumbled remains of the Hudson River expressway, Val turned uptown, remembering what he had learned from Tessler. *Place called C. Lee's . . .* Val saw the sign, so caked with grime that it was almost unreadable. *That's it.* Val stopped, put the satchel down. *Now, what will I need?* He opened the bag, staring down at an assortment of weapons and equipment, running through the stats and technical briefings that the actor had shown him. *Don't want to kill them too fast*, he thought, pushing things aside. *Want to talk first. Get some information.* He pulled weapons out of the sack, depositing them around his person. *These should do.*

He turned toward the door of the bar, the Beast naked and growling behind his eyes.

"How many did you kill?" Grimsdyke's voice was mild, without a hint of accusation.

"I'm not sure." Val let his satchel drop to the floor, wiping a hand over his eyes, driving the Beast down. *Gets harder all the time.* "Eight. Maybe ten."

Grimsdyke shook his head. "Does it make you feel better?"

Val hesitated, tested his feelings—*there's nothing there.* "I don't know."

"I feel sorry for you."

"Feel sorry for yourself." Val turned on the actor, face contorted as the Beast slipped back into partial control. "If you and the other Inconnu elders did a little killing of your own . . . "

"We'd be no better than the Methuselahs!"

Val stopped, pushed the Beast back down. *Not as deep this time.* "Maybe." He let himself drop into a chair, fatigue washing over him. "How's Acquiel?"

"Hungry." The actor smiled. "And waiting for you." Grimsdyke pointed at Val. "You have things to teach her, you know."

"Teach?" Val looked puzzled. "What could I teach her?"

Grimsdyke shook his head. "You're her sire, it's your duty to teach her the Traditions."

"Traditions . . ." Val's eyes softened; the Beast growled, was driven farther back. "Yes, I remember." He rose from the chair, headed for the door to the inner sanctum. "She deserves that much."

"She'll need to hunt, too." Grimsdyke reminded the Brujah. "And soon."

Val nodded. "I'll remember." A smile creased his lips as the Beast whispered into his mind. "I have something very special in mind for that!"

Lady Ambrosia watched the moon set. Things were not going according to plan. The boy had loosed his Beast, right enough, but he was attacking the wrong targets. *He's supposed to go after the Toreador!* The Methuselah snarled. *Why is he killing anarchs?* This was all the retainer's fault. Her eyes burned as she glared around the room. *I should have killed him sooner, before things got out of hand!*

She pulled at the drapes, closing them over the window, mindful of the movement of the hated sun. *How do I get the boy to do what I want?* She lay back in her cushions. *I can't reach his mind. . . .* Lady Ambrosia rose from her soft seat. *Grimsdyke?* her head shook. *No.* Controlling him would be too difficult. She started toward the inner sanctum. *There must be someone else.* She stopped, *perhaps . . . Yes! That might work!* She stepped into the sanctum, a smile playing about her lips. *After all, sauce for the goose . . .*

The door to the sanctum closed just as the sun touched the horizon.

*   *   *

"Do I have to dress like this?"

Val looked at Acquiel, clad in Brujah leather and denim, amused by her tone of voice. "How do you want to dress?"

"I don't know." The little blonde gestured. "Something black and slinky." She rubbed her fingers through the material of the jacket Val had given her. "Leather's cool." She held up the tails, letting them run through her hands. "But not so much of it!"

Val smiled. "So do some shopping."

"Can I?"

"Sure. You don't belong to anybody now." He shrugged. "Except yourself."

"I understand that." Acquiel looked down at the ground. "But would you come with me?"

Val's eyes darkened. "I can't, little one." She stiffened at the name. "There are things . . . things I still have to do."

Acquiel nodded, looked up at Val, eyes bright. "I understand."

"I know you do." He pulled her in for a hug. "And I know you're being brave." He gave her a kiss. "Now, let's go hunting."

"Where do we go?" Her smile was bright. "The Blood Club?"

Val nodded. "Yes, I think we will go to the Club." The Beast climbed out of its box, hung ready just behind the eyes. "There's someone I want to see there."

Acquiel saw the change, took a step back. "Who's that?" Her tone was low, frightened.

"Someone you know." Val smiled. Acquiel took another step back. "And someone who knows you."

"Who's that?"

"The Kindred who arranged the gallery show. The one who made a scene at that show." He looked at Acquiel. "A scene that separated you and me from Mariana."

Acquiel nodded slowly. "Dieter Kleist."

"Dieter Kleist."

The techno was sitting in his usual place at the Club, deep in the corner of the Treasure Room, laptop active, its screen throwing a sickly bluish glow across his face. He didn't hear them come in; the music (*noise*) was too loud.

"Dieter?"

"Ah." The laptop snapped shut. "Acquiel." He smiled, "How nice to see you." He noticed a movement behind her. "And Val." His grin widened. "How . . . unexpected."

"Kleist."

"Can I do something for you?" The Toreador motioned to the empty seats that surrounded him.

"Yes, I think you can." Val's face was bleak. "Why don't you step outside with us?"

"Oh, I don't think that would be wise." Kleist's smile disappeared. "Not wise at all."

Val shrugged. "It really doesn't make a difference what you think."

"Oh," Kleist said as he made a motion, "I think you'll find it does."

"Dieter said there might be trouble." Andy appeared through what had seemed a solid wall. He smiled, knocked on the wall. "Hidden door." Three other Toreador appeared. "The Club is full of them."

Val pushed Acquiel behind him as the four Toreador

stepped toward him. "Acquiel, why don't you wait for me outside."

Kleist looked over the shoulders of the Toreador, smiling at the blonde. "Yes, Acquiel. Wait for me there." He ran his eyes over her body. "I have some other leather you might like better."

Acquiel patted Val on the back, then hurried to the staircase. *I hope he knows what he's doing.*

Val felt Acquiel leave. He relaxed, let his body lean to one side, shoulder against a huge cabinet. "Are you sure you won't go outside with me?"

Kleist nodded. "Positive."

Val turned to the others, his Beast clawing at him for release. "You know that he helped kill Mariana."

Andy shook his head. "The fire killed her. Don't try to blame it on anything else."

Val sighed, and *moved*, the Beast loose and in command. His right hand pulled a brass trophy from the cabinet he was leaning on, swung it in a short arc, and smashed it into the side of Andy's head. Val felt the skull smash, saw the Toreador's eyes roll up. *Should have left me alone!*

He whirled as the other Toreador charged him. *They're armed*, he realized, seeing the knives in their hands. His grin turned feral as he pulled a long knife out from under his own coat. *Fools!*

He swung the blade in a blindingly fast figure eight, then ducked as his first two attackers plowed by. One of them dropped to the floor, head hanging loosely from a thread of skin. *Two down.*

Val dug his toe under the body of Andy, kicked it up and into the fourth Toreador, knocking the Kindred back, off-balance. He fell into Kleist, throwing the two of them down in a tangle of bodies. Val whirled as they fell, throwing his knife into the heart of the just-returning second attacker. The blade punched through the man's chest, flinging him to the ground, pinning him there like some grotesque insect. Val giggled, then stomped on the hilt of the blade, embedding it deeper into the cement floor of the Club. *That'll hold him!*

He turned again, just in time to grab the arm of his final attacker, stopping the downsweep of his knife in mid-move. "You should have listened to me!" the Beast snarled in Val's voice, then, with the Kindred's arm still locked in his grasp, Val pivoted, tossing the Toreador over an outthrust hip. The man hit the ground hard, his grip on the knife loosening. The Beast smiled, pulled the blade free. He righted the weapon in his hand, then plunged it down, pushing the point through the Kindred's widened eye, blasting through the other's brain.

The knife tip snapped against the floor.

The Beast turned, eyes glowing, teeth clenched. "Kleist!" The techno had backed himself into a corner, was desperately searching for a way into the secret door Andy had used. "Too late, traitor!" The Beast leaped forward, grabbing Kleist by the ears. He rolled his shoulders, snapping the techno's neck.

It wasn't enough. Val's shoulders rippled, his arms moved again.

The head tore free.

The Beast laughed, tossed the head into the corner of the room. Val struggled to regain control, failed. From deep in his own mind, he watched the Beast reach into a pocket, pull out an oval object. *Not in the Club!* The Beast didn't listen. Instead, he pulled the pin out of the object and stuck it in Kleist's mouth. The

Beast looked down at his work, nodded, and headed for the stairs, still moving with celerity. *Gotta get out!*

Val regained control just as they reached the top of the stairs, turning just as the white phosphorus grenade went off. *Too late to worry about it now!* he thought, shielding his eyes from the sun-hot glare. *Better get Acquiel home.*

"What happened?" the blonde asked as he stepped out of the door.

"Kleist isn't going to show you those leathers." Val smiled, eyes still grim. "And we'd better get out of here."

"Why?"

Val nodded back to the Club; smoke was already coming out of the doorway. "That's one reason." He headed down the street, made sure Acquiel was following him. "Besides," he said, his grin almost back to normal, "we still have some shopping to do!"

"The Blood Club is gone?" Don Cruez leaned forward, not willing to believe his ears.

"Burned to the ground." Topper stood just inside the door, face grim. "At least four Kindred destroyed so far." He shook his head. "And the fire's still burning."

"Are there a lot of havens in that area?"

Topper shook his head. "Not too many. You know the rules about Elysium."

"Somebody always breaks those rules—and, remember, this is a Sabbat stronghold!" Don Cruez got out of his chair, started pacing. "Do we know who the Kindred were?"

Topper nodded. "Some of them." He pulled out a list. "Almost everyone in the Club that early at night was Toreador. We know Dieter Kleist was in there, along with a couple of Toreador actors and the guy who plays the butler."

"Andy." Don Cruez took the list from Topper. "This is Val's work."

Topper looked at the Justicar. "How can you tell?"

"Kleist was at the gallery when the girl was killed." Don Cruez threw the list onto his desk. "Acting very oddly, now that I think about it."

"Oddly in what way?"

"I think that he was used as a diversion." The big Brujah scratched at the tiny scars still marring his forehead. "Just before the bomb went off."

Topper nodded. "Would Val know that?"

Don Cruez indicated the list. "This certainly indicates that he did."

"What do we do?"

"For now"—Don Cruez sighed—"we do nothing." He stalked back to his desk. "I'm not going to call a Blood Hunt on my own childe!"

"Don't forget the Conclave."

"I don't forget anything." Don Cruez's eyes came up, burning into Topper. "But remember, a lot can happen between now and then."

Topper nodded. "Agreed."

The Justicar leaned back into his chair, looking out at the faint reflected glow the fire left in the night sky. "Get some more of our people here. We have to make sure we're not caught shorthanded if the Sabbat start a war."

"Already taken care of." Topper headed for the door. "And Tessler should be recovered in time."

"Somehow," Don Cruez said, staring at the city lights, "I think we're going to need him."

"I've got to go out there!" Anneke paced the floor, a panther in a cage. "Toreador are being killed!"

"You can't go." Lady Singhjul sat quietly behind her Chinese desk, watching the television report of the fire downtown. "If you do, my opponent will take the opportunity to destroy you."

"How?" Anneke snarled the word. "This Brujah would have no chance against me!"

The Methuselah shook her head. "I'm sure that's what Kleist said, not to mention Tessler and those anarchs." She sat back, eyes hooded. "This Percival is drawing power from somewhere."

"It doesn't matter!"

"It does!" Lady Singhjul's eyes, purest green, turned full on the Toreador Justicar, pinning her in place. "And you will do what I command!"

Anneke stood for a moment, glaring back, then lowered her eyes, bowing her head to the elder. "As you say."

"Better." Lady Singhjul touched a control, muting the television. "You will get your chance at revenge." There was a noise like dry rocks scraping against one another.

Anneke shuddered. Is *that a laugh*?

"Why not?" The Methuselah smiled. "Look how well this Brujah is doing our job for us." Lady Singhjul's smile widened. "Do you really think the Conclave will decide against us *now*? With Kindred blood spilled in the streets." The Methuselah turned her chair, gazing out on the dark fields of Central Park. "The game is all but over."

The unsettling laughter of the Methuselah filled the room.

* * *

Val shook his head disbelievingly as he exited the big Twenty-third Street Armory building. *Amazing what kine will keep around.* He shifted the duffel bag on his shoulder, trying to keep the weight inside balanced properly. *I hope all this stuff works the way the books say.* His smile turned bleak. *It had better.*

He headed for the subway station, plans running through his mind. Inside him, the Beast waited, not so deep now, not so controlled. *I can feel it watching,* Val realized. *It knows I will loose it when the time comes.* His smile was hard, vicious. *And it knows that time will be soon.*

Acquiel . . .

The blonde's eyes snapped around. She had learned to enjoy the thrills of the hunt, but voices behind her . . .

Don't be afraid, Acquiel.

"Mariana?" Acquiel squinted, eyes peering into the depths of the park around her. "Are you here?"

I'm dead, Acquiel.

The blonde backed away from the trees, moving to a little wall, using it to guard her back.

You don't have to do that.

Acquiel reached the wall, felt the touch of cold stone through the leather of her new vest. The blonde shivered as she faced the woods. "Let me see you."

I can't. Acquiel felt sadness run through her. *I told you, I'm dead.*

"Then how can you be speaking to me?" Acquiel's head scanned from side to side, her eyes constantly moving. "How do I know you're not some Methuselah trying to use me?"

You don't. Acquiel shook her head as warmth spread through her. *But please believe that I do love you.*

The blonde sighed, let the warmth enfold her. "What do you want me to do?"

Percival is going into danger. Acquiel nodded; she knew about that. *He's going to need your help. This is what you should do. . . .*

Val checked the numbers on the buildings as he approached Central Park. *Yes, this is the one Tessler located.* He looked it over. Old. *Probably built just after the Civil War.* Val nodded. Stone foundation. Brick walls. *This one won't burn.* Good.

He turned to the other side of the street, checking mailboxes. *I need one with a single occupant.* The first three were apartments. *Too many kine.* He kept going. A shop in this one, *no.* A law office . . .

There! Two stories, one name on the mailbox. *Perfect!* Val knocked on the door.

Two hours later, Val was pulling a mattress down to the basement of the place. There were no windows down here, a fact he noted with relief. *Would have hated to board them up!*

The building's single resident had turned out to be a woman. *Not bad-looking.* Val had originally planned to simply break her neck, but he had found her entertaining. Instead of killing her, he had drained her of most of her blood, then laid her carefully down in the upstairs bedroom. *She'll be safe enough there.* With the telephone and alarm system disconnected, she posed no possible danger to him. Val licked his lips. *Who knows, I might want to visit her again.*

He could feel the sun just touching the horizon. Val put the mattress down in the corner of the cellar, checked once again for chinks in the wall, unseen holes, then, with dawn just starting, he settled down to sleep.

Tonight, he thought as he dozed off. *Tonight we see how good the kine's equipment really is.*

The Beast didn't sleep; it lay there, waking dreams of blood and death running through its mind.

It smiled.

Night fell. Acquiel *felt* the sun fall beneath the horizon. *Cool!* She rose from her bed, padded naked to the dressing table she had persuaded Val to set up for her. *Got to look my best!* She looked at her reflection in the mirror. *Don't know how Bela and those guys got along without these!* Her hair was a mess. *Too much tossing and turning.* She picked up a coarse brush and set to work.

Acquiel.

"I'm on it!" She looked around the room. "Don't worry, I'll be there on time."

Percival's life depends on it.

Acquiel nodded, put the brush down. "All right, I get the picture." She pulled underwear on, then wriggled into the tight leather miniskirt she had picked to replace the long jacket Val had given her.

"Much better!" She smiled at the image in the mirror. "Really hot!"

Acquiel . . .

The blonde nodded again, then padded to Val's side

of the bed, digging through the stuff in the bag he had placed there. "Wow, look at all this!" She pulled out an Uzi, loaded, with two clips taped back to back. "Heavy-duty!"

You don't need that.

"Right." She rummaged some more, pushed aside a Colt Python, a Browning . . . *Jim Brady would hate all this stuff.* . . . Finally, Acquiel's hand fell on something long and flat.

That's it.

"Okay." The blonde tucked the item into her belt, smoothing things carefully over and around it. "That should hold it."

Uptown. Now!

Acquiel nodded, pulled on boots—"I love leather!"— and headed for the door. The nearest subway was two blocks away. Acquiel smiled as she hit the street. *I'll just hunt uptown,* she thought. *After I save Val's butt!*

She licked her lips in anticipation. *Should be fun!*

Val awoke the instant the sun was down. *Got to work fast!* He rolled off his makeshift bed, trotted up the stairs to the building's second floor. *Better check on the owner.* He opened the door to her bedroom, found her lying on the bed, legs folded tightly to her chest. *Whup!* He rolled her over, checked her eyes. Blank. *She's gone away.* He shook his head. *Too bad.* He moved in, pushed the hair away from her throat. *Might as well drain her.* His teeth sank in. *I might need the extra energy.*

He left the body where it lay, hurried downstairs, and opened his knapsack. *I'll lay the charges first,* he decided, pulling out several packages of puttylike gray material. He ghosted out of the door, headed across the street. *Both doors.*

Seconds later, he was back, pulling long, almost flat rectangles of metal from the bag. *Where're the tripods?* He fished around some more, found the thin aluminum poles. *Okay,* he thought as he went out the door again and trotted across the street, *where do I put these for maximum coverage?* He saw a spot in front, right at the bottom of the stairs. He set up the first tripod there, mounted the rectangle, carefully obeying the THIS SIDE IN instruction on the base; then he took the second one to the back, placing it at the head of the alley. *They won't be able to run this way.* He checked his handiwork, nodded, and made one more trip back to the apartment. *Almost ready!*

The subway was crowded. *Must be a game tonight,* Acquiel thought. A young, good-looking boy brushed by her, his hand coming up to cop a feel. Her hand was there first, deflecting his. *Mustn't touch the merchandise!* She smiled as he stumbled by. Giggled as he tripped over the knees of a huge seated Hispanic. *Cute, but clumsy.* She watched as he found a spot, hanging from one of the straps, eyes on her. *I used to hang from straps, too,* she thought, eyes darkening. *But not anymore.* She looked down. *No.*

The train stopped at Forty-second Street, spilling the bulk of the crowd out. *Running to Connecticut,* Acquiel realized. Her boy was still there, still staring at her. She smiled again, looking around. *There aren't a lot of people left.* She sauntered toward him. *And I do have to feed. . . .* She sat in front of him, letting the skirt ride high on her thighs. *Might as well give him a thrill.*

The train thundered uptown.

Val made his last stop in the apartment. He pulled a stubby-looking rifle out of the bag, then filled his pockets with its short, thick ammo. *Better make sure I have the right one up the tube.* He checked the color coding. *Yes, unless someone lied to me, that's right.* He put his second planned round in his right pocket, the remainder in his left. *Okay, that's the big stuff.* The Beast behind his eyes laughed as he pulled a Browning 9mm from the bag, checked its load, and stuck it in his belt. *So much hardware!* It chuckled again. *Don't you trust yourself?* Val forced it down, pushing it back as far as it would go. *Not yet!* The Beast snarled at him, but it went.

Val took a moment to gather himself—*this is it*—then plunged out the door, into the street. The door of the brownstone stared at him as he lifted the stubby barrel of the M–79. *Let's see if Anneke is really as good as she thinks she is.* He pulled the trigger.

The grenade launcher *whuffed*, sending the round spinning toward its target. Val, his discipline active, saw the thick bullet shape inch toward the target, rotating slowly, the safety fuse unraveling as it went. *I hope there's enough room for it to arm.* The round impacted.

Boom! The street shook, Val was rocked back on his heels—and the door to the brownstone disappeared in a shower of splinters and dust. *Guess there was!* Val stared at the opening for a moment, then pulled the second round out of his pocket, inserting it into the still-cool barrel of the M–79. *Wait for them to start moving!*

He saw movement down the hall. Three, no, four huge figures appeared, rushing toward the entrance, ready for anything. *Except me.* Val raised the gun.

Whuff! The second round fired, but instead of sending a single projectile toward the door, this one sent a spray of metal balls. *Antipersonnel.* Val watched as they spread out. *Supposed to be quite effective.* The spray of metal met flesh at the doorway, and Val's view disappeared in a cloud of blood. *Seems to work.* Val stepped forward, inserting a third round.

The barrel was warmer now.

Whuff! This was another solid shot, rotating as it passed through the doorway, hitting the far wall of the hall. There was no explosion, but a bright flare of light filled the hall as white phosphorus sprayed everywhere, turning the hall into a blazing inferno in seconds. *That should flush something out!* Val fired a second white phosphorus round into the side window, watched it flare into a second blaze. *Now for the basement.* He pulled a tiny radio transmitter out of his pocket, ran the antenna out, and pressed the red button.

BAROOOOM! The shock nearly knocked Val off his feet. *May have used a bit too much.* He steadied himself, watched as the house shuddered in place, cracks appearing in the walls, around the windows. *That should do it.* He saw movement at the side of the house. *Coming up the alley.* He pulled a second radio transmitter from his pocket, flicked the switch to 2, pushed the red button. *Wumph!* The claymore in the alley fired, throwing two thousand fléchettes of metal into whatever was moving there.

Movement stopped.

"Anneke?" Val looked at the building, saw the walls settling, cracking the cellar supports. *It's going to collapse.* "Time to come out!"

Only the growing strength of his disciplines saved him.

"Aargh!" A burned and battered figure launched itself at him from the second floor window. Val didn't have time to pull his pistol, didn't have time to do anything but duck out of the way. Even so, he found himself reeling, his jacket ripped open, his chest oozing blood.

"Fool!" Anneke rolled to her feet, ready for another attack. "Don't you know who you're dealing with?"

The Beast peered out of Val's eyes; it showed his teeth. "You're the one who killed Mariana."

"Wrong." Anneke shook her head. Val absently noted that her hair was gone, burned off by the white phosphorus. "I'm the one who's *going* to kill *you*!" She leaped forward, claws arcing for his eyes.

The movement was achingly slow. *Something's wrong with her. . . .* Val ducked out of the way. *Something's interfering. . . .*

The Beast took over, its power suddenly augmented a thousandfold from the same outside source. *I'm being used!* Val submerged, held down by the newfound power of the Beast. He saw the fight in bursts. . . .

Anneke's claws were jammed into the street, her left leg was broken, the bone sticking out at an odd angle—the Beast was standing over her, eyes hard, hands moving. The Justicar tried to roll away, tried to cut at the hands reaching for her, but she was too slow. *I don't believe it!* She could do nothing but watch as the Beast reached down, caught her by the elbow, snapped the joint in hellishly strong hands.

For the first time in a century, Anneke knew real fear. *All that power! He can beat me!* She backed away from the shocking figure that stalked her, got her back against the brownstone's staircase. *Got to get away!* She tried to stand up, but her leg was broken too badly to hold her weight. Desperate, she called her own Beast out, but it was slow to emerge, lulled into overconfidence by too many years of victories.

Anneke screamed as the ancient Beast using Val's body approached. Screamed again as it snapped her left elbow, stomped on her knee, rendered her as helpless as a moth tacked to a board. She shrieked one last time as she saw the smile on the Beast's face, saw its teeth reach out to her neck. She was still screaming when the blackness claimed her.

Acquiel got off the subway at Seventy-ninth Street, carefully straightening her miniskirt. She smiled at the departing subway. *He'll have a pleasant memory in the morning,* she thought, catching a glimpse of the cute boy. Her smile widened. *And a sore hand!* She shook her head. *They always want to touch!* She skipped up the stairs, getting out in sight of the Metropolitan Museum of Art. *Gotta go there someday.* Not now, though. She got her bearings, checked to make sure she still had the weapon—*yup, still there*—and headed for the address Mariana had given her.

Even though she's dead.

Acquiel saw a glow in the sky. *Fire.* She shrugged, hurried her steps. *Dead or not, I think she was right.* She turned the corner, stopped short when she saw the ruins of the brownstone. *Yes, this is the place!* She saw blurry movement in the center of the street. *That must be Val.* A figure was hurled out of the blur, falling short of the brownstone, struggling to get up. *And I think that's*

Anneke. Acquiel started forward. *Maybe Val doesn't need my help after all.*

Val watched the fight, isolated in his own mind. The power of the Beast amazed him—and its sudden independence. *What's happening? Where is all the power coming from?* It scared him. *I've got to get control back.* He watched as the Beast broke Anneke's arm, tossed her body away like a bit of Kleenex. *If I don't, it'll destroy everything!*

The Beast laughed.

Lady Ambrosia's laughter filled the sanctum as she withdrew her essence from the battle. "Victory!" She allowed herself to roll back onto her cushions. "As if a mere Justicar could stand against me!" She turned to her new retainer, smiling broadly. "That should teach that meddling Singhjul a lesson!"

"Milady?"

"Silence."

No use letting my good mood spoil him. "I'll tell you when I want you to speak." The Methuselah relaxed into the cushions. "Prepare our cat's-paws for the Conclave." She looked out over the city, savoring the cold fire of the stars. "Everything will run smoothly, now."

"As you say, milady." The retainer bowed, backed out of the room. "I will begin work immediately."

Lady Ambrosia watched him leave. *I should have made the change months ago,* she thought. *It would have saved me a great deal of grief.* She shrugged, turning her thoughts inward. *Too late to worry about it now.* She smiled. *I have better things to think about.*

The Beast stood up from the still body of Anneke. It looked around for other enemies to kill. Inside, Val heard the sirens of the kine getting closer. *I have to leave!* He struggled to regain control, failed. *Grimsdyke was right! I'm being used!* He continued to fight, using all his will, all his intelligence.

It wasn't enough.

There was a movement in the house. The Beast turned to confront whatever still lived there, watching as an enormous mountain of a creature lumbered down the stairs, coming toward it. The Beast grinned, moved forward, claws out and ready. It attacked, raking at the hulk, grappling for a hold on one of the enormous arms.

Nothing happened. *It's a flesh golem!* Val's struggles renewed. *Grimsdyke told me about them. Very powerful servants . . .* A thought struck him. *For Methuselahs! A Methuselah lived in that house!*

The Beast slipped off the golem's arm, ducked to one side, renewed the attack. *No!* Val screamed inside. *You can't hurt it that way!* The Beast didn't respond. Instead it attacked again, slashing at neck, groin, eyes. Cutting deep into gray flesh.

The golem ignored the injuries.

How do I hurt it? Val thought, racking his memory. *Silver! I need a weapon made of silver!* The creature kept moving forward, stretching thick fingers toward Val's neck.

Val fought harder for control as the Beast rushed in,

ripped at the golem's chest—and was caught. The Beast screamed as the golem lifted it off its feet; it clawed at the golem's eyes, trying desperately to twist free.

The Beast went into frenzy, striking in every direction, biting at the mountain of flesh before it. The Beast tried everything, concentrating all its remaining energy in the attacks.

Val surfaced, gained control. The Beast growled, scarcely submerged, but lent its strength to Val's attempt to regain freedom. Again Val kicked out, but this time he put every iota of strength he had into one, carefully placed blow right to the face.

The golem took it, eyes unchanged, and began to exert force on Val's trapped leg. Val felt the muscles compress, heard the bones grate on one another. *I don't have much time left. He'll crush me if I don't do something. But what?*

"Val!"

"Acquiel?" He looked around, shocked. The blonde was a few feet away, dancing away from the two combatants, a knife in her hand. "Val, you need this!" She tossed the blade toward him.

Mariana's knife! Val caught the weapon, saw the silver ripple in the light. *The one she chased with silver!* He laughed. *I have a chance!* He swept the knife down, running the blade through the golem's face. Ichor oozed out; the golem screamed, a hellish noise like nothing Val had heard before, and released Val, both hands grasping at its wound.

"Get back!" Val yelled at Acquiel, glancing over to make sure she was out of the way. "I'm going to try something!" He raced forward, turning his body at the last minute to launch into a flying side kick. His feet thundered against the golem's injured face, staggering the monster, sending it reeling backward. Its legs hit the brownstone's staircase, tripping it. It fell, ponderously, onto the stairs.

Oh please, let it be there! Val reached into his pocket. *It is!* He pulled the little radio out, clicked the switch to the 1 position, and waited. The golem never stopped moving; grabbing at the staircase for leverage, it pulled itself upright, turning toward its antagonist. *That's right, just stand there.* Val pushed the button. *Wumph!* Two thousand metal fléchettes thundered out of the claymore, each of them hitting the golem in the chest. The monster dissolved, flesh disintegrating as the pellets thundered through it. Its head fell free, bounced twice on the stairs, and came to rest looking angrily at Anneke.

Val slumped. *No use looking for the Methuselah. She's long gone by now.* Val heard the sirens. *Getting pretty close.* He dropped the radio transmitter, walked over to Acquiel. "I think it's time to go home."

They reached the subway just as the first police car rolled by. Acquiel watched it pass. "What about Anneke?"

Val sighed. "If we're lucky, they'll take her to the hospital."

"And if we're not?"

"The morgue." He started down the stairs. "Somebody will pick her up if she gets there, take her to a safe haven." He shrugged. "I'm too tired to worry about it tonight." He looked at Acquiel. "And by the way, how did you know I'd need that knife?"

"Mariana told me."

Val stared at her. "Mariana is dead."

Acquiel shrugged. "Aren't we all?"

He thought about that. "I guess we are."

A train rolled into the station.

The New York Coliseum is a huge box of a building. Opened in the mid-fifties, it was planned as the cultural center of the city, big enough to house conventions, sporting events, corporate meetings, anything that might be required. Its location, straddling Columbus Circle, was ideal, putting it at the terminus of four subways and two major roads.

For ten years, it lived up to every promise. But gradually, problems arose. Air-conditioning that didn't work. Plumbing that backed up. Electrical systems that failed at embarrassing times. The problems were ignored by city officials intimately involved with the construction of the Coliseum. They blocked investigations, applied patches, kept the building open.

More years passed. Failures became more common, but were ignored as commonplace. Then the accidents started: seats collapsed, walls cracked, small fires started, seemingly without cause. The newspapers picked up the story, investigations were called for, and finally started.

Within weeks, the Coliseum was closed. Irregularities were found in its contracting, including the use of substandard concrete and steel in its foundation. The building was deemed unsafe, and plans were made to demolish it.

But demolition cost money, and in a city near bankruptcy, money was scarce. The building stayed in place, entrances blocked, subway access sealed, electricity off. A huge reminder of the power of corruption.

And, for the Kindred, the perfect site for a Conclave.

"Is everything ready?" Don Cruez glanced around the big room, noting the turnout.

"Ready." Topper nodded toward the bleachers. "Lots of Toreador out there."

"Yes." Don Cruez sighed. "I expected that."

Tessler came forward. "Anneke's not here."

Don Cruez's brows lifted. "Not here?"

"Nobody seems to know where she is." Tessler gestured toward the seats placed near the dais. "Masika seems to be acting in her place."

The Brujah Justicar nodded. "All right, let's get this under way." He turned to Topper. "Are the entrances guarded?"

"Doubly." The huge figure nodded toward the hall. "With the extra people we called in, and selected members from other sects."

"Good." Don Cruez gestured to Tessler. "Turn the lights on and let's get this over with." He strode out onto the stage, reaching the dais just as the lights came up.

"Members of the Camarilla!" Don Cruez's trained voice boomed through the huge arena, amplified by the excellent sound system borrowed from the ruins of the Club. "I call this Conclave to order!"

He waited for the murmur to die down, then gestured toward the front row. "In accordance with custom, I ask if anyone has a matter they wish to bring forward."

"I do!" Masika rose from the first row. "In the name of the Toreador, I demand justice!"

Don Cruez nodded. "And do you have two supporters?"

"More." Masika gestured to the audience, where a score or more of other Kindred sat.

Another nod from the Brujah. "So be it." He stepped to one side, offered the podium to the Archon. "Speak."

Masika strode to the dais. "Before I state my charges"—he turned to Don Cruez, eyes hard—"which involve the Brujah Justicar quite directly"—he looked into the audience—"I would like to request a different chairman."

Don Cruez shrugged. "Is there one in attendance who is willing to accept the responsibility?"

"I'll do it." All eyes turned to the back of the room where a shadowy figure rose. "If there are no objections."

"Who are you, sir?" Don Cruez squinted against the stage lights.

The figure stepped forward, revealed himself as Nosferatu. "I am Ebenezer Roush."

Masika looked troubled. "I had hoped that Anneke . . ."

Don Cruez smiled slightly. "Come now, my friend, surely we would *all* prefer a neutral chairman."

The Toreador's eyes searched the auditorium, finally turning to the approaching Nosferatu. "So be it."

Roush mounted the stage, taking his place at the dais. "So, Toreador, you have something to say?"

Masika stepped forward, leaned over the microphone, and began his tale.

"How's the leg?" Grimsdyke watched as Val limped into the room.

"Almost healed." Val grinned. "You know, I didn't even know it was broken until I got on the train."

"That's the way of the Beast." Grimsdyke took a sip from his cup. "You feel no fear or pain while in its grasp." He raised a lecturer's finger. "It is only afterward that wounds make themselves known."

Val nodded. "Even bad ones."

"Especially bad ones."

The two sat back in comfortable silence. Val knew he'd have to hunt soon—*and figure out my next move; I don't like being used.* For now, though . . .

The door to Grimsdyke's rooms burst open. "They've started!" Acquiel's eyes were huge, fearful.

"Started what?"

"The Conclave." Acquiel rushed to Val, sat down at his feet. "They're trying to say that you and Don Cruez want to destroy the Toreador and take over the city."

The Beast growled, rising back near the surface. "That's absurd." Val fought it down.

"They've got witnesses." Acquiel hugged Val's legs. "Someone named Tusk." She shuddered. "Who's really ugly." She looked up at Val. "Will I get like that?"

Val shook his head. "No. He's Nosferatu."

"Good." Her smile was quicksilver. "He says that he saw you killing a bunch of anarchs—for no reason."

"I had my reasons."

"And another Toreador." Acquiel wrinkled her brow in concentration. "Kallista, I think her name was . . ."

"Sculptress." Grimsdyke put in. "Good one."

"She said you tried to kill everyone in the Blood Club."

The Beast's snarl was louder. Almost audible. "Who's behind all this?"

"Someone named Masika."

"Anneke's Archon." Grimsdyke again.

"Figures." Val glowered. "Where is all this happening?"

"The old Coliseum." She gestured. "A few blocks that way."

"An appropriate choice." Grimsdyke laughed dryly.

"They're liars!" The Beast was close now, almost ready to grab control. "They won't talk like that when I get through with them!"

"No, I don't think that would be a good idea." The actor stood up, walked to the door. "You wait here for now. I'll go see what's going on."

Val snarled.

"I mean it." Grimsdyke turned to Val and the blonde. "Stay here until I get back." He smiled at the barely controlled Brujah. "Then, if it's as the girl says . . ." His smile hardened. "Perhaps it will be time for me to take sides."

The door closed behind him.

Lady Ambrosia chortled as the Conclave moved along. *It's just as I had planned!* She looked out over the crowd, using the eyes of a totally dominated thrall. *Better!* She laughed again. *I don't even have to worry about Anneke!* She watched as another witness, Hasina Kesi, told her story. *Caitiff bitch!* Lady Ambrosia's smile tightened. *I wonder who's pulling your strings!*

The Methuselah listened through her borrowed ears. *You do tell a good story, though.* Her mood brightened as the Nosferatu called Colin Flynn to the dais. *This should finish it!* She reached out with her flesh hand, pulled a thrall to her. *The city is mine!* She plunged her teeth in, closed her eyes to the constant thrill of new blood. *Finally!*

" . . . And then"—Flynn's face tightened as he looked into the audience—"I watched as this Brujah"—Flynn glared at Don Cruez—"the childe of the Justicar"—another glare—"jammed the grenade into Kleist's mouth."

"And then?" Roush's tone was neutral. He'd seen clan feuds before.

Flynn shrugged. "I ran." He looked back into his audience. "Got out before the thing went off, before the Club burned down."

"What're they trying to do?" Tessler paced backstage, growing more agitated by the minute.

"I believe they plan to put the city under Kindred control—expel the Sabbat." His face grew grim. "And the Brujah as well."

"That'd cause a war!"

Topper's tone was low, controlled, as he nodded. "Most certainly."

"What can we do about it?" Tessler pulled out a knife, absently stropping it on the leather of his pant leg.

"Nothing." Topper glared at the weapon until Tessler put it away. "The Justicar has to answer the charges by himself."

"Not if we move now!" A new figure joined the two Brujah. "We have our own people on all the doors." Dre grinned coldly. "This place has always been a death trap. If there was a fire . . ."

Topper shook his head. "That is *not* why Don Cruez sent for you and your people. He would never approve."

Dre shrugged. "Hey, what if we didn't ask him?"

"Are you prepared to deal with his anger?" Topper pierced the other Kindred with a cold stare. "Or mine?"

Dre backed away, a snarl on his face. "I was only trying to help!"

"We don't need that kind of help." Topper turned away. "Not now."

On the dais, a Gangrel, Bear Paw, had appeared. He was saying something about rats. Topper watched. *It would, however, be nice to have some kind of help.*

Do they really blame me for all this? Don Cruez stood on the dais, looking over the audience as witness after witness described the atrocities committed by Val and the anarchs. *Or is this all being played out by some ambitious Archon*—his gaze fell on Masika—*and his Justicar.* Don Cruez's eyes searched the darkness at the back of the auditorium. *Where is Anneke? I'd have thought she'd be here to ensure her triumph.* His gaze darkened. *Or is it the triumph of a Methuselah controlling her.*

He looked backstage, noted the heads conferring there. *Dre will be advocating an immediate attack.* Don Cruez's lips creased in a dry smile. *On the Conclave.*

He shook his head. *He may not have been our best choice as a backup.* He watched the gestures, saw the moment when Topper dealt with the would-be conqueror. *I'm glad the big guy's on my side.*

He turned to the Conclave. *It's almost over.* He glanced at Roush, the Nosferatu.

That one's already made up his mind. Don Cruez pulled down on his jacket, made sure it was straight. *I wonder what he's going to decide?* He looked at his own people, still talking backstage. *And I wonder what I'm going to do about it.*

"Well,"—Grimsdyke came into the haven, face carefully neutral—"it's over."

"What did they decide?" Acquiel was almost ready to jump up and down, her face a mass of conflicting emotions.

"There was a Nosferatu acting as chairman." Grimsdyke moved to the sideboard, lifted the top off a carafe. "Good man." He poured some red liquid into a glass. "Fair."

"What did he say!"

"He judged that Don Cruez had been remiss in his duties." Grimsdyke looked at Val, sitting silently in the corner of the room. "He said the actions of Don Cruez's childe proved that."

Val shivered, the Beast clawing at his control.

"What else did he say?" Acquiel ran back to Val, anxious to give him what comfort she could.

"He said . . ." Grimsdyke took a sip of his drink. "He said that the city should have a ruler." Another sip. "A prince from the Camarilla."

"Who?"

Grimsdyke sighed, sank into his own chair. "That's the rub. As there are so many of them in the city, he suggested a Toreador prince."

Val's shudders became more pronounced. The Beast was gaining control.

"He said Anneke could choose one." Grimsdyke looked at Val. "But nobody knows where Anneke is."

Val fought for control, pushed at his inner self, tried to cage it.

"So he proposed that Anneke's Archon become prince." His mouth hardened. "Masika."

Got to hold on!

"Don Cruez objected to that, said Masika was unworthy of the position. Tessler and Topper agreed." Grimsdyke smiled. "Loudly!"

Push it down!

"Finally"—Grimsdyke shifted in his seat—"Roush, the Nosferatu, told Don Cruez that there was only one fair way to resolve the issue." The actor looked at Val. "Trial by Ordeal."

Chain it!

"What kind of Ordeal?" Acquiel sensed there was something wrong here, something Grimsdyke was avoiding.

The actor took another sip of his drink, then, looking at the level in the glass, drank the remainder in one gulp. "Don Cruez is to hunt down and destroy his insane childe." He looked at Val. "Percival."

"Me?" *Keep it under control*! Val shook his head. "My sire has to try to kill me?"

Grimsdyke nodded.

"No." The Beast leaped to the surface. "I won't let him kill me." Clawing, fighting for control. "I won't let anybody kill me.

"An Ordeal!" Lady Ambrosia's claws bit deeply into the thrall next to her, evoking a shrill cry of pain. "Have they all gone mad?"

"Perhaps not, milady." The retainer's look was one of deep thought. "After all, this Percival has proved himself to be quite formidable."

The Methuselah nodded her head in sudden agreement. "And he *is* Don Cruez's favorite childe. . . . " She leaned back across her cushions, ignoring the look of fear in the eyes of the thrall next to her. "This *might* work out for the best." Another nod of the head, more decisive now. "But we have a way to *ensure* our victory."

*   *   *

"Where is he?" Don Cruez's voice was flat, controlled.

"I don't know." Tessler snarled. "If I did, he'd already be dead!"

"One of you would be." Don Cruez looked across his desk at Tessler, eyes candid. Dre, sitting to one side, snickered.

"Hey!" Tessler leaped to his feet, started to pace. "He took me by surprise! Confused me with all that Methuselah crap . . . !"

"Enough." The Justicar raised a placating hand. "I don't need you to prove that you're better then he is." He looked the angry Kindred in the eye. "I just need you to find him."

Tessler nodded. "I can do that."

"Let the others help you." His gesture included Dre, Topper, and the rest of the assembled Brujah. "Find him as quickly as you can." His face hardened. "That damned Nosferatu only gave us two nights."

"I'll find him."

Don Cruez smiled at Tessler, a genuine smile, full of trust and approval. "I know you will." He signaled to Topper, who opened the door. "And when you do, you'll tell me where he is." The smile disappeared, replaced by a steel-hard gaze. "Nothing else."

Tessler hesitated, then nodded once. "Nothing else."

Percival . . .

Val awakened instantly from his uneasy sleep, rolling off the bed, coming to his feet ready to fight. "Who's that?"

It is I, Mariana.

"It can't be you." Val's eyes scanned the room. The

Beast, never far away now, rose in the back of his mind, searching for something to fight, something to kill. "You're dead."

We're all dead.

The Beast caught a hint of motion in the corner of the room, growled somewhere deep inside, and propelled Val's body forward, hurling it at a tiny spark of life.

It's only a spider.

Val looked at the dead arachnid in his hand, pushed the Beast back down, forced it to relinquish control. "Where are you?"

Somewhere else.

"What do you want?"

I want you to think.

"You can't be real." Val shook his head, sat down on the edge of the bed. "You must be another trick." His eyes came up, the Beast inside again. "The Methuselah!"

I'm not the Methuselah.

The Beast snarled at the empty room, searching for something, anything to kill.

"I found him!" Tessler almost ran into Don Cruez's office. "He's uptown. Near Lincoln Center."

"Interesting." Don Cruez nodded slowly. "That's Toreador territory."

"He's staying with that actor." Tessler's mouth curled in distaste. "Grimsdyke."

"So . . ." The big Justicar stood up, pacing the room as he thought. "Peter has given him sanctuary . . ."

"There's a girl there, too." Tessler's face turned sour. "A childe *he* sired."

"Percival broke the Traditions?" Don Cruez paused in his pacing, his mind racing. "I find that hard to believe!"

"It's true." Tessler sank into the chair in front of the desk. "She's living there with him."

"So." Don Cruez touched the signal on his desk. Almost immediately, the door opened and several Kindred walked in, ushered by Topper. "You all heard?"

Dre nodded. "Yeah. What are we going to do?"

"I'm going to fulfill the letter of the Ordeal I agreed to." Don Cruez sank into the seat behind his chair. "But the rest of you are going to see to its spirit."

"What do ya mean?" Planning was not Dre's strong suit.

"Idiot!" Tessler sneered at the other. "The Justicar wants us to clean up the undesirables in the city."

"Just so." Don Cruez nodded at the others. "If the Conclave wants things to be safer, we will make them safer."

"The anarchs!" Dre's smile showed *very* sharp, very bright teeth.

"I want them utterly destroyed."

"Val's already started that job." Tessler leaned out of his chair, toward the others. "The anarchs are scattered."

"Will that create a problem for you?" Don Cruez gestured to the assembled Brujah. "The best hunters in the city?"

"We'll find them!" Dre was enthusiastic now that he knew what he was supposed to do.

"We certainly will." Tessler smiled. "I've been waiting a long time for this!"

Don Cruez nodded. "Yes." He turned away. "Now I have my own job to do." The Justicar shook his head sadly. "My Ordeal." He gestured to the others. "I'll confront Percival tomorrow." His mouth quirked. "When I'm done, I want to walk home through a city scoured of anarchs."

"It will be!"

Don Cruez rose, walked to Tessler, who sat quiet in his chair. "Will *you* do as I ask, Tessler?"

The Brujah nodded. "Yes." He looked up at the Justicar. "I'll do whatever you say."

"Good." Don Cruez leaned against his desk as Topper reappeared with a tray full of glasses. "A toast, then." They each took a glass, held it up in response to Don Cruez's motion.

"To the Brujah!" Don Cruez smiled. "And *our* city!"

Don Cruez glanced up at the sky. *It'll be spring soon*, he thought. *The city will be full of life.* He smiled gently. *And unlife.* He looked around at Lincoln Center. *I remember when this was new.* He smiled. *Started as pork for some city councilman, turned into something better.* His eyes wandered over the side of the library, noting the broken windows, barely covered with plywood sheets. *Now the bastards in the street seem determined to destroy it.* The big Justicar sighed. *Somebody is always trying to ruin the good things.*

His eyes moved to the sky again. *Getting late.* Don Cruez shook his head. *Maybe I should have confronted him when he left to go hunting.* He sighed again. *No, too many humans around. The Masquerade might have been jeopardized. And I can't allow that.*

There was movement to his right. *Percival?* Don Cruez shifted position slightly, making sure the fountain was behind him. *Don't want anyone sneaking up on me.* More movement. *I'm glad I got the others out of the way.* Closer.

Wouldn't do to have anyone else help me in this. Almost in sight. *It's supposed to be a personal trial.*

A human appeared out of the shadows, walking slowly through the square. *Damn!* Don Cruez watched as the man passed his position. *Drunk.* The footsteps wavered, the man staggered. *Keep going.* He staggered some more, turning his head, looking for a place to rest. *Not here!*

The man stumbled over to the fountain, tried to sit on its rim, slipped, fell down beside it, rolled over, and started snoring. *No danger of him revealing any secrets!*

Another sound. Close. Don Cruez whirled, stepping to one side to clear the edge of the fountain. His eyes searched the square, peering into shadows. *There!* The Justicar moved swiftly. *He should come out.* . . . Noiselessly, Don Cruez ran to the mouth of the little alley formed by the side of the Vivian Beaumont and the library. *Right here!*

"Hello, Percival." Don Cruez let his body fall into a relaxed position, arms hanging to the side, legs slightly bent, weight on the balls of the feet. "I've been waiting for you."

An animal stared back at him.

He's loosed the Beast! Don Cruez realized, just as the thing that had been Val growled and attacked.

Percival . . .

"What do we do now?" Acquiel watched as Percival launched himself at the Justicar.

"We let them fight." Grimsdyke was grim. "And while they do . . ." He led the blonde to one side, to the door of the library building. "Follow me."

Grimsdyke unlocked the door with a key he produced

from an inside pocket. "Got it from the first director. When was that?" He walked through, motioning Acquiel to follow. "Fifteen, twenty years ago."

"Where are we going?"

"Up." He moved through the lobby, past the check-out desks, up a short flight of stairs. "The elevators are off, we'll have to climb."

"Where?"

"I told you." They reached a door marked PRIVATE Grimsdyke used another key to open it. "Up."

The stairway was narrow. "Private staircase," the actor said as he began climbing. "Just for the staff." He smiled down at Acquiel. "And people who don't like crowds."

Acquiel shook her head and followed. Percival had told her to trust the elder, and Percival was her sire. I *hope he wins*. Two flights passed. Three. Four.

"Here, I think." Grimsdyke gingerly pushed at the door's release, whispering. "Try to be quiet." The door opened silently, swinging into a dark hall. Grimsdyke held a finger to his lips and headed to the right.

Acquiel followed. *Where are we going*? She was worried about Val, afraid of what would happen if her sire was killed. *According to those stupid Traditions, I'm illegal!* She smiled. *Now, if they said I was immoral* . . . She stifled a giggle. *That I could accept!* The smile faded. *They could destroy me!* Grimsdyke had disappeared from sight. *Shit!* She hurried forward. *Where did he go*?

Acquiel raced ahead, turned a corner. *There's a window open up there*! She headed in that direction. *I wonder who* . . .

"Tessler!" The Brujah was kneeling beside the open window, a long rifle in his hands, his eye pressed to a telescopic sight. "What are you doing?"

"He's planning to kill Don Cruez." Grimsdyke's voice was mild. "And salvage the Methuselah's plan."

Tessler didn't seem to hear them, just moved the rifle barrel slightly, hand coming up to adjust the scope.

"I saw him from down below." Grimsdyke smiled. "To tell the truth, I expected to see him." The smile disappeared as Tessler tensed. "He's almost ready."

Acquiel stood on tiptoe, looking out over the top of the rifle. Far below, she could see Percival and Don Cruez, locked together, rolling on the ground. "What do we do?"

"We stop him." Grimsdyke shrugged. "After all, that's what we came up all those stairs to do."

Don Cruez tried desperately to parry Val's attack. *He's faster than I am!* The Justicar watched skin peel from his arm, torn by Val's claws. *And he's getting help from someone of tremendous power!* Don Cruez rolled away from another attack. *It must be one of the Methuselahs!*

Val moved closer, hand poised to rip at Don Cruez's throat. *Now!* The Justicar grabbed his opponent's arm, pulled him closer, wrapping Val's smaller body in his big arms. *Got him!* Val writhed, tried to shift away. Don Cruez held on, riding the other Kindred like some wild stallion. *Use my strength now, no Methuselah can take that away!* The big Justicar squeezed as hard as he could, trying to smash Val's ribs, drive the splinters into his heart. He felt cartilage pop, muscle soften. *Harder!*

Suddenly Val moved, his body sliding to one side, his hip suddenly under Don Cruez's. *No!* The Justicar was thrown to one side, spilled onto the concrete. Val whirled toward his momentarily helpless opponent, teeth bared, claws ready. *Can't let him get on top of me!*

Don Cruez rolled to one side, then, with all the speed he could muster, pushed himself to his feet. He came upright just in time to meet Val's charge. *Damn!* Again the two men were locked together, but this time, it was the Justicar's arms that were trapped. *He learns fast!*

Don Cruez felt the terrible pressure begin, felt his ribs creak. He fought with all his strength, all his skill, but the Beast, reinforced by the Methuselah, was too strong, too fast.

I'm going to lose!

The thought had never crossed his mind before.

"Don't do that." Grimsdyke pulled up on the barrel of the rifle just as Tessler put first pressure on the trigger.

"Huh?" Tessler's eyelids fluttered wildly.

"Tessler?" Acquiel moved closer. "Why are you doing this?"

Tessler rolled backward, a knife appearing in each hand. "What are *you* doing here?"

"I might ask you the same thing." Grimsdyke held up the rifle. "And I might also ask where you got this."

"That's not mine."

"Then why were you about to shoot Don Cruez!" Acquiel's voice was indignant at the other's pretended innocence.

"Why would I shoot Don Cruez?" Tessler's eyes were wide with shock.

"Why indeed." Grimsdyke ran the bolt of the rifle, pulled out the round in the chamber, tossing it aside. "And why did you set fire to the gallery that night."

"I didn't do that!" Anger flared through Tessler, righteous fire that caused his Beast to stir.

"Yes, you did." Grimsdyke's voice was calm, unrelenting. "I was there." His voice lowered. "I saw you."

Tessler sat back, shocked. "You *saw* me?"

Grimsdyke nodded. "Just as Acquiel and I saw you aiming this rifle, preparing to kill Don Cruez."

"But . . ."

"Think, Tessler, remember!" The actor's voice was forceful, commanding. "You'll never be free if you don't throw off this Domination now!" He stared into Tessler's eyes, projecting calm power. "You can do it."

Tessler stared into Grimsdyke's eyes, his own reflection staring back at him. He thought back to that night in the Village, saw himself watching the gallery. . . .

I *saw Kleist go in*. Tessler remembered. *He had something under his arm. . . .*

"No, Tessler." Grimsdyke's voice cut into his mind. "You didn't see Kleist."

The picture shifted. N*o, it wasn't Kleist*. . . . Tessler saw the door to the basement open, saw a hand reach out to an incendiary bomb.

It was his hand.

"You're right." Tessler's voice was strained, he looked at Acquiel with new eyes. "It wasn't Kleist." He shook his head in wonder. "It was me."

He turned to Acquiel. "But I didn't do it on purpose. I didn't even want to do it!"

His head came around, eyes falling into the blue depths of Grimsdyke's gaze. "I didn't want to do it!"

Grimsdyke nodded. "We know." His tone hardened. "It was the Methuselah." He gestured to the square below. "The same Methuselah that's making those two fight."

"What do we do now?" Acquiel stepped to the window. The two figures sprang apart for an instant, then blurred into a single form again.

Grimsdyke joined her. "We wait."

Percival.

The Beast reveled in the battle. It was *winning!* It ignored the voice in its mind, hardly noticing, so intent was it on destroying his opponent.

Percival. You must listen to me.

The Beast snorted, reached deep into stores of offered blood, immeasurable ancient power. It could feel power rushing into it, while its opponent's power drained away. Soon bones would crack and then . . .

No, Percival. Louder. More insistent. Somewhere, deep inside, something awoke, listened. *You cannot kill him.* The listener heard, pushed against the layers of blackness that held him helpless.

PERCIVAL!

Val broke through the blackness. Suddenly he was looking through shared eyes, ignoring the Beast's inward growl of resentment. *I'm in Lincoln Center.* He saw the night unfold around him, saw the fountain. *But why . . . ?* Another growl, ignored again. Val put out tendrils, felt his muscles straining, felt the struggles of an opponent. *I'm fighting!* He tried to look down, tried to see his enemy. *Who . . . ?*

Something fought him. His eyes wouldn't move. They remained in the control of the Beast.

You're fighting Don Cruez.

Val's mind leaped with recognition. *Mariana?*

He felt her nod, felt her smile. *Yes, my love, it is I.*

Why am I fighting with Don Cruez? He fought for control

of his vision, was pushed back, the world grew dark again.

Because the Methuselah wants you to kill him.

Val's mind recoiled at the thought. *Why?*

So she can take over the city.

Val's mind reeled. Kill Don Cruez? Help a Methuselah take over the city? *What can I do?*

You must overpower the Beast.

Val nodded inwardly, felt the cold heat of Mariana's kiss. *I'll try.* He gathered his strength, thrust out against the blackness that surrounded him. He had to fight the Beast off, take control of his own body, his own destiny.

Even if that destiny was final death.

"Don Cruez is losing." Tessler looked down from the heights of the Lincoln Center Library. He saw Val clamp the big Justicar in his arms, saw the struggle become more intimate as each fighter fought for the upper hand. "Val's got him in a bodylock." He turned to the others. "It's only a matter of time."

"Val's winning?" Acquiel's smile lit up the big room. "That's great!"

"No, it isn't." She turned at the sound of Grimsdyke's voice. "It means the Methuselah will get its way, the city will fall under its power."

"We won't stand for a Toreador prince," Tessler snarled. "The Brujah will fight!"

Grimsdyke shook his head. "It won't matter. It'll just speed things up. Eventually, the anarchs will take over. The city will fall into chaos." He sighed. "Only Don Cruez could have prevented that."

"I could still make sure Don Cruez wins." Tessler reached for the rifle, started to pick it up.

Acquiel's hand stopped him. "You'll have to kill me first!"

The actor's voice came between them. "Even if you did shoot Val now, would Don Cruez thank you?" He turned to Tessler, eyes piercing. "Or would he denounce you for your action?" The eyes grew weary. "And leave the city in self-exile."

"You're right." Tessler nodded. "He *would* leave."

"And the Methuselah would still win."

Tessler got to his feet, started pacing, back and forth down the length of the room. "What can we do?"

"Nothing." Grimsdyke looked out the window at the struggle below. "Nothing at all."

I *can't beat him*. Don Cruez tried trick after trick, technique after technique. Nothing worked. *My own son!* He knew that it was Val's Beast in control, using its ferocity and untamed force against him. But *it's the power of the Methuselah that's beating me!* He thought of loosing his own Beast, of going into Brujah frenzy.

No. I won't die like an animal!

Don Cruez allowed himself to go limp, hoping that his opponent would become overconfident, allow him to break free. *Even if he does, I don't know if I can beat him.*

Val struggled for control. He beat back the darkness surrounding him, forced his way to the forefront of his brain. He could see now, could feel the world around him. *Almost there*! All around him, the Beast exulted, delighting in the fight, celebrating the victory. *Over my own sire!* Val redoubled his efforts. *Not if I can help it!*

He felt again. *Just a little more!* His arms continued their frightful application of power. He could feel Don Cruez's ribs crack, feel the bones break. *No!* Don Cruez went limp.

The Beast bared its fangs, victory certain—and Val exerted all his force of will. *It's my body!* There was a brief, vicious battle, and Val was in control. *Thank God!*

Immediately, he released the pressure on Don Cruez's body. *I hope he's still alive!* Val began to place the body on the ground, lowering it gently, respectfully . . .

And found himself suddenly falling, arm held at shoulder and elbow, unable to stop himself. *He was pretending!* Val struck hard, felt his arm twisted to the side. The bone snapped, the joint crumbled.

Again the Beast leaped up into Val's mind, fighting for control of the body, ready to defend, to kill, to maim. . . .

No! Val fought internally, ignoring Don Cruez's continuing attack. He diverted all his attention inward, keeping the Beast at bay. *I will not kill my sire!*

The Beast snarled, snapped, then disappeared, withdrawing to cower deep inside.

Val opened his eyes—and found Don Cruez towering over him, arm lifted for a final, killing stroke. "Father."

"Percival?" The other hesitated, fell to one knee alongside the broken body of his childe.

Val tried to nod, found he couldn't. *Neck's broken.* "I've beaten the Beast." He smiled.

Don Cruez let his arms fall, let himself relax into a crumple of arms and legs. "Percival, I've got to . . ." The Justicar's eyes met Val's. Sad eyes. "I must survive the Ordeal." Sadder still. "To do so, I must destroy you."

"I understand." Val again tried to nod, still couldn't. "Do one thing for me."

"Anything."

"I've sired a childe." Val smiled. "In a way, she's both mine and Mariana's."

Don Cruez nodded. "She will be claimed as my own." His face hardened. "None will harm her while I live."

Val's eyes closed. "Thank you."

Don Cruez straightened himself, brought his hand back for the killing blow. "I'm sorry . . . son." The hand came down, driving deep into Val's chest, bursting the heart, allowing the vitae to flow freely.

Val felt nothing. The world grew dark around him. *Mariana?* He fell into a vortex of darkness, whirling away from Don Cruez, away from the world he had known all his long life. *Where are you, Mariana?*

He died the final death.

"It's over." Grimsdyke put his arm around Acquiel. "It ended as it had to."

"Percival?"

"He's gone." The actor smiled sadly. "Gone to where we all must eventually go."

"We've got to go down." Tessler headed for the staircase. "Don Cruez may need our help."

Grimsdyke nodded. "Yes." He helped Acquiel to her feet. "We should speak to him."

As Tessler opened the door, Grimsdyke broke the rifle in half, tossing the bits to either side of the big room. "But we don't have to tell him everything."

Tessler nodded, gratitude in his eyes. "Thank you."

They headed down the stairs.

"It's over." Lady Singhjul relaxed back into her chair. "That fool Lady Ambrosia has lost again." She smiled.

"And the boy never realized he was being used?" Anneke looked at her mistress with something like worship.

"Never." The Methuselah giggled. "He actually thought he was talking to his dead lover!"

Anneke shook her head. "Amazing."

"Not really, my dear." Lady Singhjul called for her new retainer. "We Kindred are quite a romantic lot." She paused as the hulking figure entered the room, bearing a tray with two glasses. "That's what makes us so vulnerable."

"And Lady Ambrosia?"

"She will try something new." The Methuselah took a sip of her drink. "That is the nature of the game." She smiled. "That is what keeps us alive."

Anneke nodded. "And me?"

Lady Singhjul gestured. "I have plans for you, my dear." The Methuselah took another sip of her drink. "Major plans."

Anneke nodded. "I see."

"Not yet." Lady Singhjul laughed. "But you will. You will!"

"I've failed!" Lady Ambrosia turned from the window, hands rending the pillow she leaned upon into tiny bits of cloth and padding. "Failed!"

The new retainer retreated to the doorway, keeping

as much of the room between them as he could. "What will you do now?"

Lady Ambrosia allowed herself to sink into the remaining cushions. "Think of something else." Her brow wrinkled. "Something that will rid me of that damn Brujah!" She looked out the window. "Something that will *avenge* me on Lady Singhjul."

"Is there anything I can do?"

The Methuselah shook her head. "Not yet." She turned back to the window. "But soon . . ." The moon was high, the darkness inviting. "Soon."

Grimsdyke, Acquiel, and Tessler reached the fountain just as Don Cruez came to his feet. The body of Val lay beneath him, chest ripped open, heart at his feet, already dissolving in the rapid dissolution of all Kindred elders.

"Don Cruez!" Tessler rushed forward. "Are you all right?"

The big Justicar frowned at the other's approach. "What are you doing here?"

Tessler stopped in his tracks, unsure of his answer. "I . . ."

"He came with me."

"Grimsdyke!" Don Cruez blinked into the night. "And the lady?"

"This is Acquiel." The young Kindred made a pretty bow. "Val's childe."

"Ah." Don Cruez nodded. "She is the one." He gestured Acquiel to join him. "Percival spoke of you." He put his arm around her, pulled her to him. "He asked me to take care of you." Dark eyes stared deep into eyes of clearest blue. "I promised I would claim you as my own." Don Cruez suddenly smiled, lighting up the plaza like the rising of the sun. "And I will, happily." The smile disappeared. "You are all I will have left of my son."

"And you are all I have of either Val *or* Mariana." Acquiel's voice was unsteady.

"So be it." Don Cruez nodded, pulling the girl closer. "We will be family." The Justicar motioned to Tessler. "And this one will teach and protect you."

Tessler's head went down. "Sir, I don't know if I am worthy to . . . "

"Nonsense!" Don Cruez's voice had regained its old strength, its power of command. "You will do what I tell you." He gestured Tessler to join him. "Come. Take her hand. You are cousins now."

Grimsdyke nodded. "It's all right, Acquiel. He's beaten the Methuselah." He smiled. "I don't think he'll ever let anything happen to you."

"Never." Tessler's voice was shaken but firm. "Not while I exist."

"So be it!" Don Cruez pushed Acquiel toward Tessler. "Now, find us a taxi." He took a step, grimaced as his leg gave out. "I think I'm going to need one."

"Will you join me now?" Grimsdyke moved to Don Cruez's side, sure now that the two younger Kindred were out of earshot. "Make sure this"—he gestured at Val's rapidly vanishing remains—"never happens again."

Don Cruez looked down at the remains of his childe, then shook his head. "No, Peter. I won't join you." He began to limp forward, toward Broadway, toward the city. "I can't."

"Why not?"

"This is *my* city now." The Justicar gestured toward

the tall buildings, the broken windows, the cracked sidewalks. "I've fulfilled the Ordeal; I now hold the power!"

Grimsdyke nodded. "So you do."

"As such, I have even more responsibility than before." Don Cruez glanced behind him. "I have to force the Sabbat out—without forcing an open war."

"That won't be easy."

Don Cruez faced forward. "No. But I'll do it."

"And the Methuselah?" Grimsdyke stayed close.

"If I find the one responsible for this," Don Cruez said, his face turning fierce, "I will destroy it."

"And if you don't?"

"My city"—they changed directions slightly, headed for the taxi that Tessler had waved down—"will be very uncomfortable for Methuselahs." He smiled. "Perhaps they'll leave, head for friendlier climes."

"That's quite a dream." Grimsdyke's smile was rueful. "I hope you can fulfill it."

"They will help me." He reached the cab, gestured toward Tessler and Acquiel. "And others like them." He smiled at Grimsdyke. "They will fight." The smile disappeared. "Not just observe."

The actor nodded, sighed. "I hope you're right." He turned away, heading back into the plaza. "I really do."

Don Cruez watched him go, then climbed into the taxi. "Are you two going to join me?"

Tessler shook his head. "Acquiel and I are going to walk for a while." He smiled wanly. "Maybe get a bite to eat."

Don Cruez nodded. "I'll want to talk to you tomorrow."

"We'll be there."

The cab drove off.

*   *   *

"Not going to find much to hunt here." Tessler looked around. Central Park was quiet after midnight. Out of bounds to ordinary citizens, who had learned that it was dangerous to enter the dark wilderness. Too many gangs. Too many predators.

"We'll just walk through." Acquiel pointed to the East Side. "Percival used to go over there a lot." She pushed a bush aside, climbed out onto a path. "There's a temple in the museum there." She smiled sadly. "It meant something to him."

They reached the Tavern on the Green, deserted now, only the cleaners present. "We could eat there." Tessler pointed at the workers.

Acquiel shook her head. "Nah. Too simple."

They kept going, past the almost-deserted roadway that wandered through the park, staying on the footpaths, watching the night around them.

There was a sound. "There!" Acquiel grinned. "Let's check that out!"

The two moved silently, bypassing bushes, placing feet with a hunter's certainty. Finally, they reached the center of the park—and the zoo. They looked over the wall.

"What we gonna do with you two?"

Acquiel smiled. "This looks like it!"

The trapped ones were boys this time. Youngsters caught in the wrong place at the wrong time. "Leave us alone!" One of them was about fourteen, scared but not willing to show it. "We don't have any money!"

The gang that faced them was small. Four members, but they had the courage of numbers.

"Did we ask for money?" Their leader was average-sized, the sort of teenager you wouldn't look at twice if you passed him on the street. Here, with a knife in his hand and other blades backing him, he was twelve feet tall. "If we wanted money, we'd ask."

The others were the same. Punks. Young men who believed in no law but their own, no rights except those made by might.

"Let me go first!" Acquiel stood up, smoothing down her miniskirt, strutting through the zoo's gates.

"Hey!" One of the gangers noticed her at once, eyes widening at the sight. "Lookit this!"

"You boys want a little action?" Acquiel's smile was broad, not reaching her eyes.

"Yeh, Mama!" The leader stepped forward, knife still in his hand, but mind in other places. "We sure do!"

"Good." Acquiel stepped forward, laid her small hands on the leader's shoulders. "Me too." She kissed him then, touching her lips to his, then moving them to his cheek, his ear, his neck. . . .

Acquiel fed while the leader stood there, transfixed with ecstasy. To the others, it looked as if he were having some incredible orgasm, but Tessler knew what was happening.

He was being drained.

The Brujah smiled, admiring the other's style. "When do I get my turn?" he muttered, voice low.

Acquiel finished with the leader, then, with a casual twist, she snapped his neck, letting his lifeless body fall at her feet. "All right, who's next?"

The other punks looked at her, astonished. What had this tiny girl done to their leader, their brother? The bravest of them moved forward, looking down at the fallen man.

"He's dead." Acquiel's voice was right beside him. "And you're next."

The punk spun in terror, knife thrusting up, aimed at Acquiel's voice. But she wasn't there, just a steel-hard hand that grabbed his knife arm, snapped the wrist.

Tessler arrived just as the punk started to scream. He disposed of one of the others quickly, snapping the punk's neck before he could turn. The final one he took his time with, feeding to satiation before ripping the punk's throat out.

Acquiel watched, smiling. "Had enough?"

"For now."

"So let's go home."

They started out of the park, heading to the Fifth Avenue side now. "By the way," Acquiel asked, turning to face her new partner. "Where is home?"

"Wherever you want it to be." Tessler smiled. "If you want, I'll show you one of Val's places."

Acquiel nodded. "Good enough."

They walked down the street. "You know . . ." Tessler glanced over at her.

"This could be the start of a beautiful friendship."

Somewhere, a Methuselah laughed.

A lifelong fan of science fiction and fantasy, **DOUG MURRAY** spent the early years of his life writing articles about horror movies for magazines like *Famous Monsters*, *Monster Times*; *Millimeter*, and *Steranko's Mediascene*.

In the mid-eighties, he turned to the comics field, creating and writing the award-winning *The 'Nam*, a historically accurate story of one unit's experiences during the Vietnam War. Later he moved on to lighter fare, scripting such diverse comics as *Conan*, *Nick Fury: Agent of Shield*, *Batman: Digital Justice*, and even *Darkwing Duck* and *Roger Rabbit*.

At the same time, he was moving into the prose field, selling anthology stories to *Confederacy of the Dead*, *Tales of the White Wolf*, *The Fleet*, and many others.

Now, with *Blood Relations*, Doug Murray finally makes the move to novel-length work—a move he hopes will bring pleasure to all those who have followed his career to this point.